THE PAIN SCALE

A Long Beach Homicide Novel

Also by Tyler Dilts:

A King of Infinite Space

THE PAIN SCALE

A Long Beach Homicide Novel

Tyler Dilts

THOMAS & MERCER

Text copyright © 2012 Tyler Dilts
All rights reserved.
Printed in the United States of America.

Published by Thomas & Mercer
P.O. Box 400818
Las Vegas, NV 89140

ISBN-13: 9781612186023
ISBN-10: 1612186025

For Nicole

PART ONE: COMPLAINT

———————— , ————————

Absent thee from felicity awhile,
And in this harsh world draw thy breath in pain,
To tell my story.
  —William Shakespeare, Hamlet

Eight

WHEN I SLEEP I DREAM OF PAIN.

―――――― · ――――――

"On a scale of one to ten," the new doctor asked, "with zero being no pain at all and ten being the worst pain you can possibly imagine, how would you rate your current pain level?" He was young, not far past thirty, with thinning red-blond hair and freckles tinged green under the fluorescent lights. Wore surgical scrubs under a white coat and a fake smile. An ID badge identified him as Dr. Ballard. It was maybe the ten-thousandth time I'd been asked the same question in the previous thirteen months.

"Did you read my file?" I asked.

"Of course, Mr. Beckett." He looked confused, as if I were accusing him of something. Must have been the edge in my voice.

"Do you know what I do for a living?"

"You're a police officer."

"A homicide detective."

"Oh. Well." He didn't follow.

I wanted to tell him my problems with his question. Why it was meaningless. Why I was so sick of it I could barely keep myself from screaming. I wanted to tell him about the things I'd seen. It would only take a few examples. To tell him the kind of pain I could imagine. And that the reason I could imagine it was because I'd witnessed the actions that caused it with my own eyes. To tell him, for example, about a woman who'd been flayed alive by her husband after she had asked him for a divorce. About a six-year-old boy who'd been immolated by his welder father with an oxyacetylene torch because he'd gotten up to ask for a glass of water after bedtime. About an elderly woman who'd been dismembered by her meth-addled grandson because she wouldn't surrender her Social Security check. I wanted to tell him about dozens of cases I'd worked, about the bodies of people who had experienced pain so extreme it would be beyond the imagining of anyone who hadn't beheld its victims for themselves.

I wanted to tell him I could imagine pain that would make him weep.

I wanted to tell him that it felt like I had a bear trap tearing into my wrist and my arm was plunged shoulder-deep into a vat of boiling oil.

Instead, I stared at the FDA food pyramid poster on the wall and said, "Eight."

He examined the scar tissue that, but for a quarter of an inch on the top of my forearm below the base of my thumb, formed a shiny pink band around my wrist, just about where my watchband used to be. More than once it had been mistaken for one of those charity cause-of-the-month rubber bracelets.

He poked at it a few times, then began typing into a computer on a rolling cart tethered to an outlet in the wall. "It's been, what, eight months since the last surgery?" He didn't look away from the monitor.

"That's right."

"And you'd like a refill of your prescription?"

"Yes."

"You know Vicodin can be habit forming."

"You don't say."

He still didn't look at me. I couldn't tell if he didn't get the sarcasm or if he was just ignoring it.

"Have you thought about Advil or Tylenol?"

I was glad the nurse had already taken my blood pressure, because I imagined it rising every time he opened his mouth. The deep breaths I took didn't help.

"Look at me," I said.

"I'm sorry?"

"Quit typing and look at me."

He did. Mouth hanging open, green eyes wide with confusion, as if he didn't know what to do with a patient who was going so far off the script. Didn't they cover that in med school? Wasn't there a handout or something?

I let him stew in the awkwardness a few seconds before I spoke. "I'm only here because my old pain management specialist moved to Idaho and the HMO said I have to start from scratch."

He didn't answer. I don't think he knew what to say.

Across the room, I heard my partner's ringtone sound from the cell phone in my coat pocket. She knew where I was. It could only mean one thing.

"Look," I said, "I know you're just trying to do your job and all, but you need to understand something. The things that I've seen, that I've experienced, have taught me more about pain than you'll ever know. That ring you just heard means someone's dead and I'm all out of time to sit here and chat with you. Either write me the fucking prescription or refer me to the new pain-management doctor."

He did both.

———————— / ————————

As soon as I was in the hallway, I speed-dialed my partner, Jennifer Tanaka. We were next up in the case rotation, so she'd stayed behind at the Homicide Detail's squad room downtown while I came to my appointment.

"What's up?" I asked.

"I hope you're ready to get back in the saddle."

I'd only returned three weeks before from a yearlong medical leave, and the first cases we'd caught had all been rubber stamps—a murder-suicide (an out-of-control husband and his unfortunate wife) and a convenience store robbery in which the clerk and the fourteen-year-old gangbanger trying to rob him both wound up dead. They all required the reams of paperwork inherent in any homicide investigation, but little more.

"Something interesting?"

"Yeah. It's bad. Mother. Two kids. Bixby Knolls. Looks like a home invasion. I'm on my way now." There was a waver in her voice I couldn't remember ever hearing before.

I wrote the address in my notebook and told her I'd meet her there.

They used to call Bixby Knolls "uptown." They don't so much anymore, but its Los Cerritos neighborhood is still one of the oldest of the old-money sections of Long Beach. While most of the city has grown denser and taller, with cutting-edge architecture and designs to meet the ever-increasing upmarket demands of gentrification, Bixby Knolls is still the place to go for a traditional starter mansion with half an acre to call its own. Bordered by the concrete channel of the Los Angeles River on the west and hemmed in by the 405 freeway on the south and the Virginia Country Club on the north, it's a quiet neighborhood, still clinging to the notion that ostentatious bragging about wealth is just plain bad form. The homes there are luxurious enough that they never took the hit the rest of the real estate market did. The prices start at just under two million.

Driving up Pacific, I watched the neighborhoods grow more expensive and expansive with each passing block. It doesn't take long after the street passes under the San Diego Freeway to reach those seven-figure price tags.

It turned out I didn't even need to check the address. By the time I got there, there were already three cruisers, two unmarked cars, and the Crime Scene Detail's van.

Something was off. There was way too much activity for such an early stage of the investigation.

I parked my Camry across the street in the shade of a hundred-year-old oak and got out. Half a dozen uniforms were hanging around the sidewalk in front of the house. I knew most of the names and faces, but nobody spoke. Just a few nodding heads. The house was a large colonial-style two story, white with very well-tended landscaping and a sprawling lawn at least fifteen yards deep, bisected by a stone pathway. As I was walking up, Jen came out of the front door and met me halfway.

"What's up with the crowd?"

She didn't answer. That surprised me.

I softened my tone and said, "What's inside?"

Her eyes narrowed, and her jaw tightened. She'd taken her coat off and wore a sleeveless black silk blouse. There was an uncharacteristic tightness in her back and shoulders as she ran a hand through her spiky black hair.

"Don't know yet. Just had a quick look at the bodies, then I saw you pull up. Thought I'd let you give them the once-over before we dig in."

"You all right?"

She bit her lip and gave her head a single shake. "Just fine," she said, her right fist clenching and unclenching as she spoke.

I didn't believe her.

On the last major case I'd worked, I was attempting to apprehend a suspect when he attacked me with a knife. Not just any knife, but a Gurkha kukri, which has a large and heavy downward-curving blade that's designed to maximize chopping ability. If it hadn't caught on the stainless-steel band of my watch, the doctors assured me, I would have lost my left hand. Instead, I'm told how lucky I am, and five surgeries later, I'd recovered 90 percent of my pre-injury function.

The pain, though, remained.

The double front door was ten feet high and opened onto a two-story foyer. A wide, marble-treaded staircase curved up the wall to the right. Cops and criminalists moved up and down it with room to spare. I followed the trail of uniforms.

At the upper landing, I found Lieutenant Ruiz, the LBPD Homicide Detail commander. He was the most solid boss I'd worked for in more than a decade and a half with the department. The Texas Rangers had trained him back in the eighties, and he had risen quickly through their ranks. But in those days, Latinos only advanced so high, and he'd had to migrate west to head his own squad. Rumor had it that the Rangers' brass was concerned that they might not be able to distinguish between a Mexican lieutenant and the coyotes and narco mules they faced off against on a daily basis. "The tortilla ceiling," some called it. Ruiz never said anything about it, though, and the whispered stories spread. But he had left Texas in the past, all but for a slight vocal inflection he was never quite able to shake. I heard it when he greeted me.

"Danny."

I nodded back at him. "Hear it's bad."

"Yeah. Mother, two kids. Sara Gardener-Benton, Bailey and Jacob. Six and three."

It was unusual for him to be on the scene at all, especially before the detectives. It meant that someone had bypassed the normal protocol and he'd already sounded the bugle for the cavalry. I wondered if the family mass killing on its own was enough to raise the case's profile so high.

There were uniforms and criminalists at each end of the hall.

"Different rooms?"

"Mother in one"—he nodded toward one doorway—"and kids in the other."

"Which is worse?"

"Depends how you think on it."

I didn't know what he meant. But I'd find out soon enough.

Whoever killed Sara Gardener-Benton had done a real job of it. Her body was spread eagle on a four-poster California king in a master suite so large it made the bed itself seem small. Each of her limbs was tied taut to a corner post with three-quarter-inch synthetic mountaineering rope in knots that looked like they must have been tied by professional sailors. She was naked, and it was obvious even from twelve feet away that she'd been tortured extensively. Her body was deeply bruised, and she had bled profusely from her genital area.

The ME from the coroner's office was examining the body. He was a small man in his fifties. Bald and hard.

"Carter," I said. "What do you know?"

"They beat the shit out of her, then raped her with a broken broomstick."

"They?"

"Yeah. I'm fairly certain you'll find it was a two-man job. Beat her first, then one held her down while the other tied. After that, fuckers probably took turns."

I looked at the puddle of blood between her legs. The top surface had begun to coagulate. The comforter had slid or been pushed off to the far side of the bed. I squatted and lifted the dust ruffle with a gloved finger.

"Hasn't bled through," Carter said. "Probably won't. This mattress is a top-of-the-line Simmons. Got this extra pillow-top layer of padding here on top. Synthetic fiber and memory foam. Not completely waterproof, but close." He looked up at me. "You're wondering how much she bled."

"Yeah."

"Too early to know for sure, but I'm betting it was the blood loss that got her. She probably passed out while they were still working on her."

He didn't bother mentioning the shock or the pain, either of which might have hastened her loss of consciousness. I wondered if she really was lucky enough to have passed out.

———————— , ————————

Bailey and Jacob were in another room down the hall. From the Barbie and Disney princess decor, I had to guess this one belonged to the girl.

Her body was face up on the floor, with her face twisted toward her left shoulder. A dark-red-black tangle marred the corn silk smoothness of the hair on the side of her head. She wore blue jeans with an elastic waistband and a pink polo shirt, the collar stained with blood. She'd been shot twice behind the ear with a small-caliber weapon, probably a .22. Another round had left a crimson stain in the center of her chest, just about where she would have held her hand while reciting the Pledge of Allegiance.

Jacob had been hiding in the closet. His jeans were just like his sister's, but he wore a *Toy Story* T-shirt on top. He had been shot three times in the face and once in the chest. It was hard to see through the blood-soaked fabric, but it looked like the slug in the torso had gone right through Woody's left eye.

I couldn't guess what he had done to warrant the extra bullet. He'd held his hands up to protect himself, but they'd done nothing—from the angle of the wound, it appeared that one of the shots had pierced his left palm and continued on into his skull.

What does a three-year-old feel when looking into the barrel of a gun?

———————— , ————————

A second door led out of the bedroom and into a large bathroom. Bright colors, double sinks, separate shower and tub, a toilet behind its own door, and finally, another exit into the next bedroom. It was more luxury than any child could need, but at least they shared. Maybe there was a lesson or two in that. Not that it would do them any good now.

Through the second door, a *Thomas and Friends* theme dominated the room. The little tank engine was everywhere—curtains, sheets, and pillowcases, and especially in the wooden-track toy train set laid out on what I'm sure was a custom-made table. It was a full-size sheet of plywood framed by white pine one-by-sixes and mounted on short four-by-four legs that raised it about eighteen inches off the ground. A perfect height for a three-year-old engineer. I couldn't help imagining Jacob grinning as Thomas chugged around the yards-long loops and curves of track through the village of plastic buildings.

I swallowed at the catch in my throat and tried to rub some of the pain out of my wrist. Neither action had much effect.

———————— , ————————

Downstairs, I found my way into what was either a family room or den. It always seems to me that one of the great challenges of wealth must be coming up with names for all the rooms in your house. I supposed it didn't really matter what the Bentons called the room. What I found most interesting was the display of family photos that covered most of one wall. Something struck me as odd.

Ruiz and Jen came into the room behind me. He spoke first. "The man in the pictures is Bradley Benton the Third."

That's when I got it. He was in almost every picture. I scanned the rows. Bradley Benton III with guys in suits. Bradley Benton III on skis. Bradley Benton III on a boat with a big fish. Bradley Benton III in many places with many people wearing many outfits. There were even a few pictures with Bailey and Jacob. And, all the way on the left, a single image of him with Sara. A wedding photo. The one thing that was completely clear from the array was that Bradley was the star of the show.

"Bradley Benton?" I asked. "Any relation?"

"Yeah," Ruiz said. "The victims are the daughter-in-law and grandchildren of our congressman."

"Terrific," I said.

That explained the high profile.

I looked back at the photo of Bradley and Sara. She was beaming like most brides on their wedding day, but he wore a smug expression on his face, and an overweening arrogance emanated from his eyes. Just the kind of look that made me want to Taser someone.

"What?" Jen asked me.

"I don't like him."

"No surprise there."

"What do you mean?"

"When's the last time you met a rich guy who didn't make you want to puke?"

"Funny," I said. "We have any idea where he is?"

"Yeah," Ruiz said. "He's on an airplane flying in from DC. His old man's coming, too."

"Does he know?" I asked.

"His attorney does. I imagine he's spread the word."

"You made the notification to the lawyer?"

"That's the play they dealt. Told Benton's chief of staff I was a cop; he put me straight through to the mouthpiece. He hemmed and hawed so much I just gave up and spit it out."

"This is going to be a peach," Jen said.

Ruiz's cell rang. He checked the caller ID display and took it out of the room.

I went back to the photos on the wall. In one of the few that didn't include Benton, Sara was standing on a playground between two swings. On her left was Bailey, on her right, Jacob. Her arms were open, and she had one hand on each child's back and was just beginning to push. The family resemblance shone in their smiles, and the three of them seemed to share some deep and secret happiness.

———————— , ————————

An hour and a half later, we reconvened in the den. The lieutenant had called in the rest of the Homicide Detail to back us up. Marty Locklin and David Zepeda were the old hands, with almost fifty years on the job between them. Patrick Glenn was the newest addition to the squad. He'd been on loan from Computer Crimes while I was out on medical leave, and Ruiz was trying to make the reassignment permanent. We'd all torn the house apart on the assumption that the Bentons' attorneys would get in the way once they arrived. We assumed Bradley probably had a whole host of things he'd rather not have the police looking at. The house's status as a crime scene gave us quite a bit of latitude. Until someone protested, we were allowed to search just about anything. And we wanted to find out as much as we could before we had to start justifying our actions.

Ruiz eyeballed us. "Impressions?"

"It's a mess," I said. "The first thought is home invasion. The back door's been forced. Looks like a safe's been ripped out of one of the master bedroom closets with pry bars and a sledgehammer. But if you go with that, why torture Sara?"

Jen spoke next. "The combination to the safe?"

"Maybe," I said. "But it was pretty hard core for that. Looks like these guys enjoyed what they did to her."

Marty took a turn. "Coincidence? A couple of pervs who take scores see the chance to combine work with pleasure?"

Jen shook her head. "Crossover like that's pretty rare. Usually the deviants aren't big on multitasking. Too much of a distraction from the real business." She'd spent three years in Sex Crimes before transferring to Homicide.

"And what about the kids?" Ruiz asked.

"Looks like a mob hit," Dave said. "No wits."

"It does," I said. "But that doesn't fit, either. They don't usually kill kids. Too much heat—the percentages don't add up."

"Well," Ruiz said, "nothing adds up here." He looked down at his shoes. I thought a speech might be in the offing, but I was wrong. He went for terse. "Figure it out. There's a storm coming, and it's moving fast." Well, terse and clichéd.

"Marty?" I asked.

He hooked a thumb at Dave and said, "We'll get started on the canvass."

Patrick held up an external hard drive. "Two computers. I copied both. Going to take them back to the squad and start digging."

"Should you do that?" I asked.

"Well," he said, "I *can* do it." He shrugged.

I let it go.

After everyone else made their way out of the room, Jen and I were left alone.

My gaze drifted back over the photos of Benton. Twenty-two of them. Benton himself in twenty. What kind of man, I wondered, had more pictures of himself than of his children? What kind of ego did that indicate? What kind of narcissism? I moved my eyes down the rows and studied his face. His eyes. His smile. There was something missing in every one.

A slicing pain wound its way up my arm like a twisting chain. I knew.

I didn't know how or why, but I knew.

Jen was watching me. "What?" she asked.

"He's guilty," I said.

"Well, good," she said with mock relief. "That'll save us a lot of work."

I was working on a comeback when we heard the scream.

Four

I SUPPOSED THE REAL PROBLEM WITH THE PAIN SCALE ITSELF AS a diagnostic tool was the patient's capacity for imagination. At one support group for chronic pain sufferers I attended, we spent the first twenty minutes complaining about the folly of the scale and about the incredible extremities of pain we could imagine. Anyone who has dealt with the medical establishment's treatment of chronic pain in the last few years has encountered this phenomenon. We're asked to rate our pain on a scale of one to ten. To assign it a numerical value. One: no pain at all. Ten: the worst pain imaginable. So you can see why what we are capable of envisioning is a significant factor in our estimation.

Pain does strange things to you. Chronic pain especially so. It changes you. Your feelings. Your thoughts. Your beliefs. Even your imagination. Things that were once abstractions become tangible. Suffering, true suffering, becomes something that is no longer an only vaguely considered possibility but a palatable, day-to-day reality.

You learn to imagine the unimaginable.

And to live in pain is to encounter the darkest possibilities of your imagination.

When you did what I did every day, those possibilities were very dark indeed.

It turned out that the scream had come from the nanny. By the time Jen and I made our way to the kitchen, she was sitting rigid on a chair at the corner of the breakfast nook. Ruiz was next to her, a fatherly hand on her shoulder and comforting words trickling out of his mouth. We stood back as he eased her into the requisite questions.

Her name was Joely Ryan, and she'd been working for the Bentons for a little over a year. She was blonde and cute, early twenties, and she seemed like someone accustomed to being in the presence of wealth but not someone born to it. Her demeanor held too much deference to the lieutenant's authority for it to have developed in any kind of excessive privilege. And her distress was almost surely genuine.

Ruiz motioned Jen and me to the table. "Joely," he said, "this is Detective Tanaka and Detective Beckett. They're going to ask you some more questions."

She nodded and removed a fresh tissue from the box on the table to dab at her cheeks.

Jen took Ruiz's spot at the table as I leaned back against the large granite-topped counter that dominated the kitchen. I noticed a large Post-it note on the stainless refrigerator door. In large black handwriting, it read:

DON'T FORGET!

LUNCH W/CAT

WED 12

I looked at my watch. It was after 2:00. Sara missed her lunch. I made a note and turned my attention back to the table.

"I know this is difficult," Jen said. "But can you think of anyone who might have wanted to hurt Mrs. Benton or the children?"

Joely shook her head.

"How about Mr. Benton?"

She looked up at Jen. "No."

17

"Have you noticed anything unusual or out of the ordinary recently?"

"Like what?"

"Changes in anyone's behavior, changes in schedules or the way the Bentons liked to do things, new people around, strangers. Anything at all."

"No." Joely shook her head again and wiped her nose.

Jen let things sit for a moment.

"Well," Joely went on, "just tiny things. Like today."

"What happened today?"

"The kids were supposed to be in school. Sara hardly ever keeps them home, but they both had that bug that's going around, so she asked if I could come early. I wouldn't even be here yet—" Her voice caught in her throat.

Jen gave Joely time to compose herself, asked her a few more questions, then told her we'd probably need to talk to her again. Gave her a business card in case she thought of anything in the meantime.

We were back in the den before either of us said it out loud.

I said, "Looks like the kids are dead…"

"…because," Jen continued, "they had a cold."

We had the run of the house for another half an hour. Then the weather changed and a cold front blew in. Brad's lawyers showed up.

The alpha had short, well-tended hair glistening with some sort of product and a gunmetal-gray suit that looked like it cost more than my car.

Ruiz led him and a quarter dozen of his minions out onto the back patio, where Jen and I were tossing out some preliminary ideas. He introduced us as the leads on the investigation.

"I'm Julian Campos," he said, extending a hand. "I'm the Bentons' attorney." His handshake felt like he'd been working on it with a personal trainer. "These are my associates from Sternow and Byrne. We're here to help in whatever way we can."

"Is Mr. Benton with you?" I asked.

"Presently, he's understandably distraught. He's seeking assistance from the family's physician."

"We'll need to talk to him as soon as possible."

"Of course. In the meantime, is there any way we can be of assistance?" The pergola overhead cast zebra-striped shadows across him.

"You can stay out of the way."

"Of course."

The gaggle of lawyers melted into the background. But as soon as Campos closed his mouth, they spread out through the house and started taking photos and writing down everything they saw.

Jen and I split up and walked the house one more time to make sure we'd caught everything there was to catch. Although they were smart enough to stay away from the rooms in which the murders took place, it seemed like I couldn't turn around without seeing another attorney.

After we had covered the entire scene again, we met up with Ruiz in the foyer.

"Well?" he said.

"I think we're covered," I said. "But I don't like all the lawyers."

"Why?" He looked at me. "You got something to hide?"

———————— , ————————

While I'd been on leave, I'd read an article in *Los Angeles* magazine about a new trend among high-end Southern California legal practices that the author referred to as "megafirms." These were top-of-the-line, spare-no-expense organizations that had battled the economic downturn by offering their clients a full array of luxury legal services. They also provided private security, investigative services, and just about anything else imaginable within the realm of on-demand law and order.

Sternow and Byrne was one of these firms. If you signed up with S&B, they'd not only handle all your business's legal needs, but they'd also do a background check on your potential trophy wife, draft a bulletproof prenup, follow her when she started cheating on you, provide stellar representation during the divorce, and probably even offer up someone to intimidate her when she violated the restraining order. And they'd do your taxes. Not bad if you could afford it.

We leaned against the hood of Jen's 4Runner as I ran down what I remembered from the article. It seemed to ring a bell for her.

"Sternow and Byrne," she said. "They're the ones who got all the press for buying that private military firm that was operating in Afghanistan, right?"

"Yep. They reorganized it and turned it into their new security and investigation division."

"Nice. Benton's lawyers have actual mercenaries on the payroll."

———————— , ————————

We left the scene and decided to rendezvous back at the squad. None of us had eaten, and by the time we got back it would be close to quitting time. Jen and I would be working through dinner. The overtime had already been approved. I volunteered to take a detour on the way back and stop by Enrique's for takeout.

"The usual?" I asked as she climbed into her 4Runner.

"You still remember?"

"I'm crushed you even asked."

Before I started the car, I phoned in an order for carne asada, chicken veracruz, mixed-bean soup, steamed rice, and chips and salsa.

It had been more than a year since my partner and I had worked over dinner. Driving south down the 710, I hit the *PLAY* button on the steering wheel. Springsteen started in on "Further On (Up the Road)," and I felt like I was going home.

PART TWO: PRESENTATION

—————— , ——————

Severity is in the eye of the sufferer...Pain is pain.
—David Foster Wallace, Infinite Jest

Three

PAIN IS RELATIVE. IT'S BEEN YEARS SINCE I'VE BEEN ABLE TO sleep through the night on any kind of a regular basis. Even before I nearly lost my hand, I was already in a kind of pain. My wife burned to death in a car accident a few years earlier. I've killed two teenagers in the line of duty. And as I've already mentioned, I've been obsessing over homicides for more than a decade. None of these things has ever treaded lightly on my psyche. I was on close personal terms with Grey Goose a good long time before I ever had any major surgery at all.

On occasion, I consider the two varieties of pain I've experienced—the physical and the psychological. And I often believe that I prefer the physical. It's tangible and palpable in a way that the ghosts that haunt my sleepless nights never are and never will be. There's a hope, too, in the physical pain, a hope of some cure or remedy, of some relief, no matter how distant, that is forever absent in the other. What hope is there, for example, of forgetting the last time I saw my wife, on a stainless-steel autopsy table, her body burned and blackened, her face charred almost beyond recognition?

———————— , ————————

A few years earlier, the brass had wanted to update the furniture in the Homicide Detail squad room when the building got a top-to-bottom refurbishing. They had planned to install cubicles and fabric-covered partitions to "delineate workspaces" and "facilitate a professional atmosphere," as they were doing throughout the department. Ruiz hemmed and hawed, stomped his feet, and just generally made a stink until the Detective Division commander threw in the towel and let him keep the traditional squad arrangement—three clusters of two WWII-era steel desks, each facing one another, in the large open space.

I looked at Jen over our gray wood-grain Formica desktops. She'd changed into jeans and an LBPD T-shirt before I'd made it back with the food.

Over dinner, we'd talked about Jen's hunt for a house. She'd never owned one before but had some money in the bank and thought the time was right to get into the market while home values were bottoming out. She was looking at places in California Heights and even Lakewood. I was pushing her toward Belmont Shore.

"That's where all the cool people live."

"I know," she said. "That's why I'm looking on the other side of town."

A few hours later, the wastebaskets were full of empty Styrofoam takeout containers, the leftovers were secured in the coffee room fridge, and we were wrapping things up for the night.

It was after nine, and the rest of the squad had drifted out, one by one. We'd spent the last few hours putting together the murder book, setting up the bulletin board that would keep the most significant details of the case in plain sight, running MOs through ViCAP and NCIC to check for possible hits, and probably most importantly, using Sara Gardener-Benton's calendar and phone and bank records to establish a preliminary record of her movements for the last days of her life. None of it was terribly exciting, but it was the legwork that would, if anything at all did, most likely lead to a break in the case. And so far, there were none of those in sight.

I looked up from the local usage detail report from Verizon with a listing of all of Sara's calls and text messages for the last month and thought I caught Jen smiling at me.

"What?" I asked.

She looked at me and shook her head but couldn't completely hide the grin.

Back in the saddle.

Whoopie-ti-yi-yay.

———————— , ————————

Sometime past midnight, Jen had called it a night and headed home for a few hours of sleep. I was tacking the night's final crime scene photo on the board when I felt a twinge of pain shoot through my wrist.

"Motherfucker," I said to the empty room.

———————— , ————————

In my seventeen sessions with the pain psychologist, we worked on things like creative visualization and guided imagery and mindful meditation. The purpose of these activities was to find a technique that could be successful in occupying my conscious mind to such a degree that it might be possible to direct my thoughts away from focusing on my chronic pain and down more serene and pleasant paths.

"So basically the point is to distract myself," I said.

"Well…" She danced around the phraseology a bit but ultimately agreed that I was right about the basic idea.

So we imagined peaceful streams and secluded beaches and snow-kissed mountains and tropical islands and suns setting over distant horizons.

Pretty stuff.

It never occurred to either of us that pretty stuff was the exact opposite of what I needed.

———————— , ————————

I thought back over the previous several hours. The last time I remembered thinking about my pain was early in the evening, picking up dinner at Enrique's. I had stretched my neck while I was waiting for the takeout. And before that? On the way to the crime scene.

As I felt the awareness of the pain wash over me again, I couldn't fathom the sensation. I think I might have smiled.

Five hours. Maybe six. Hours I'd spent losing myself in the Benton investigation. With almost no awareness of my pain.

That was the best I'd done in over a year.

Son of a bitch.

The psychologist was on to something, after all. It wasn't the technique that was wrong. It was the imagery.

———————— , ————————

I live in the lower unit of a duplex in Belmont Heights, on Roycroft, a block from Warren High School. The tenants before me were a graphic designer and his family. He had a flair for color, and the way he'd painted the place was the reason I moved in. The kitchen is done in bright primary colors—red and blue and yellow—with a Caribbean flair. The dining room, living room, and master bedroom are finished in textured plaster, each in a different earth tone, with the ceiling molding and accents in perfect contrasting colors. The detail that really sold me, though, was the bedroom that had belonged to his daughter. From the doorway, the wall on the left is painted a deep blue, highlighted with a night full of white-gold stars surrounding a smirking crescent moon over which jumped one very happy cow. As your eyes travel up the wall and onto the ceiling, the colors gradually fade, perfectly blending together in imitation of the growing dawn, becoming lighter and lighter until day breaks on the far right wall in a rainbow of bright colors, with a glowing yellow-and-orange sun that beams out from behind a perfectly detailed pair of Ray-Ban sunglasses. Even now, I like to stand in the middle of the room and let my gaze slowly drift from one wall to the other.

When my wife, Megan, died, she was pregnant and hoping for a girl.

I moved in about six months later.

———————— , ————————

The night of the Benton murders, I tried to sleep, but as is often the case, I couldn't. I went into the spare bedroom, spun the desk chair away from the computer in the corner, and stared at a grinning star painted by a man I've never met. As I massaged the pain in my left forearm, I thought about the day and all that had happened. I couldn't help wondering if it was a twinge of guilt I felt as I smiled back at the sun and imagined the coming day.

Five

I MANAGED A FEW HOURS OF SLEEP AND WOKE TO THE PAIN DULL and throbbing in my wrist and forearm. It seemed like a good sign. I do better with that than when it's sharper and more piercing.

Most days I have to make a choice. Usually I know shortly after I wake up whether the day will end with Vicodin or with vodka. If the pain tends toward the sharper side, the narcotic usually works better, but if it's duller and more generalized, the Grey Goose is usually more effective. Either way, just to take the edge off, I have to get so wrecked that I wind up in a near-drooling daze.

At that point, I'd manage with just one or the other, but most days I figure it is just a matter of time. It is all about the Vs.

———————————— , ————————————

Even with a solid four hours of sack time, I still managed to beat the lieutenant into the squad room by more than an hour. When he arrived, he helped himself to one of the donuts I'd brought. He went for his regular—a maple bar. Me, I was on my second vanilla cruller. And I had serious designs on a third. That's the thing about picking up the pink boxes yourself. It's really the only way to make sure you get enough crullers. Nobody ever gets enough crullers. And nothing starts the day off worse than having to settle for some strawberry-coconut piece of crap.

"Rise and shine," Ruiz said around his first bite. "You get any sleep?"

"A little." I didn't sleep much. The previous night's discovery about the case's effect on my pain hadn't allowed me much rest. But I couldn't deny that I'd woken that morning feeling more enthusiastic about going to work than I had in a long time. Would I be able to get lost in the case again? What would happen to my pain? Now that I was aware of the phenomenon, would the relief disappear?

"What's the game plan?"

"I'm hoping we can talk to Bradley Benton today. We've also got a friend who Sara canceled lunch plans with yesterday to interview. Beyond that, Jen and I are putting together Sara's last seventy-two hours and working the victimology. Anything about the rush on the autopsy?"

"Paula's doing it herself."

Paula Henderson is the lead medical examiner for the southern region of the LA County's coroner's jurisdiction. "The chief asked her to move the Bentons to the head of the line. So make some time for the prelim this afternoon."

"Will do." I couldn't help but wonder what kind of strings had been pulled on the congressman's behalf. "When's the press conference?"

"Sometime this morning. Probably around ten so it'll be less likely to be picked up live. The brass are happy as pigs in shit. None of the media's caught wind of anything yet. They can't stop talking about 'managing the story.'" Los Angeles had local news coverage on one station or another all day long, but the 9 to 11 a.m. window had the fewest live broadcasts going on. "They're hoping to break it before any media does. You get any calls yet?"

"Not so far."

"The chief wants something planned before the congressman gets involved."

"Think he'll want to be at the conference?"

"I can't imagine a politician missing a chance to make a speech."

"Better make it quick, then. You want Jen and me for the stand-up?"

"I'll get you out of it if I can, but don't count on it."

"Might be a good chance to lasso some of the family."

"Good idea."

The brass would want the two lead investigators on the case to appear at the press conference disclosing the Benton murders. It was standard procedure. We wouldn't speak or be spoken to. Our job would be to just stand there looking sad and competent. If Jen and I had to dance our jig, we'd lose a few hours of prime investigative time. But it might be worth it if it gave us an opportunity to interview the family.

It was quarter to eight when Jen arrived. She eyeballed the donuts but didn't take one.

She studied me.

"What?" I asked.

"You look rested," she said.

I thought about telling her what had happened last night, telling her about the relief the case seemed to be bringing me. But I didn't know how to say it. I'd been trying to play down my pain levels. I knew she saw through it to some degree, but I didn't know how much. I didn't want to admit how much I had really been hurting, and I would have to do that for her to understand.

And even more importantly, I was afraid talking about the case's effects would diminish them.

So I filled her in on the developments in the investigation and left everything else I was thinking about unsaid.

When I finished, I asked how she thought we should prioritize the morning.

"Talking to Benton's number one," she said.

"I figured I'd wait until eight to call Campos. Then badger him into the soonest meet we can get. A little luck and it'll be the same time as the press conference."

"How about the 'Lunch with Cat' note?"

"I cross-referenced the address book, e-mail, cell, and land-line records. Smart bet is that 'Cat' is Catherine Catanio. In the last month, Sara's talked to her more days than not. After the family, I think we should make her number two on the list."

At 8:05, I called Campos's office number, identified myself to the receptionist, and was told he was unavailable. I called back every two minutes. On the fifth try, she decided it would be all right to transfer me to his cell.

"Campos."

"Hey, Julian. Danny Beckett, here. LBPD Homicide. Remember me?"

"Yes." I thought I could hear traces of annoyance in his voice, but that might have been wishful thinking. "What can I do for you?"

"A couple of things. First, we're going to need to talk to Bradley Benton today."

"I'm not sure that will be possible."

"Why not?"

"He's having a very difficult time. His doctor has medicated him very heavily. It doesn't seem he'll be up to seeing anyone today."

"How about the rest of the family?" Now it was my turn to try not to sound annoyed.

"That's certainly more of a possibility."

"The chief and Media Relations have scheduled a press conference for ten a.m. The congressman and any other members of his family are certainly welcome to attend."

"Yes, we've been informed. Mr. Benton's father and mother will both be in attendance."

I wasn't surprised. The chief's office had probably cleared it with the family before they bothered to tell us. You get even more perks for being a congressman than you do for being just plain rich.

"Perhaps we could speak to them briefly afterward."

"I'm certain we can arrange something."

To nearly everyone's surprise, the congressman was, in fact, able to pass up an opportunity to make a speech. He didn't even make an appearance on the platform with the chief and the rest of us. He sat in the back of the room with his wife, Campos, and a small entourage. I kept my eyes on him for most of the duration of the press conference. He was wearing a dark suit, his hair was coifed in perfect anchorman fashion, and he seemed to be holding up well. I wondered how strong a wind would be required to dislodge it. His wife, Margaret, was taking it much harder. Even with the obvious face work and Botox, the grief still found its way into her expression. As the talking heads spoke, she closed her eyes, and her lips tightened into a subtle grimace that seemed her only defense against an overwhelming emotional onslaught. Even from thirty feet away, I could see her pain.

First the chief and then Captain Hemmings from Media Relations made vague and general statements about the crime; then they took questions from the press, which they answered with more vague and general statements. It all amounted to them saying we don't really know anything and maybe we'll tell you something when we do. Maybe.

Ruiz thought it best to give as much of the appearance of preferential treatment to the senior Mr. Benton as possible, so he arranged for the interview to be held in the administrative conference room on the sixth floor. That's the one in which the chief and his deputies gather to hatch their plans for world domination. There's a lot of teak.

Jen and I were already seated at the large table when Ruiz and DC Baxter escorted Congressman and Mrs. Benton and Julian Campos into the room, followed by a bald man with a shiny head and a much younger woman who seemed to be burdened more by the proceedings than anyone else in the entourage. The lieutenant led the congressman to the seat at the head of the table, and the politician sat there without an apparent thought about it. The deputy chief made the introductions. The two we hadn't seen before were Roger Kroll and Molly Fields, the congressman's chief of staff and his assistant.

Jen began. "We can't begin to express how sorry we are for your loss."

The congressman said, "Thank you."

It was a foregone conclusion that Jen would take the lead in the interview. She has a way of conveying empathy that I am never able to manage. And we'd been ordered by Baxter to use the utmost sensitivity with the Bentons. He'd sighed with relief when Ruiz had told him who'd be asking most of the questions.

"We know this is very difficult," Jen said. "Can either of you think of anyone who might have wanted to harm Sara or the children?"

The congressman said, "I thought this was a home-invasion robbery. That it was random. Are you saying it's something else?"

"No, sir," Jen said. "We just need to consider everything at this point. There is some evidence to suggest robbery as the motive, but it's not conclusive. So we need to look at every possibility."

"Why would anyone want to hurt Sara or the children?" Mrs. Benton asked.

"No one would," her husband said. "At least no one I can imagine."

Jen went on. "I know your son is an attorney. What type of law does he practice?"

"He used to do contracts. Now he's consulting with a lobbying firm in Washington. That's why he was away when it happened."

"How much time was he spending away from home?"

"One or two weeks a month. He still has an office here in Long Beach that he works out of the rest of the time."

"Do you think it's possible that someone might have wanted to hurt him through his wife and children?"

"Well," the congressman said, shaking his head, "politics can be pretty vicious, but I can't imagine anything like this." He seemed to get lost in his own thoughts for a moment. "No," he said finally, "not like this."

Jen shifted her body slightly to be more inclusive of the congressman's wife. "Do either of you know Catherine Catanio?"

"Yes," Mrs. Benton said. "She was Sara's maid of honor. They've been friends since college. Why?"

Just to feel useful, I answered her question. "They were going to have lunch yesterday." For some reason, that statement triggered her tears, and she tugged a tissue from the box on the table in front of her.

Jen let her have a few seconds to compose herself, then asked, "How were Brad and Sara doing?"

"What do you mean?" Mrs. Benton asked.

"Well," Jen said, "he'd been away a lot." She offered a slight smile and made sure there was nothing harsh or accusatory in her tone. "Was that, or anything else, causing any strain or stress in their relationship?"

"Neither one of them was too happy about him being out of town so much," Mrs. Benton said, "but neither of them thought it was a long-term situation. And I can't think of anything else. Sara seemed so happy the last time I talked to her. She was excited about being back in school, and the kids were doing so well." Her voice trailed off as she reached for another tissue.

Congressman Benton continued for her. "Brad told me—in confidence, of course—that they were even thinking about another baby." He rubbed at his eyes and cleared his throat. "Excuse me," he said.

"You said Sara was back in school?" I asked. "Yes," Mrs. Benton said. "She's working on a master's degree in art history. It's something she's been wanting to do for quite a while. She just started in the fall."

Jen asked a few more questions, but we both knew we'd gotten all we would from them for a while. We thanked them for their time and once again offered our condolences. The deputy chief escorted them out of the room.

"Any insights?" Ruiz asked.

I shook my head and looked out the window. The sky was the crisp and clear Southern California blue we usually only see the day after a winter storm. But it hadn't rained in weeks.

Five

"**G**OT SOMETHING FOR YOU," MARTY SAID AS WE CAME back into the squad.

"Something good?" I asked.

"Nothing earth-shattering, but it might be useful." He flipped open his notebook and went on. "On the canvass, we came up with two people who spotted a white van in the neighborhood. This morning, we got a confirmation from Criminalistics. There was some dirty water in the gutter outside the Bentons' driveway. Left a tread pattern when they drove through it. Matches the OEM tires on a GMC commercial van from '02 through '05. No plates or anything else, but it's something."

Jen asked, "They get enough of a print to match the tire?"

"Maybe," Marty said.

"Got to be stolen or rented," I said.

"Dave's downstairs now checking with Auto Theft."

"Good," Jen said. "Maybe we'll catch a break."

―――――――― ⸰ ――――――――

We parked an unmarked department cruiser in the beach lot on the peninsula across from Naples Island and ate chicken tacos from Cocoreno's. The February crowd was sparse, and the day was beautiful. For a moment, I thought of how nice it would be to take the afternoon off and just watch the sunlight play on the waves. Then I felt a twinge of pain in my forearm and got back to business.

I couldn't be sure, but I thought Jen noticed me noticing my pain. Her expression changed, and I thought I saw a flicker of concern in her eyes. There must have been something I wasn't aware of in my voice or body language that she was picking up on.

"Find out anything about Catherine Catanio?" I asked.

"Teaches art history at Cal State. According to the university website, she's published a bunch of stuff about Picasso. She's up on her cubism."

"That's pointy people with two eyes on one side of their head, right?"

"Could be. There weren't any pictures."

"Just so you know, I was going to make a crack about her being abstract, but it was too lame, even for me."

"There are cracks that are too lame for you?"

I let her have the point. I didn't have a comeback.

With more than thirty-five thousand students, California State University, Long Beach, is one of the largest institutions of higher learning in the state. It's also my alma mater. I graduated with a double major in criminal justice and English. My father was an LA deputy sheriff who died in the line of duty when I was still young enough to believe in giant-killers. From the time I was six years old, I knew that I would be a cop when I grew up. My mother hated the idea. She told me my father's only wish for his sons was that they never went into law enforcement. So when it came time to decide about college, I picked one subject for myself and one for her. She's still hoping I'll someday wind up teaching poetry to teenagers.

Aside from the ginormous blue pyramid visible from the 405 freeway a mile to the north that housed most of the school's athletic events, and the two new science buildings perched on the hillside of the upper campus, things looked pretty much the same as they had when I graduated way back in the last millennium.

The students, at least, had fewer mullets.

As a courtesy, we checked in with the university police. They gave us a parking pass and a token that would let us through the security gate into one of the staff lots. There weren't any open spots in the lot they'd told us to park in, so we did laps up and down the lanes waiting for someone to leave. It took about twenty minutes for a tweedy-looking fellow to back his Prius out of a nice shady spot under a eucalyptus tree.

The faculty offices for the art department were in a row of aged two-story metal-and-stucco rectangles tucked along the east edge of the campus behind the larger buildings that housed the classrooms, studios, galleries, and workshops. We climbed an exterior staircase with a wobbly railing and found FO4 203. The door was open. We'd called ahead.

"Professor Catanio?" I asked.

"You must be Detective Beckett," she said.

I told her who I was and introduced Jen. The office was small and filled with furniture even older than what we had downtown. The carpeting was rust colored and worn smooth in spots by years of use. The paint was fresh, though, and the art on the walls livened up the atmosphere. I assumed it was good, but there weren't any starry nights or water lilies or little angsty guys with their hands on their ears, so I wasn't able to tell for sure.

She gestured to two steel-and-vinyl chairs across from her desk. "Please," she said. Either force of habit or simple politeness compelled her to say, "It's nice to meet you." Of course it wasn't. It's a very rare thing when it's actually a nice thing to meet two homicide detectives. At least she'd heard about the deaths from the Benton family, so we were spared the difficulty of the notification.

I said it for both of us. "We're very sorry for your loss."

"Thank you." She didn't look like an art professor. At least not what I'd expected an art professor to look like—no nose ring, or black turtleneck, or indoor sunglasses. Maybe art history was different. She was wearing khaki pants and a pale-yellow sweater, and she had her brown hair pulled back into a ponytail. I made her for midthirties, but sadness and the circles under her eyes might have been adding some years. Sara Benton had been thirty-three.

"Professor Catanio," Jen began, "you knew Sara well?"

"Please, call me Catherine," she said, as if she found the formality embarrassing.

"Catherine," I said, softening my voice. "You and Sara were very close?"

She nodded. "Since college. We both majored in art history at UCI. Took a year off after graduation and went to Europe to see the great art. We couldn't believe we were both accepted into the graduate program at Irvine." It was clear she was relishing the memories, but her voice dropped as she continued. "But she met Brad and quit school. I went straight through the PhD, and here we are." She tried a smile, but it didn't quite take.

"She was coming back to school, though," I said.

"Yes." Catherine paused a moment. "She thought I got her into the grad program here. I'm not even on the committee." She shook her head. "She never really believed in herself like she should have. There was never a doubt she'd get in here. I encouraged her to go to UCI or UCLA and go for her doctorate. She insisted on starting smaller."

Jen said, "Why did she decide to go back now?"

"A few reasons, I think. The kids were getting older. Jacob started preschool. Mostly, though, I think she really needed something that was just hers."

"How do you mean?" I asked.

"Well, you know how Brad is."

Neither Jen nor I really did know how Brad was, but we let her go on.

"Everything in their lives has been about him for so long I think she felt like she was getting lost. I don't know how she managed as long as she did. He was the star, the congressman's son, the up-and-comer. She needed something that wasn't part of the Bradley Benton the Third show."

I said, "You don't sound like you're a fan."

She looked from me to Jen and back to me again, and for the first time since we'd sat down, I saw the teacher in her. In three seconds, she evaluated us and made a decision that transformed her expression. The pain and sadness that had seemed permanently imprinted there vanished and were replaced with something new and raw. Anger.

"Brad wanted a trophy wife. Sara was too good for that. But he never saw it. He never respected her. I'm not even sure he ever loved her."

Whoa.

"Why do you say that?" Jen asked.

She didn't answer right away. We waited.

"Well, aside from his attitude," she said, weighing her words carefully as she spoke, "he cheated on her. More than once."

Ding, ding, ding.

"You say cheated," Jen said. "Past tense?"

"As far as Sara knew. He swore he'd stopped. But there had been at least three affairs. Probably more." There was a kind of satisfaction in her voice. She was grieving her friend, but she was also glad to be nailing Brad to the wall.

"Do you know with whom?" I asked.

"Two were women he worked with. I don't know their names. But the third time was with one of their former nannies. The first one they'd hired after Bailey was born. She worked for them for two years. And she worked him for almost that long."

I said, "Do you remember her name?"

"Michelle something. I don't think I ever knew the last name."

Jen and I both made notes, and I knew she was wondering the same thing I was—had Bradley ever tried to put the moves on Joely?

"But he stopped cheating?" I asked.

"He said he did," Catherine said. "And Sara believed him."

"Did you?" Jen asked.

"No. But I never believed much of anything that Brad had to say. I made him for a politician the first time I met him, and he hasn't ever done anything to change that opinion."

Jen asked, "What did Sara see in him?"

"He can be charming when he cares to. It took her a long time to see through that."

"But she did," I said, "see through it."

"Not until after Bailey was born."

"She stayed with him for the kids," Jen said.

"Yes. She thought it would be better for them. That she and Brad could work things out. As romantic as she was, she had a pragmatic side, too. She saw a better future for the kids with him than without him. She was willing to sacrifice."

"Sounds noble," I said. "Did she ever cheat on him?"

I thought I noticed a slight hesitation before she spoke, but I might have been mistaken. If it was there, it was subtle.

"No. And she was noble. That's not a word I use very often, but she's probably the noblest person I know."

"That's high praise." Jen made a quick note in her book.

"Then again," Catherine said, "I suppose it didn't hurt that he's good-looking and rich." She finally managed that smile, but it was so sardonic and bitter it almost made me wince.

———————— , ————————

"See," I said on our way back to the car, "told you he was a douchebag."

"It's a long way from douchebag to murderer." She thought about that for a dozen or so steps. "You really like him for this?"

"I don't know. We might get an idea if they ever let us talk to him. Maybe we should front Campos again."

"Couldn't hurt."

In the passenger seat of the Crown Vic, I hit REDIAL on my cell. "Detective Danny Beckett for Julian Campos." His assistant told me he was in a meeting, and I asked her to have him call me. "At least his secretary's getting sick of me."

"Well," Jen said, "we take what we can get."

We took Seventh Street back toward downtown. As we got close to the public golf course at Recreation Park, I saw a few FOR SALE signs on the residential side streets.

"Got some houses for sale. Want to take a look?"

"Alamitos Heights is a bit out of my price range," she said.

"Let's just drive around the block and check it out."

She turned left on Terraine Avenue, and the first sign we saw was in front of a huge colonial-style house that seemed both too big and too grandiose for the neighborhood. The real estate agent's sign in the front lawn had flyers in a plastic flip-top box mounted on the post.

I told Jen to pull over.

"No way."

"Come on."

"There's no way I'm even looking at that."

"I know. I just want to see."

She gave up and pulled over to the curb. I hopped out of the car and grabbed a flyer.

"Five bedrooms. Four and a half baths. Open kitchen and great room. Swimming pool and large landscaped—"

I hadn't come close to finishing reading the glossy flyer when she interrupted me. "How much?"

"You're missing the point. You can't put a price tag on"—I looked down at the brochure to make sure I got the phrasing just right—"'luxury living at its finest.'"

"How much?"

"Two million, four hundred fifty thousand."

"I knew I shouldn't have told you until I actually found something."

"No, come on. I can help. I'll be good at this."

She gave me one more wary glance at the stop sign on Sixth and Havana before looping back up to Seventh and our route back downtown.

Seven

"**N**O BIG SURPRISES," PAULA SAID TO JEN AND ME, LOOK-ing down at her clipboard over the top edge of her glasses. Carter had called it correctly at the crime scene. Sara had died of blood loss, although she had a subdural hematoma that would have done the job itself if she hadn't bled out first. Bailey and Jacob had died of gunshot wounds. "There is some good news," she continued. "Sara fought back. We found skin under her nails—enough for a DNA match of at least one of the suspects. We'll run it." Theoretically, at least, if a match were found, it could break the case and give us one or both of our murderers. With even the highest priority, though, the lab's backlog would mean waiting weeks or even months for the results. I'd worked on a dozen cases in which the suspect was already convicted by the time the DNA came back. Still, the results could help us to confirm or eliminate suspects we came up with through other leads. The latter was the most likely. Even on a high-profile case like the Bentons', we knew we'd have a long wait on our hands.

But still, things were moving.

It was a simple and straightforward autopsy report. It had seemed that way as we watched. Often, Paula would explain things we'd had no hint of during the procedure. Not this time. The bodies still lay covered on three parallel tables, Sara on the far left, then Bailey, then Jacob. Their shapes under the clean white sheets troubled me more than most of the victims that I had seen. The smallness of the children's outlines on the large tables left a knot in my stomach. "Thanks, Paula," Jen said. She watched me stare at the bodies. "Ready?"

"Not quite." I stepped in next to Sara and turned down the sheet to expose her face. Then I did the same for each of the children. They were purple white in the fluorescent glare. Sara's face was bruised and swollen, but Bailey and Jacob looked surprisingly peaceful. Troublingly so, in fact. A sharp pain ran up my arm, and the air-conditioning felt suddenly too cold.

———————— · ————————

During one of my sessions with the pain psychologist, I had said, "Sometimes it seems like I just can't get out of my own head." She'd nodded in understanding.

Jen drove as we left the morgue and headed back down the 110 to the squad. I looked out the window. The bright sun reflected off of an Infiniti in the next lane, and I squinted behind my sunglasses.

"What's up?" Jen asked.

I thought again of telling her about my previous night's epiphany, about my temporary escape from the pain, but I was still afraid to speak of it out loud, as if giving voice to the experience might break the spell. Undo the magic. I needed to see if I could find that place again. Something in me resisted, but I forced my mind back to the autopsy room and to the faces of Sara Benton and her children. The more I focused on them, the less I focused on myself.

"I'm trying to get out of my head," I said.

She looked like she understood what I meant, but she didn't say anything more.

———————— · ————————

"This is Special Agent Young," the feeb said, "and I'm Special Agent Goodman." We were all in the lieutenant's office: Ruiz, the two feds, Jen, and me. There weren't enough chairs, so we stood in a loose circle around the desk. We exchanged handshakes.

"The bureau's here at the request of the congressman," Ruiz said.

"That's right," Goodman said. He was the older of the two—midforties, maybe—with a bit of gray at the temples. But aside from the age difference, the two agents might have been brothers—both had solid frames, an inch or so over six feet, strong jaws, medium-brown hair, brown eyes, and a general all-around white-breadiness. But then again, all feds look alike to me. "Congressman Benton's asking that you keep us in the loop in terms of your investigation."

"Must be nice to have connections," I said. Ruiz and Jen both shot me disapproving looks, but Goodman's demeanor was all warmth and reassurance.

"I know how it must sound, Detective," he said. "But I want you to know we have no intention of interfering here or stepping on any toes. We just want you to provide as much information as is prudent. You can understand the congressman's position, can't you? He's not used to feeling powerless, and this situation has him tied in knots. He needs to feel like he's involved in some way, and that's why we're reaching out and asking for your help."

I wasn't used to that kind of candor from representatives of federal law enforcement agencies, and I almost regretted my snide comment.

Goodman was slick. I didn't know what to say, but Ruiz didn't wait. "Of course we'll be happy to give you anything we can," he said, matching Goodman in feigned sincerity. "Danny, Jen, why don't you take the agents to the conference room and fill them in on the details?"

"Sure thing," Jen said.

I seemed to be the only one lacking the requisite cordiality. One more thing to work on.

―――――― · ――――――

Half an hour later, we'd run down every significant detail of the case. Since we were also handing over copies of all of our reports, we didn't give them anything they couldn't have read for themselves. The satisfaction of holding out on sharing our own hunches and suspicions was limited by the fact that we didn't really have any to keep to ourselves. Well, none aside from my virtual certainty that Bradley Benton III was a colossal dick. And I wasn't ready to share that with one of Daddy's lapdogs. Not yet, anyway.

"That's everything we have with any apparent aesthetic value."

"Aesthetic value?" Special Agent Goodman asked.

"Long story," Jen said.

"Thank you." He extended his hand. "We appreciate your help."

"You're welcome," Jen said, shaking his hand.

"Special Agent Young," I said. He gave me a quizzical nod, which I returned.

After they left, I asked Jen, "Why do you suppose they call all FBI agents 'special'?"

―――――― · ――――――

"Julian Campos, please."

"Just a moment, Detective."

"Detective Beckett?"

"That's me, Julian."

"How many times is this today?"

"More than a few, less than a lot."

"I think we might define our terms differently."

"Maybe so."

"What can I do for you?"

"I assume Mr. Benton the younger is still incapable of speech?"

"Just as he was an hour and a half ago."

"Figured as much. But I have a question for him."

"I can attempt to pass it on. Of course, I can't guarantee anything."

"Of course."

"What's your question?"

"We need to know what was in the safe."

"Ah."

"Yeah. 'Ah.' Can you run that by your client between the sedatives?"

"Detective, I'm not certain I appreciate your tone."

"I'm fairly sure you don't. I'll see what I can do about that."

"Do. And I'll ask Bradley your question and get back to you."

"Or you can just tell me when I call back in an hour."

It was after five when Jen and I sat at our desks and reviewed the case. We talked through the few concrete facts we had so far, attempting to reinterpret the details in such a way that something might break free and emerge as a relevant piece of information.

Nothing did.

"So I guess we're waiting," Jen said. She was right. We were. Waiting for ballistics, for the interview with Benton, for the GMC van, for anything.

In my left hand, I squeezed the racquetball I keep next to my phone. My physical therapist told me it was beneficial for my injury, but I also find it a good way to pass the time while I am thinking. I just have to remind myself to switch hands every now and again so I don't wind up looking like a left-handed professional bowler.

"What do you think?" she asked.

"I think you should hang it up for today."

"Just me?"

"You've got your thing, don't you?"

Jen has a third-degree black belt in aikido and volunteers as a teacher in a city program for at-risk youth. I once saw her give a demonstration to a group of teenage gangbangers and wannabes from some of the poorest areas of Long Beach. She held up a PR 24 side-handle baton in one hand and a hundred-dollar bill in the other, promising the money to anyone who could hit her with the nightstick. Half a dozen of them lined up to take their shot. Each and every one wound up pinned facedown on the mat, hoping she'd stop before breaking bones. The only thing she did break was the C-note, buying me fish and chips for lunch at E. J. Malloy's.

She's studied enough Shotokan to break bricks, too. I know she could kick my ass without raising her heart rate.

"Isn't this a big one?" I asked.

"It is. Hector's testing for his brown belt tonight."

He'd been one of her first students, and one of her proudest achievements. He was the first of his three brothers to stay out of the East Side Longos.

"How long has it been?"

"Almost since the beginning. Four years."

"Think he'll make it?"

"I hope so." She shut down her computer, turned off her desk lamp, and picked up her bag. "Don't work too late," she said.

"I won't. Have a good time."

Patrick called it a day soon after. As he left, he handed me a Post-it note that read, BAILEY0426.

"What's this?"

"Sara's password."

"Password? For what?"

"Facebook, Gmail, and just about everything else, it looks like."

"Bailey's birthday," I said. I'd had to type it into forms several times already in the course of the investigation.

"Yeah. Bad enough to use such a predictable password. But to use it for everything?" He looked at me and thought he saw something. "Danny, you don't use the same password for everything, do you?"

"Of course not."

He didn't look like he believed me.

I knew we'd probably have to comb through Sara's e-mail at some point, but I decided to look first at her Facebook page. I'd only been out on sick leave for a bit over a year, but in that time, dissecting a victim's Facebook page had gone from being something you did when you started running out of things to do to one of the first steps in building a victimology.

I opened up Sara Gardener-Benton's account and started with the basics. Under her name it said, *Went to Marina High School * Lives in Long Beach, California * Married to Bradley Benton III * Born on November 24.* Bradley's name wasn't highlighted. No page for him. Did that mean the rumors about him running for office were true and he didn't want any drunken exploits from his college days showing up online? Or just that he'd managed to avoid being bitten by the social media bug infecting just about everybody else? Her privacy settings were set to the highest levels, which I found, for some inexplicable reason, to be reassuring.

On Sara's profile page, I discovered she liked the music of Neko Case and Wilco, listed her political views as moderate, her favorite quotation as "You're gonna need a bigger boat," and when it came to TV, preferred *Arrested Development.* So aside from the questionable politics, she had good taste.

I clicked on her Friends list. She had 172 of them. Aside from several family members whose names had come up so far in the investigation, only Catherine Catanio's name rang any bells. We might need to dig deeper into the list at a later point, but for now, we could leave it.

There were more than two hundred photos and two dozen videos. I didn't look at all of them, but from my cursory examination, it appeared that they were more or less the same files as those stored on her computer and phone. Again, something we might need to investigate in more detail later.

I spent a few more minutes examining Sara's Wall. Fortunately, she wasn't a prolific poster, and her status updates tended toward the straightforward: *Sara Gardener-Benton is hoping her sweeties get well soon. Sara Gardener-Benton is wishing she picked up the Costco lasagna instead of making it from scratch.* Going back a few days, I found one gem: Black Swan *Best Actress? WTF?*

I kept poking around for a while, but without going deep and doing a comparison with the other case materials—a task that would take a very long time to complete—I wasn't going to find out much more about Sara.

Logging off, I thought about Jen. It was ten minutes after eight. I wondered if she'd think that I'd worked too late.

———————— · ————————

I picked up a six-pack of Sam Adams at Ralphs, parked my car at home, and walked six blocks to Harlan Gibbs's house. He was an LA County deputy sheriff who'd retired after thirty-five years on the job. We'd met the previous year during the case on which I'd nearly lost my hand. He'd lived across the street from the victim, a high-school English teacher with whom he'd formed a fatherly bond. Her loss was a hard one for him to bear, and I'd taken to visiting him every week or two for lunch or an evening drink.

I rounded the corner and saw him sitting on his front porch, the fringe of thin white hair around his bald head backlit by the bare hundred-watt bulb next to the door. He raised a hand in greeting as I crossed the lawn.

"Harlan," I said, "good to see you."

"Saw you on the news today."

"Yeah?" I sat down in the empty white plastic chair next to him.

"Yeah. You did a real nice job of standing there behind all the important people." He didn't smile, but there was a hint of playfulness in the gravel of his voice.

"Least I'm on the job. Could just be spending all my time sitting on the porch and spying on the neighbors."

"You just go ahead and make fun. We haven't had a crime on this street since…" His voice trailed off, and I knew we were both thinking about Elizabeth Anne Williams.

We gave her a moment of silence.

"Who's renting the place now?"

"Nice young couple. Just had a baby. They won't be there long, though. They'll need another bedroom." The guesthouse Beth had lived in had only one.

"I ran into her sister a few weeks ago."

"The lesbian?"

"Yeah. She's doing well. Their mother moved out here. Got a little house up by City College. They're picking up the pieces."

We were quiet a while. Harlan opened two beers and passed one of the bottles to me. I wondered what he was thinking. Was he picking up the pieces? How much time did he spend sitting on the porch and staring at her house? But who was I to be critical? How many sleepless nights had I spent thinking about Beth? And I hadn't even known her. Not while she was alive.

"I wasn't going to say anything," he said, looking off into the distance. I tried to follow his gaze, but I was unable to tell where it fell, if anywhere at all. He didn't finish the thought, and I didn't push him to.

So we sat. I didn't check my watch, but it seemed like a long time.

Finally, he spoke. "Went to the doctor last week."

Uh-oh.

"Been having stomach problems."

"You mentioned that the last time I was here."

"Yeah. It's been getting worse."

"What did the doctor say?"

"Says I have a 'mass.'"

"What does that mean?"

"Means I see the oncologist tomorrow."

Shit. "You want some company?"

"Got some. Cynthia's coming in from Ontario."

I'd never met his daughter, and he didn't talk about her often. My impression had always been that he cared deeply about her but that their relationship was distant and maybe more strained than he would have liked.

I didn't know what to say. So I settled for "Fuck."

"Yeah."

Another long silence. A cricket started chirping somewhere on the side of his house. Pinpricks of pain climbed my arm.

"You worked Homicide," I said.

"For a bit, yes."

"Then you know what I'm about to say isn't bullshit. It's just going to sound like it is." Every death investigator I have ever known has uttered the phrase "I'm sorry for your loss," or some variation of it, literally more times than they can count. It sounds trite and clichéd and insincere. The truth is that it is rarely any of these things. It is virtually always said with honesty and earnestness. We say nothing more because the sentiments we want to express can't be given voice. Words simply can't capture them in any meaningful or satisfactory way. So I hoped he understood when I said, "I'm sorry."

"I know, Dan." The corners of his eyes wrinkled when he spoke. "You didn't even need to preface it."

Nine

As soon as I left Harlan, the pain worsened. The sharp, needling sensation began in my palm and shot up my arm and into my shoulder and neck. I stretched as I walked, pulling my left hand this way and that, rolling my shoulder to the front and back, angling and twisting my head from side to side. Other than making me look odd, it didn't accomplish much.

At home, I stood in the kitchen and held the Vicodin bottle in my hand. I'd only had two beers at Harlan's. (Two beers really isn't that much, is it? No, two beers is nothing at all. Doesn't even count, really.) I thumbed open the bottle and shook two pills into my hand. They were white and oblong, and when I held one up to the light, I could read its name spelled out on one side. The other side had one of those little lines for cutting it in half. I couldn't imagine many people wanting to do that.

I put the pills back into the bottle, screwed on the childproof cap, dropped it next to the multivitamins I never take, pulled a shot glass out of the cupboard, and crossed the kitchen to the freezer.

The Grey Goose went down like hot ice. It melted the tension in my stomach, and I felt warm waves radiating out from my center. I poured another and drank it down. Then I did it one more time. Not long after, I took one more glass into the darkened living room and sank into the couch.

For a few moments, the sensation pulled my attention away from the burning ache, and soon, when I began to settle into the drunkenness, I found myself in sort of a middle place between the pain and the inebriation.

The drapes were usually drawn on the picture window in the front of my duplex. That night, though, I'd left them open, and I nursed my glass of vodka and stared at the palm tree across the street in the neighbor's yard. A frond was hanging low and swaying back and forth in the light breeze. I thought if I watched long enough, it might lull me to sleep.

It didn't.

I keep a hydroculator—a kind of hot pack filled with a clay-like substance that's designed to give off moist heat—in a pot of water on my stove. It has to stay wet all the time. I put it in the microwave for four minutes, wrapped it in a kitchen towel, took it into the living room, and slung it over my shoulder, high on my neck, as I reclined on the sofa. If the scalding sensation didn't exactly relieve the pain, at least it made it feel different.

I knew sleep wouldn't come easy, but a few hours later, I tried going to bed. Over the years that I've suffered from insomnia, I've taught myself to relax in bed, even when I can't sleep. It doesn't always work, but most nights, I manage to lie there, breathe deeply, calm myself, turn down the volume on most of the anxieties and neuroses that bounce around the inside my head, and actually get some small amount of rest. In all honesty, sometimes I feel better after these nights than after one of my fitful and dream-filled nights of sleep. Like so much else, it's a crapshoot.

I knew shortly after my head hit the pillow, though, that it wouldn't be a peaceful night. After an hour of tossing and turning and thinking about things I didn't want to think about, I got out of bed. I watched the last three-quarters of Craig Ferguson, about an hour of CNN, and then tried to find something interesting to read. Waiting on the coffee table was the previous week's *New Yorker*, unread except for the cartoon, which I always read as soon as the magazine arrived, saving the articles for nights like these. Sometimes I even got desperate enough to read the short fiction.

Seymour Hersh had a new piece that filled an hour or so; then I skimmed some of the other articles, then gave up on reading altogether and worked on an iTunes mix I'd been making for Jen. I hadn't given her a new one since I'd been back at work, but I couldn't decide whether Sparklehorse's "Painbirds" should be the first track or the last. Sooner or later, I'd figure it out.

When there were less than three hours left until I'd have to get up to start the day, I turned off the lights, turned on the radio to *Morning Edition* for a bit of background sound, and went back to bed. I was able to keep my eyes closed for most of the time.

The next day, Jen had to testify in court on a gang killing that had occurred when I'd been out on sick leave. While I was working on my own, the plan was for me to coordinate the statements from the canvass that Marty, Dave, and the uniforms had conducted, go deeper into the victimology, arrange a few more interviews, and try to look for common threads in the various bits of evidence we'd acquired so far.

Before I got to any of that, though, I decided to spend a bit of time online researching the congressman. When I thought about it, I realized I knew quite a bit less about him than it seemed like I had. Aside from recalling a minor financial scandal from a few years earlier, I couldn't really think of anything specific about him.

The first thing I discovered was how fucked up the gerrymandered congressional district lines are in Long Beach. I knew the city was divided turf, represented by two different people, but I'd never looked at just where the dividing line was. Benton's district, the 46th, was shaped like a dumbbell in an old cartoon, with one of the larger ends encompassing the Palos Verdes Peninsula and the other Huntington Beach, Newport, and Fountain Valley areas. Through most of Long Beach, the dividing line was only two or three blocks from the ocean, separating those who could afford million- and multimillion-dollar homes from everyone else. The part of the city north of the district line shared representation with Carson and Compton, two towns on the opposite end of the socioeconomic spectrum. It made me think of the crime and gang activity maps that frequently circulated around the department. Guess which side of the line got the most ink on those.

I tried not to let any of this prejudice my opinion of the congressman. As I visited the different pages on his website, I kept reminding myself that he wasn't necessarily a bigger fuckhole than anyone else in Congress. He toed the party line on every major issue—health care, global warming, immigration. The only thing that really surprised me was that nothing surprised me.

The bio was brief and uninformative. Southern California native. Grew up on the beach. College. Air force. Law school. Family. Blah, blah, blah.

Truth be told, though, I didn't expect the Twitter feed that told me @RepBenton had not only been to Home Depot recently but would "speak soon on House floor about Reagan on the centennial of his birth CSPAN" and that I should "take a moment to sign up for the House Natural Resources Committee's weekly e-mail newsletter—new edition today!"

But was any of this relevant to the case? I needed to find out more about the congressman's son to figure that out. So far, I didn't have anything solid on his background. The rumor was that he was being groomed to follow in his father's footsteps, but there weren't enough "Bradley Benton III" Google hits for me to make the same sort of half-assed assumptions I was making about his father.

I knew Patrick would be doing online background for everyone of interest in the case. His history in Computer Crimes made him the squad's go-to person for any kind of Internet research. Nobody I knew was better than he at finding every rock that could be looked under. After all, it had only taken him ten minutes to figure out Sara's Facebook password.

Not wanting to cover the same ground he would be going over, I called Patrick. He didn't answer his cell, though, so I left a message.

I stopped Googling and opened Marty's notes on the canvass. There were only half a dozen with any substance at all, and aside from the van, none shared any common details.

I decided to let that go for the time being and see if I could find out about Bradley. I wanted to find out just what the official story was on Bradley's political aspirations was.

"Roger Kroll's office," the young woman who answered the phone said.

I identified myself and asked, "Is this Molly? Molly Fields?"

"Yes, Detective, it is." She sounded surprised. At her place in the pecking order, she probably wasn't used to people remembering her name. "How can I help you?"

I thought about asking for Kroll as I had intended, but I figured Molly would know the story as well as anyone and be more forthcoming with additional details.

"I wanted to ask you about some things I've been hearing in some of the news reports."

"Okay." There was an edge of uncertainty in her voice that I hoped might work to my advantage.

"Well, I've heard a few reporters mention that Bradley is thinking about running for office himself. They've been mentioning the thirty-seventh district. Is he planning to run?"

With a practiced confidence, she said, "The congressman and his son are exploring options in that regard."

"That means yes, doesn't it, Molly?"

"Well…"

"It's okay, Molly. I'm not the media. Whatever you tell me is just between us. I promise you that."

"Yes, he was planning to run. Now, though, nobody seems to know what's going to happen."

"That's understandable. Things have changed. Bradley seems to be struggling very much with everything that's happened."

Molly didn't say anything in response to that.

"Just one more question," I said. "Would he get your vote?"

There was just enough hesitation to confirm my suspicion. If I hadn't been listening for it, I would have believed her when she said, "Of course."

Then, just for grins, I called Campos again.

———————— , ————————

Fortunately, the trial that Jen was testifying on was in Long Beach, where the courthouse was just across the street from the police station, so we met for lunch in the squad room. Marty had been out most of the morning following up on the canvass, and on his way back, he brought us take-out sandwiches from Modica's Deli. Pastrami for me, mozzarella veggie for Jen, and turkey for himself.

As he unloaded the bag, Jen asked if there were any developments in the case.

"Nothing so far," I said. "I learned a bit about Congressman Benton, but probably nothing relevant. I am following him on Twitter, though."

"You thinking there's some political angle?" Marty asked.

"Not necessarily." I unwrapped my sandwich. The grease from the meat had seeped through the paper along the edges.

The hunger didn't really hit me until the smell did, and the first bite tasted every bit as good as I had expected. "But we don't want to rule anything out."

"A political conspiracy?" Marty said. "You do know that Lee Harvey Oswald acted alone, right?"

"Not according to James Ellroy and Oliver Stone," I said.

"I stand corrected," Marty said. Then he tore into his sandwich.

"How's the trial going?" I asked Jen.

"It's not. Not yet, anyway," she said. "They didn't even get to me. Sat around all morning. Waiting."

I didn't know much about the case. Only that it was another Asian Boyz gang murder. It occurred to me that it was sad that I felt like I didn't need to know any more about it.

———————— , ————————

Late that afternoon, I had an appointment with my physical therapist. Her name is Brookes Little, which I always find amusing because she stands an even six feet tall. I've never mentioned it, though, because I'm afraid she would hurt me.

"How are you, Danny?"

I like answering that question for her because she is one of the very few people who seems like she is hoping for an honest answer when she asks it.

"Better, a bit." I wasn't sure how much to share with her. "I think going back to work is going to be good for the pain."

"Good. I'm glad to hear it."

I spent forty-five minutes on her table, and she stretched and contorted my arms, shoulders, and neck in ways that still surprised me, even after nine months. Then she had me demonstrate several of the daily exercises she'd prescribed for me to check my form.

"Have you thought any more about getting a guitar?"

"I suppose I could get one."

She'd first made the suggestion several weeks earlier, and it was becoming clear that she wouldn't be letting up. I knew her husband was a musician of some kind. Maybe that had something to do with her enthusiasm. "I just can't imagine myself playing. I'm not very musical."

"You'll play it."

"What makes you so confident?"

"Because you always do what I tell you to. You're good that way. Get the guitar. It'll improve your hand strength and dexterity."

"Okay."

"Don't just say okay and then not do it again."

"Okay."

———————— , ————————

After my appointment, I took a drive to the congressman's neighborhood. Was Bradley really as homebound as Campos kept telling us he was? I didn't have any illusions about how much I might be able to see. But I thought I might be able to get a glimpse of Bradley's car. Even that wouldn't be definitive, but I wanted to see it parked there with my own eyes. That wasn't exactly true. I wanted to see it *not* parked there. I wanted to confirm my suspicions that Bradley was in much better shape than we'd been led to believe. I wanted to be able to call Campos a liar to his face.

I drove up and down the street twice. The gate and the wall obstructed the view from the street completely. There was a chance that if I got out and walked up to the gate I'd be able to get a look inside, but I knew there was a camera on the gate; I'd have no chance at seeing what I wanted to see without someone inside having a chance to see me.

The alley was my best chance. I circled around the block in my Camry and drove up the small lane behind the estate. There was no mistaking the rear of the congressman's property. The wall matched that in the front, down to the swirl pattern in the stucco. The garage actually had its main entrance off the front drive, but its back wall stood only a few yards away from the rear wall of the property. As I had hoped, just past the garage was a service gate. Of course. It just would not do to have caterers and plumbers and other riffraff coming in up the main drive. At the edge of the gate, facing back the way I had come, was a single hooded video camera. It looked quite a bit older and less secretive than that in front. They'd want anyone approaching the back gate to know they were being watched.

I turned left out of the alley and parked on the street two long blocks away from the house. On foot, I went back up the alley. If the camera I had seen really was the only one back there, I would be able to approach the back gate and get a look over the fence without entering its field of view.

The wall was eight feet high, and even though it had been a long time since I'd scaled one like it, it was still relatively easy to take hold of its top edge and pull myself up to get a look. Which I did three times as I got closer to the gate. There was a fairly large concrete area off to the side and out of view of the house, about the size of two or three average suburban driveways. There was nothing in the space at the moment, and the moonlight lit it up in bright contrast to the sliver of yard I was able to see at its far edge.

There was just enough light to make out the passenger side of a Porsche parked in front of the garage.

So he was probably holed up inside.

Unless he caught a ride with someone else. The congressman had to have drivers on call 24/7, right?

As I reached up and put my hands on the sharp edge of brickwork topping the wall to pull myself up again, the folly of what I was doing hit me.

What did I really think I could find out here?

Bradley might be there, and he might not.

Had I thought I might look over the fence and see him in the act of burying the body of some as yet undiscovered victim?

I brushed the grit and dirt off my hands and started back toward my car.

As I approached the mouth of the alley, I heard the sound of a car moving slowly behind.

No lights. Just the tires on the asphalt and the low growl of the engine.

Maintaining my pace, I let my hands float out away from my hips and made sure they were open wide.

The high beams hit me from behind, and I could see the dark emptiness in exactly my shape that they carved into the mist in front of me.

There was only enough time to wonder if I should have drawn my gun and dove for cover before the cruiser's candy bar lit up the alley in flashing red and blue, the tires ground to a stop, and the unit's door opened.

I didn't recognize the uniform's voice, but there was the unmistakable tone of cop in it. "Please stop where you are."

The drill was familiar. In my own uniform days, I'd been on the other end of it hundreds of times. I knew enough to do exactly as I was told. My adrenaline levels had peaked and were beginning to fall; his were still on the rise.

"Turn around slowly."

I did, careful to keep my arms and hands in plain view.

When he saw my face, there was a moment in which I thought he might have recognized me, but I wasn't sure. There was no chance of my recognizing him. The high beams and flashing lights were working exactly as they were supposed to.

"What's your business here, sir?"

"I'm on the job." I gave it a moment to register with him. "Homicide. LBPD."

"What's your name?"

"Beckett."

"ID?"

"Right back pocket. Right underneath my gun."

"Sorry to do this, sir, but would you turn around and place your hands on the back of your head?"

He believed me. It wouldn't have been a question if he didn't.

"Yes, certainly." I heard him approach and stop two feet behind me. He was looking at my gun. Raising my arms would have lifted the bottom edge of my jacket high enough for him to see the muzzle, and it was never too late for something like this to turn into a horrible mistake.

"I'm just going to reach into your pocket for your badge, all right, Detective?"

"Yes, go ahead."

He had to dig a bit to get a grip on the badge holder, but he found it, read it, and said, "I'm sorry, Detective. I just had to be sure."

"No worries. I would have done the same." I wouldn't have needed to, though. By the time I was riding solo, I knew every detective on the Homicide Detail by sight. There was never any doubt for me about where I wanted to end up. I hadn't thought about that hunger in a long time.

"Who put in the call?" I asked.

"I've got it on the screen."

I followed him back to his cruiser, and he got in and moved the laptop mounted to the dash, articulated to a better angle for me to see. It was a name I didn't recognize and an address that wasn't the congressman's.

Had I been in less pain, or even a little less tired, I would have gotten the uniform's name and tried to connect with him for a few minutes. But I didn't. I didn't have it in me. Just told him to have a good night and went back to my car.

It seemed a lot later than it had when I'd gotten there.

―――――――― , ――――――――

"A guitar?" Harlan said. He hadn't mentioned his medical situation, and I hadn't asked.

"Yeah." We were in his living room. I tipped the Sam Adams bottle back and drained the last drops.

"You don't seem like the guitar type."

"That's what I said. She didn't really care, though. I think it's just about the therapeutic value."

"Gonna do it?"

"I don't want to spend the money."

"Never pegged you for a tightwad."

"Who brought the beer?"

He studied me for a few seconds, then got up and went into his bedroom. He came back out with what I first thought was a guitar case. When I got a closer look, though, I could tell it was the wrong shape. Not enough curves. "What's that?" I asked.

"A present." He practically tossed it into my lap, then sat down right where he'd been and picked up his beer. "Open it up."

The case was much heavier than I'd expected. I searched around the edges for the clasps and undid them, one by one. Inside, cradled in dark-blue velvet, was a banjo. It looked like a good one, too. It was made from a dark wood that appeared to be aged mahogany, with mother-of-pearl inlays in the neck and polished brass encircling the round part on the bottom. It was worn from play but obviously well cared for.

"What am I supposed to do with this?" I asked him.

"Play it," he said with a seriousness that surprised me. "For your therapy."

His tone took all the argument out of me.

"I didn't know you played the banjo," I said.

"I don't anymore. Can't do it with the arthritis." That was the first time I'd ever heard him mention that ailment. I thought about questioning him, but I let it go. "If you're not hung up on the guitar, that'll be just as good. Probably even better for the dexterity."

I looked down at the instrument in my lap.

Then back at Harlan.

Then back at the banjo.

I couldn't guess exactly what he made of my expression, but I could tell that, somewhere deep below his stern countenance, he took pleasure in my bafflement.

"What?" he said.

I didn't know what to say. I had no idea what to make of it. I couldn't even recall giving any thought at all to the banjo since my brief teenage fascination with the stand-up comedy stylings of Steve Martin. And perhaps the occasional *Deliverance* reference.

Harlan was enjoying the moment, but I felt like it was a delicate situation nonetheless.

I said the only thing I could think to say. "Thank you."

———————— , ————————

My first estimation of the banjo's weight was about fifteen pounds. By the time I had carried it home, though, I was convinced it was twice that. The pain in my shoulder felt like a dull knife, and it pulsated all the way down my arm. Along the way, I stopped half a dozen times to switch the shoulder strap on my briefcase to the other side and transfer the instrument from one hand to the other. As counterintuitive as it seemed, it was actually more comfortable to carry the load in my left hand. I think the weight helped to stretch some of the tightness and ache away.

At home, I put the case down on the couch in the living room, hung my coat and shoulder holster over the back of one of the chairs at the dining table, then went into the kitchen. I poured myself half a glass of Grey Goose and topped it with orange juice, thought about grabbing something to eat, decided against it, and went back into the dining room. I spread photos, notes, and reports across the table.

I started with their faces.

Sara.

Bailey.

Jacob.

The question was the same one we'd been asking for two days. Why?

We had the missing wall safe as a possible motive for Sara's murder. But why, then, the children? It was hard to believe they'd been murdered to eliminate them as witnesses. But what else was there? The MO matched that theory. But the kids couldn't have testified. They wouldn't have been any threat at all. Didn't the killers know that?

Maybe not. Contrary to what is depicted in popular culture, murder is rarely committed by geniuses, evil or otherwise. Killers are often shrewd but not highly intelligent. Almost all of the time, the simplest explanation is the one that turns out to be the truth.

What was the simplest explanation here?

Thrill killers, just in it for the visceral pleasure provided by extreme violence? Then why not torture the kids?

A heist targeting the floor safe? Why, then, the extremity of what was done to Sara?

Could it have been some combination of the two, as Marty had suggested?

I wound up staying up most of the night searching for other possible theories. There was nothing else viable that I could put together with the evidence at hand. I couldn't make sense of the story. Not yet.

———————— , ————————

My father died when I was five. Among the things he left behind was a garage full of tools. For years after he was gone, I would nail and hammer and saw and generally destroy just about anything

I could get my hands on. For some reason I've never fully understood, I particularly loved sawing wood. Tree limbs, two-by-fours, broken broomsticks. Any scrap I could find, I would clamp in the vise on the workbench and cut. There was one old wood saw that was my favorite. I had no idea of its true age, but when I was a boy, it seemed older than anything I'd ever held in my own hands. Except for the teeth, which were polished to a fine gleam by constant use, the blade was the deep dull gray of aged steel. The handle was worn around the gripping surface, the bare wood itself almost as smooth as the varnish still adorning the corners and sides; and I took particular joy in imagining that it had been my father's hand that had done the rubbing and wearing, and that my own hand was continuing what he had begun. I realize, of course, that the memory of the scent of sawdust, the soreness of my shoulder, and the tremendous sense of accomplishment I would feel as another piece of two-by-four clacked to the cement floor are stand-ins for the real memories I never had the chance to form.

But I still have that saw.

Late that night, after I'd turned the case over in my head as many times and in as many different ways as I could, I finally drifted off into a fitful sleep. I dreamed, as I often do, of pain. In the dream, my arm and shoulder and neck feel as though they are being rent by dozens of dull and jagged claws. The pain is greater than any I have ever felt and greater than any I can imagine, and in the disturbing logic of the dream, I will do anything to make it stop.

Anything.

I stumble out of my bedroom and into the garage of my childhood memories. From above the workbench, I pull my father's saw from its place on the Peg-Board, rip my shirt off, and begin sawing at my shoulder. The teeth bite into my flesh, and somehow I know that this is the only answer for the agony. As I cut, the pain doesn't worsen, but it changes. Each stroke of the blade causes another burning surge that makes me scream louder than the last, but I continue.

With each stroke, the blade rips deeper into my flesh. Blood spurts forward and back with the motion of the saw. Ragged bits of muscle and sinew clog the teeth.

Even when the edge of my father's saw catches on the bone of my shoulder and sends a violent jolt down my spine, I continue.

It goes on and on and on.

Finally, my arm falls to the floor. It's only then as I look down at it, flopping and twitching on the cold concrete, that I see how much blood I've lost. A huge deep-red pool. I fall into it, splashing, fully aware that I am bleeding to death. My gaze drifts up into the rafters, and I begin to fade.

And then the most horrific moment of the entire dream comes upon me.

The saw has worked.

The pain is gone.

Six

THE NEXT MORNING, A LITTLE BEFORE SEVEN, I CALLED Goodman. Something told me he'd be awake. "Can I buy you breakfast?"

I was at The Potholder waiting for him a few minutes after they unlocked the front door. I sat at the small table in the back corner of the front room and started reviewing my notes. When the waitress came, I told her I was waiting for someone but went ahead and ordered an omelet with corned beef and bacon that they called "The Rancher" and a cup of coffee.

The walls of the place were hung with hundreds of pictures taken of people all over the world holding up handwritten signs that said, *Eat at The Potholder*. Years ago, when I'd first been promoted to Homicide, I was assisting on a domestic murder on which Dave Zepeda was the principal. He was taking photos of the vic—a middle-aged woman who had been beaten to death by her husband—and he told me to squat next to her. It was one of my earliest cases with the detail, and I'd been as anxious to please the vets as an adopted Jack Russell on his first day out of the pound. Once I was down on my haunches, he handed me a piece of cardboard and told me to hold it up to the camera. At the time, I didn't realize how careful he had been to let me see only one side of it. He snapped several pictures and told me I'd done a good job. I didn't think any more about it until a new eight-by-ten showed up on the squad room wall of me kneeling down next to the bloody and bruised woman, holding up an *Eat at The Potholder* sign.

I'd never seen Dave as disappointed as he was when The Potholder refused to hang it on the wall even long enough to "get" me with it. Every time I took it down off the wall of the squad room where it had found a final resting place, a day or two later a new copy would appear. Eventually, when I had developed a sense of gallows humor strong enough to win the old-timers' approval, I gave up and it disappeared, leaving me grateful that the Homicide crew thought that was hazing enough for a new D3.

I considered sharing that story with Goodman. We'd only spent a few minutes together, but my instincts told me he'd see it as a tactic deployed to ingratiate myself to him. Which, of course, was what the whole breakfast meeting was. The only question was how obvious I should be about it.

When he came in, I waved him over to the table. He looked sharp and alert. His suit was either freshly cleaned and pressed or an identical match to the one he'd been wearing when we'd met at the station.

"What's good here?"

"Anything with grease."

He ordered an omelet, too. "The Irisher." Potatoes, cheddar cheese, and bacon. Another of my favorites. It made me want to trust him. Yogurt and berries or egg whites would have concerned me.

"I'm sorry I was kind of a dick at the squad."

He let the stern facade he'd been projecting ease and raised an eyebrow. "Your partner tell you to do this, or your lieutenant?"

"Neither one. This is all me."

He wasn't buying it.

"But I am trying to head them both off at the pass."

That satisfied him enough for us to ease into a few minutes of small talk about Long Beach. He'd worked a joint task force investigating harbor smuggling a few years before but hadn't met anyone from Homicide until this case.

When the food came, I said, "Now, there's some apparent aesthetic value."

He took the bait, but I couldn't tell if he knew it was bait. So I told him the story of how the phrase had entered the LBPD lexicon.

"A couple of months back, two uniforms picked up a guy with a camera taking pictures of the Edgington oil refinery. They figured he must have been some kind of terrorist, because why else would he be taking pictures of a dump like that? Turns out he's just a reporter, but when they asked him what he was doing, he said he was an *artist*."

Goodman let out a little chuckle at the word.

"So, of course, that was enough to freak the unis out even more. One thing leads to another, and finally the chief has to make a statement. Says that it's the responsibility of the LBPD to question anyone taking photographs 'of no apparent aesthetic value.'"

"And next thing you know..." he said.

"Right. Every cop in town is using it to describe anything from the crappy evidence in his investigation to how his wife's ass looks in those pants."

We'd fallen into an easygoing rapport. Just two old cops shooting the shit. Of course, the "No apparent aesthetic value" line had peaked in its popularity weeks ago, and the first time I had ever uttered the phrase was in the station with Goodman and his partner.

After we traded a few more war stories, I asked him how the congressman was doing.

"Seems to be holding up well. Mrs. Benton, too. The son's a basket case, though."

"That's what it looked like to us. The lawyer won't let us get close to Bradley. Anything you can do about that?"

"I'm not really as deep in that circle as you probably think. I just give the congressman a report every day. Usually not even to him. Kroll gets it. But I'll see what I can do."

We finished eating, and he asked me for directions to the courthouse, which I was fairly sure he didn't really need.

On my drive downtown, I saw a small Craftsman for sale that I thought had real potential. There were no more flyers in the box on the signpost, so I wrote the real estate agent's name and the address down in my notebook and made a mental note to tell Jen about it.

———————— , ————————

As I was telling Jen about breakfast with Goodman, Ruiz called us into his office.

"Have you seen this?"

It was a video recording of the Bentons playing at a park I didn't recognize. The kids were next to each other in two swings, and Sara was taking turns pushing them. First Bailey with her left hand, and then Jacob with her right. She'd found a perfect rhythm, and her smile was as wide and bright as those of the children.

"We don't have this," I said. "Where did it come from?"

"Channel Four. It led every local news segment this morning."

"Where'd they get it?"

"Go find out," Ruiz said.

Before we were even back at our desks, Jen was on the phone. Her first call was to a sergeant in Media Relations.

"Hank? This is Jennifer Tanaka from Homicide. You gave Lieutenant Ruiz the new video of the Benton family from Channel Four?"

She listened as she sat down and began scribbling on a yellow legal pad on her desk. "And that's the producer?" She wrote some more, made vaguely affirmative verbal noises, and hung up.

"Want to go to Burbank?"

———————— , ————————

"Where'd you get the video?" I asked the assistant producer a second time. Her name was Marisol Vargas. She was midthirties, with a bad face job that left her cheeks too high and her mouth too tight. When she'd introduced herself using a heavy Latino accent for her name and an uptight Brentwood parlance for everything else, I couldn't help but wonder if, at some point, she'd aspired to be on-air talent and had settled for this.

"As I said, Detective, I'm not at liberty to reveal our source." Her eyes didn't move when she spoke.

"Who is?"

"Please, you must understand that journalistic ethics prevent us from sharing that information."

"Is this your decision," Jen asked, "or is someone else ultimately responsible?"

"It's really not going to make any difference, Detective." Marisol seemed to be enjoying taking a stand on moral grounds. She behaved as if she were the only thing standing between jackbooted thugs of the LBPD and the First Amendment. "Whoever you ask is going to tell you the same thing."

"Oh, we're done asking," I said. "Now we just need to know who's getting arrested for obstruction of justice."

I thought that made her eyes widen half a millimeter or so, but it might just have been wishful thinking.

She left us alone in the office we'd been speaking in. We weren't sure if it was hers or someone else's—there wasn't a name on either the desk or the door.

"Want to sit?" I asked Jen. There was a couch opposite the desk.

"No," she said. Neither of us wanted to be seated when we met whoever Marisol was bringing back into the room.

After ten minutes, I said to Jen, "How much longer should we give them?"

"I think we've given them long enough."

I smiled and we both took our badges and left the office. There was a row of cubicles that followed the hallway in the direction Marisol had gone when she'd left us.

The first person I saw was a guy who looked like he was fresh out of college.

"Marisol Vargas," I said to him with as much dick in my voice as I could muster. "Where did she go?"

He looked down the hallway, then back at me. "I'm not sure. Let me just call—"

"No. Stay here. Don't leave your desk."

We started off toward the bigger offices in the back, badging everyone we passed. As we approached the end of the row of cubicles, I said very loudly, "Marisol Vargas."

She stepped out of an office at the end of the hall, and even though she had no discernable facial expression, her body language told me I'd rattled her.

"Stop there," I said.

I could feel their eyes widening around me as I reached under my coat for my cuffs.

"Extend your hands," I said in the tone I usually reserve for rousted gangbangers.

"What?" she said. "I don't understand."

Just as I flicked open the first bracelet, a short balding man began speaking in the office she'd just come out of. "Wait!" he said, joining us at the doorway. "What's this about?"

"You know what it's about," Jen said. "Marisol had plenty of time to fill you in while she left us waiting. Your news organization is obstructing justice. You have material evidence in an ongoing homicide investigation. Was withholding information your decision?"

His mouth opened, and he raised his eyebrows. No Botox for him. Too old-school. I made sure he was looking at his own wrists while I held up the cuffs.

"I think there's been some kind of misunderstanding," he said. "Won't you have a seat?" When neither of us moved, he added, "Please?"

———————— , ————————

"Did you think they'd cave that easy?" Jen asked as she drove us south on I-5 toward Long Beach.

"Of course. They're local TV news. Have you seen the shit they put on in the mornings? The BBC they are not."

The producer had given us the name of the man who'd sold them the video of Sara and the kids. They hadn't bothered to do any background on him or get anything from him other than a cell phone number and an e-mail address.

I called Patrick. "Did you hear about the video on the news this morning?"

"Yes. The lieutenant told me you guys were on it. Get anything?"

"A name. Oliver Woods." I spelled it for him, then gave him the phone number and e-mail address. "See what you can do."

By the time I'd made a fresh pot of coffee in the break room, Patrick had found some basics on Oliver Woods. We had all of his personal information and knew that he didn't have a criminal record.

"I got you into his Facebook account," Patrick said. "Here you go." He put a notebook computer down on my desk with a Firefox window open to Woods's profile.

He had dozens of video clips, hundreds of photos, and thousands of friends. This was going to take a while.

I started by clicking on the Friends tab under his profile picture, which was standard fare—a modest smiling face in front of a woodsy background. Scrolling down the long list of names and photos, the first familiar name after Sara's I came to was Catherine Catanio. I made a note. We'd need to talk to her again. On my quick perusal, I didn't see any other familiar names or anything connected with the case. The Info section told me he had studied art history at Cal State Long Beach and UC Irvine. Apparently he moved in the same academic circle as Sara and Catherine. He didn't seem to have any other connection to the Bentons, though, so it seemed odd that he'd have a video of the kids playing in a park.

I searched through the videos he'd posted on the off chance that I would find the clip that he had sold to Channel 4 or another of Sara or the children. But I didn't.

———————— , ————————

"Woods might be a dead end," I said.

Before Jen could reply, her phone rang. She answered it, listened a moment, then started knocking on her desk to get my attention. I listened to the rest of her end of the conversation. "No, that's great...And the ID is positive? Could you spell that?" She scribbled on a legal pad on her desk as she spoke. "That's fantastic. Thanks." She hung up her phone and shot me an odd stare.

"What is it?"

"We got a match on the DNA."

"What the fuck?"

"I know," she said. "It's only been three days."

It was scientifically possible for DNA results to come back in as little as seventy-two hours. We both knew that. In reality, though, we routinely waited months for the information.

"What's the quickest you've ever seen results come back?" I asked.

"Two weeks."

"What case?"

"About five years ago," she said. "Remember when the mayor's niece got raped?"

"And we got these in three days."

We both stood up and took the walk to the lieutenant's office. His door was open, and he looked up when we came in.

"What?" he said.

We told him about the DNA.

"Somebody's got their fingers in our pie," he said.

"Whoever it is, they're one step ahead of us," I said.

He looked like he had something in his mouth that he didn't like the taste of. "Nothing we can do about it. Work the lead."

———————— , ————————

An hour later, we gathered the squad in Ruiz's office for a rundown.

"We've got a match on the DNA," Jen said.

"Bullshit," Dave said. "How could there be a match already?"

"Divine intervention?" Marty asked.

"Congressional," I said.

Jen passed a mug shot around the table. "Oleksander Turchenko."

"Turchenko? What is that?" Patrick asked. "Russian?"

"No," I said. "Ukrainian."

Jen continued. "He's been here eight years, arrested nine times. Extortion, assault, attempted rape. Nothing but misdemeanors have ever stuck, so he hasn't done any real time."

"How'd he manage that?" Ruiz asked.

"Looks like good lawyering," I said.

"So he's mobbed up?" Dave asked.

"Must be," Jen said. "But we don't know yet with who. With all the Eastern European outfits around the port, they're almost as hard to keep straight as the Latinos."

"Checked with OCD yet?" Ruiz asked.

"No," I said. "We wanted to bring you up to speed before we headed downstairs."

"Let me call Lansky," Ruiz said. He picked up the phone and dialed the Organized Crime Detail's extension.

They were notoriously tight-lipped when it came to sharing information, especially on their open cases. And given the fact that most criminal organizations were ongoing enterprises that stayed in business after all but the most significant and sweeping police operations, most of the OCD's investigations stayed open indefinitely. The players sometimes changed, but the organizations rarely did. A little grease from the lieutenant would go a long way toward helping us get a handle on the crew we were dealing with.

"Mike," Ruiz said into the phone, turning his Texas good-old-boy charm up to full-tilt boogie, "I need a little favor."

———————— · ————————

Across the table sat Mike Lansky, the Organized Crime Detail's own lieutenant, and one of his detectives, Efram Kennedy. Lansky was tall and thick, with a high-and-tight haircut that always looked a little too jarhead for the expensive tailored suits he routinely wore. Kennedy, on the other hand, was small and wiry, with a twitchy energy about him that made the department's running gags about OCDs—obsessive-compulsive detectives—seem less like jokes and more like casual observations. I didn't like him the same way I didn't like Chihuahuas. He always made me feel vaguely queasy and irritated. But Lansky kept him on the leash, so he wasn't as annoying as he might have been.

"Turchenko's affiliated with a family outfit," Kennedy said. "Uncles and cousins once removed and such. Ukrainians, mostly, but a few Russians, too. They're not too hierarchical, and they've got a bit of independence from the shot callers."

"Who runs them?"

"A Russian named Tropov."

An alarm bell rang in my head. A hard-core button man with the same name had tried to shank Jen with a screwdriver a year earlier when we arrested him for suspicion of murder. She saved his life by being forgiving enough to talk me down when I was about to take his head off with a Remington 870 riot gun.

"Yevgeny Tropov?" I asked.

"No," Kennedy replied. "Anton. His cousin." He did something with his mouth that made him look like a rodent. "But your pal's in it up to his knees with these winners." A sound came out of his nose that I thought was some sort of laugh.

"Efram," Lansky said, "settle down and go over the rest of the file with them."

He did, and just like that, we were on our way to the first arrest in the Benton case.

———————— , ————————

Turchenko's last-known address was a small house in a run-down neighborhood on the border of Long Beach and Wilmington. We didn't bother with that one, though, because Lansky and Kennedy had more up-to-date intel on him and his whereabouts. For the last month and a half, he'd been living in a down-market condo north of downtown that belonged to one of his many cousins.

Marty, Dave, and three uniforms met us in the lobby of the building. Bob Kincaid, a deputy district attorney, had expedited the arrest and search warrants on Turchenko and the condo, and we were about to execute them. We rode in two elevators to the sixth floor and circled up and down the hall from the door to unit 608. Fortunately, we didn't bump into any residents on the way up. Nobody likes seeing a gang of cops with shotguns and a portable battering ram in their lobby.

Jen dialed Turchenko's landline on her cell and snapped it closed when he answered. She nodded, and we moved down the hall and flanked the door.

With my back to the wall, I reached to the side and pounded on the door. "Police!" I yelled. "Open up!"

We gave him about three seconds; then I motioned for the uniform with the ram. He heaved back, swung it forward, and the door burst open and slammed against the wall.

Zero

IF DR. BALLARD HAD BEEN THERE, RED HAIR AND FRECKLES gray in the dull light of the hallway, to ask me about my pain, I would have had to think before I answered. Then I would have said, "One." I knew much of the relief had to do with the adrenaline rush, but that wasn't all of it. It was being on the job. Or as Jen had referred to it, being back in the saddle. *This*, I thought, *is what I need to be doing.*

And then I pushed through the splintered doorframe and started screaming.

"Oleksander Turchenko!"

We didn't need to go far. In front of us, on a decades-old rust-colored couch, a man sat in a wife-beater tank top and NASCAR boxer shorts eating Fruity Pebbles from an enormous olive-green plastic bowl. He didn't bother to stop chewing, but he did divert his attention from *The View* to the crowd forcing its way into his living room. He swallowed, milk running down his chin, then sat still. Only the fact that he didn't even glance down at the Sig P226 on the coffee table in front of him saved his life.

"Turchenko?" I asked, the muzzle of my Glock not more than seven feet from his chest.

He gave us a slight nod.

"Put the bowl down on the couch next to you, then put your hands on top of your head."

He did.

"Now push the table toward me with your right foot."

As he extended his leg, the table inched away from the couch toward the middle of the room. I stepped forward, still watching him over my front sight, and picked up the Sig.

As soon as I was clear, Jen and Marty were in front of me, shoving Turchenko's face down into the sofa cushions and cuffing him.

———————————— · ————————————

Less than an hour later, he was Mirandized and uncuffed in the interrogation room. He sat there with the same dull glare he'd had on his face since we'd burst through his door. He said only one word. "Attorney."

———————————— · ————————————

Turchenko's lawyer was slick and smelled of expensive cologne. He introduced himself as Michael Weathers, and just to see if he'd rattle, I asked him if he was some kind of Russian mob fixer.

"My client's not Russian, Detective."

"No?" I said.

"He's Ukrainian. With all the difficulties in that part of the world these days, I'm sure you understand why this fact is important to him."

"Oh, yeah. I'd get all bent out of shape if somebody thought I was Canadian."

Jen and I were in the interrogation room with the two of them. The lieutenant was on the other side of the glass.

"We're sorry if my partner's slip of the tongue offended your client," Jen said. "The truth is that we have his DNA at the murder scene, and unless he has anything to share about his accomplice, we can finish this up right now."

Turchenko grunted, and Weathers said, "A moment alone?"

We gave them the room.

Ruiz met us in the hall. "Think he'll give us anything?" he asked.

"I doubt it," I said. "What's in it for him? Best the DA can do is life without instead of the needle. Not much to bargain with."

"Is Kincaid the DDA?" Jen asked.

"Yep," Ruiz said.

Jen smiled, but not enough that she wouldn't have denied it if I said anything. "Well," she said, "let's talk to him and see what he'll go for. There's the political angle to deal with, too."

"And maybe the lab will turn up something else on the samples from Turchenko's apartment," Ruiz said.

Things were falling into place. If we could implicate his partner, we'd have a major win on our hands.

Almost too easy, I thought as I began to massage the ache out of my left arm.

Six

I WAS LOOKING AT A REAL ESTATE WEBSITE CALLED CALBUNGALOWS.com that had some great Long Beach listings when Patrick said, "Check this out," and motioned me over to his computer screen.

"What am I looking at?" I asked. On the monitor was a string of text messages and replies. I leaned in and began reading.

"Turchenko sends a lot of texts to a guy named Taras Shevchuk. He's got a sheet just as long as his pal's. They're all over each other's call logs. And get this—they've been looked at for the same cases twice in the last three years."

I scanned the back-and-forth texts until I saw the line from Shevchuk that had caught Patrick's attention. It said, *Everyting readdy 4 Bixby. C you a.m.* It had been sent the night before the Benton murders.

"Am I the only one who proofreads text messages?" I asked.

He let that go and said, "I think we've got the accomplice."

———————— , ————————

Ruiz looked at the photo in the folder Pat had handed him. "Shevchuk? Is that how you say it?"

"Your guess is as good as mine," I said.

"He'll be expecting us. We'll need to go in heavier for this one."

"Should we scout it first?" Jen asked. "If he's not already in the wind and we do the search before the arrest, we'll spook him."

"Good idea. You and Danny go take a look while I get a team ready to go."

———————— , ————————

We checked in with the OCD and got a copy of Shevchuk's file. His most recent known address was a 1930s bungalow a few blocks outside of the East Village—a neighborhood on the edge of downtown named with a misguided sense of New York envy—where he was shacking up with a girlfriend. The house wasn't much to look at, but it wasn't a shithole, either. The beige stucco was old but well maintained, and the lawn was a semi-healthy pale green. There was a BMW in the driveway, and like the house, the car was fading but not completely past its prime. The place had all the requisites of typical lower–middle class Long Beach.

We parked Jen's 4Runner a few doors down on the other side of the street, and while we watched, I called Patrick and had him run the Beemer's plates. The car was registered to someone named Tiffany Molina, no wants or warrants.

"Could be a girlfriend," I said.

"Yeah. Or it could be he doesn't live there anymore."

"Or never did."

"How do you want to play it?" I asked.

"Let's just watch for a while. If nothing happens, we can knock on a door or two."

Jen is better at sitting and waiting than any cop I've ever worked with. For hours at a time, she can remain calm and attentive and seem free of any trace of the numbing boredom I always feel in similar circumstances. She credits years of martial arts training for her Zen-master serenity.

So the only thing I had to help me cope was trying to crack her shell. As much as I wanted to, though, I couldn't think of anything that might rattle her.

My hand tingled. I wiggled my fingers and noticed Jen noticing. I waited for her to speak, but she didn't. A few more minutes and the tingling had devolved into a deep burn. The more it hurt, the more obvious my movements became. Finally, I decided to say something.

"It's been doing better."

"But it's not better now?" Jen said.

"Not at the moment, no. But working helps."

"I'm glad." She put her sunglasses on and turned her attention back to the house.

—————— , ——————

We only waited an hour or so before Tiffany came out onto the driveway, approached the driver's door of the BMW, then stopped as if she'd forgotten something and went back inside.

"Did she make us?" I asked.

"I don't think so." Jen leaned forward and looked over the top of her sunglasses. "Let's give her a minute."

Soon Tiffany came back out, a cell phone pressed to her ear, and got in the car.

"We should front her," I said.

"Let's let her drive a bit first. No point in giving the neighbors a show."

Tiffany turned on Sixth, then took Alamitos up to Seventh, where the one-way street ends and you can drive east.

"She knows the neighborhood," I said.

A few minutes later, she stopped at the Starbucks on Seventh and Park, and we had our chance. We let her go inside and get her coffee while we split up and each moved a few cars away from her BMW. Jen took a position by the entrance and faked a text message, and I went down the block toward the trees that lined the residential portion of the street.

We were only about two blocks from my house. If Tiffany didn't cooperate, we could work her over in my garage. As if he had read my mind, a squirrel emerged from a hedge and gave me a disapproving look before moving on up the trunk of a eucalyptus.

Tiffany came out of the Starbucks with a venti something or other in her hand, and I started walking toward her car. We'd get there at just about the same time. Jen fell in behind her, just in case Tiffany didn't like the look of my badge.

It was obvious she was aware of me even though she avoided making eye contact. Her shoulders tensed, and her movements became smaller and less fluid. I couldn't tell if she made me for a cop or just realized that our paths were going to intersect, and I didn't have time to figure it out. We were about ten feet apart when I reached into my chest pocket, pulled out my badge holder, and flipped it open.

"Ms. Molina?" I said.

Turning just enough to see Jen over her right shoulder, she sighed and seemed to deflate an inch or two. "Yes," she said.

"What can you tell us about Taras Shevchuk?"

At the mention of his name, her eyes widened and her exasperation was suddenly layered with trepidation.

"Who? Who is that? I don't know him."

But, I thought, *you know Ukrainian names well enough to know Taras is for boys.* Maybe she just liked Gogol. Or Yul Brynner movies.

"Are you sure?" Jen asked. "Because if you say you don't know him and it turns out that he just, oh, slipped your mind? That could make things very complicated for you."

"This is not cool." Tiffany looked at Jen. Then at me. "He owns the place I'm staying at."

"That much we know," I said.

"Is he there now?" Jen asked.

"No."

"Where is he?" I asked.

"I don't know."

I studied her face. My best guess was that she was telling us the truth. "When was the last time you saw him?"

"Three days ago."

———————— , ————————

Tiffany was waiting for us in the Homicide Detail interview room. She'd agreed to come in voluntarily to answer more of our questions. We hadn't threatened her with any charges yet, but she seemed to sense the depth of the water she was treading. Jen and I ran it down for Ruiz.

"Keep it easy," he said.

Jen and I hadn't discussed an interview strategy yet, but I knew we'd both been thinking the same thing. She was cooperating. There was no reason to start playing hardball until that changed. The question was how much information to give her. The more we told her about our lock on Turchenko, the more we could use her own fear of prosecution for involvement in the multiple murders to our advantage. But it was very unlikely we'd be locking her up, and once she walked out the door, the more information she had, the more she could potentially share with Shevchuk when we released her.

"What's your take on her?"

"She was actually more forthcoming than I expected," Jen said.

"Me too," I said. "I thought she'd shut us down before we even got started. I think she knows how bad these guys are and is looking for an out."

"Then give one to her," Ruiz said.

———————— , ————————

"Can we get you anything?" Jen asked, pushing the interview room door closed behind her. "Something to drink? Are you hungry?"

Ruiz and I were watching through the mirror.

"I'm fine," Tiffany said.

There were only two chairs at the table—the one Tiffany was sitting on and another facing her on the other side of the table. Jen approached Tiffany on the right and reached out for the empty chair. Instead of pulling it straight back, she pulled it sideways and took a seat at an angle to the table so there was nothing between them. She did this with such a practiced fluidity that it seemed normal and natural. If Tiffany noticed the unusual nature of Jen's movements, she didn't give any noticeable signs. But I knew Jen had planned it down to the last motion. She wanted to provide the least amount of physical opposition to Tiffany that she could, to make her as comfortable as possible.

"Thanks again for coming in," Jen said. "We really appreciate your help."

"You're welcome," Tiffany said. There was a hint of a question in her statement. Jen knew she needed to make it disappear before she asked anything about Shevchuk.

"I know this is awkward and uncomfortable for you," Jen said. "If you can just answer a few more questions for us, we'll have you on your way as soon as we can."

"Okay." Tiffany looked down at her hands on the table.

"Oh," Jen said, following her gaze, "that ring is really cool. What kind of stone is that?"

I hadn't even noticed Tiffany was wearing any jewelry.

"Amethyst."

"Is that your birthstone?"

"Yeah," Tiffany said.

"So this month is your birthday?" Jen said, letting a bit of excitement edge into her voice.

"Next week." Tiffany moved her hand so Jen could see the ring.

"Have any big plans?"

"Well, T said—" She pulled her hand back an inch or two.

"T" had to be Taras Shevchuk. I couldn't tell whether Jen had just lost her or if she had actually set the hook.

"T?" Jen said. "Taras?"

Tiffany nodded.

"What did he say you'd do for your birthday?"

"The gondola boat ride around Naples Island and L'Opera for dinner." She looked down at her hands again. "I always wanted to go on the gondola boats. I never did."

"You don't think he'll still take you?"

"He's in deep shit, right?" Tiffany's face had hardened, but she wasn't closing up. "We wouldn't be talking here if he wasn't."

"No," Jen said, "we wouldn't."

They spent an hour and change in the interview. Jen pulled every bit of information she could out of Tiffany, who seemed only then to be realizing just how bad a guy Shevchuk really was. It was clear from her story that he was slicker and probably sharper than Turchenko. Or at least had better social skills.

After we kicked her loose with a warning not to tell anyone she'd talked to us and Jen's number programmed into her phone in case she had any contact from Shevchuk, we parked at our desks to go over what we'd gotten from Tiffany. We were getting some good background, but aside from a few names and regular hangouts, nothing concrete that might help us find him. If he was even reasonably intelligent, he'd be avoiding anyplace and anyone Tiffany had just given us.

We knew Shevchuk had been linked both by the OCD and by legitimate employment records to Anton Tropov's front company, Allied Consolidation, which was located on an acre of asphalt just a parking lot and a quadruple railroad crossing away from the northernmost edge of the Port of Long Beach. Compared to its harbor-industry neighbors, it was tiny—only a single small corrugated-steel warehouse situated in the rear corner of a lot with two unmarked, dirty green shipping containers and room for half a dozen more, all surrounded by an eight-foot-high chain-link fence topped with rusted barbed wire. There was a black Mercedes SUV parked near an open rolling door on the front side of the building.

Jen was driving, and we'd parked at the curb across and down the street.

"Can you get the plates?"

I couldn't make them out, so I took Jen's digital camera out of the glove compartment and turned it on. When the screen came to life, I hit the ZOOM button. The magnification was good enough for me to see the digits, so I read them off to Jen, who then called them in for a DMV record check.

I took a dozen pictures while we waited the few seconds for a reply.

She took the phone from her ear and said, "It's Anton Tropov's."

"How should we play it?"

"We front him and he's sure to tip Shevchuk."

"Think there's anything to be gained?"

"I'd like to get a look at Anton."

"Me too."

"What if we hit him for background on Turchenko?"

"He'll know we've already got him in custody."

"We could say we're checking an alibi."

"I like it."

Jen started the 4Runner and drove up the street and through the gate and parked behind the Mercedes. Along the front wall of the warehouse was a window too dirty to see through and another door that was painted red and coated with a thick layer of dust. It didn't look like it got much use. I was guessing the crew used the roll-up door the majority of the time.

We made a wide curve to get a look inside before we got too close to the door.

A white Ford panel truck was parked inside, with its nose facing the open door. It was a different make than we expected, but I wondered if the tires might match the imprint we found outside the Bentons' house. To the right of it was an interior wall that bisected the space. There were two doors. The one closest to the front of the building was open and led into a dimly lit office. Behind a computer screen, with his back to the wall, sat Anton Tropov. He looked up as we got closer to the office door.

"Hello," he said. "How are you? What can I help you with?" He'd jettisoned most of his Russian accent somewhere along the way and was doing a respectable job of imitating an average, everyday, run-of-the-mill harbor business monkey. He met us halfway and extended his hand. Jen and I each gave it a perfunctory shake. If I hadn't read his file, his shtick would have been good enough to stop me from thinking about drawing my gun.

I badged him and said, "I'm Detective Danny Beckett, and this is my partner. We're with the Long Beach Police."

"Yes, Detectives," he said. "Please come into the office and have a seat." He showed us in. Along the wall that separated the office from the interior of the building was a leather couch. It was a bit worn on the arms but still quite a bit nicer than any furniture I'd ever seen in an office setup like this one. Everything in the office, in fact, was in better shape and of a higher quality than I would have expected. The desk looked like solid oak, and there was a matching return and bookshelf, too. The file cabinets in the far corner looked brand-new.

"This is a nice office," Jen said.

"Not what you expected it would be?" Tropov said. "That's what most people think. The furnishings are a bit better than is usual in this neighborhood. I believe a businessman should maintain a comfortable working environment. I spend a bit more to do this."

I nodded, pretending I appreciated his comments.

"Plus," he went on, "it helps to make a good impression on clients."

"You have a lot of clients here in the office?" I asked.

"Not many," he said. "But sometimes."

"It's always good to be prepared," Jen said.

"Yes, Detective Tanaka, it is."

I'd never told him Jen's name. He knew who we were. That didn't surprise me.

"What kind of business do you do, Mr. Tropov?"

"Importing and exporting. Consolidation," he said.

"I don't know much about that kind of thing," I said. "What exactly is 'consolidation'?"

"We work with our clients to help coordinate the shipping services of the much larger importers and exporters here at the port. We help to meet the specific needs of individual and smaller businesses with a degree of specialization not possible with major shipping companies," he said, sounding as rehearsed as an actor on opening night.

Jen nodded, and I said, "I see," as if what he had just said had actually explained something. We could have pushed some more, but we knew Tropov would be able to keep it up as long as he wanted to.

"We need to ask you about an employee of yours," I said.

"Of course," he said, his voice rich with concern.

Jen began. "What can you tell us about Oleksander Turchenko?"

He took a deep breath and lowered his eyes to his desk, as if he were remembering the loss of a favorite puppy. "I have heard something about his trouble. He was arrested, yes?"

I nodded.

"This is a great disappointment. I do not know Oleksander well, but he is a distant relative. I hired him at the request of my uncle, as a personal favor. To find out he is charged in such a horrible crime is a great shock to me and my family."

"I'm sure it is," I said.

Jen asked, "What kind of work did he do for you?"

"He was a freight handler and occasional driver."

"And he worked here full time?" I asked.

"Oh, no," Tropov said. "We have only three full-time employees. Myself, my secretary, and one driver. Most of the people who work for us are temporary contract employees."

"And that's what Turchenko is?"

"Yes," Tropov said. "Rather, what he *was*. I'm afraid it's unlikely we'll be able to employ him again."

"Well," I said, "he is innocent until proven guilty. What if he's not convicted of the charges?"

"If that is the case, there is a possibility. But appearances are very important in my business. People's judgments and opinions have a great impact on our concerns. The perceptions of him, unfortunately, may be too much to overcome. I'm sure you understand."

"That would be a shame," Jen said.

"Yes," Tropov said, "it would."

"Would you be able to tell us if he was working for you on the evening of"—I paused and pretended to consult my notebook—"February twenty-first?"

"Of course," he said. He swiveled his desk chair, punched some keys, and pretended to consult his computer files. "No, he was not working for us that night. I wish he had been. My uncle would be much happier if he had been."

"I think that's everything." I looked at Jen, and she agreed. "Thank you very much for your help, Mr. Tropov."

"You are most welcome," he said as we all stood up. "Let me show you out." He led us back onto the asphalt lot. "Please let me know if I can be of any more help to you."

"We will," Jen said. "Thanks again."

We stood there and looked at him until he blinked at the bright sun, turned, and went back inside.

In the car, as she turned back out onto Eleventh Street, Jen said, "That was fun and all, but did we get anything we could use?"

"Oh yeah."

"What?"

"We know Tropov's the brains."

"Think he's in this?"

"He's in something." I looked out the passenger-side window at the colossal cranes along the water's edge. Docked at the closest of them was a giant freighter with dirty red-and-blue containers stacked ten high on its deck. They made me and the tightening muscles in my neck feel very small.

———————— , ————————

When we got back to the squad room, I went through my voice mail messages and, surprisingly, found one from Julian Campos. "Mr. Beckett," he said, deliberately using "mister" rather than "detective" in what I was sure was an attempt to irritate me. He might have been a good lawyer, but he was out of his league when it came to trading petty, thinly veiled, passive-aggressive insults. "If you can clear some time in your schedule today, Bradley Benton is prepared to speak briefly with you and Detective Tanaka. Please call me back to make the arrangements."

I said to Jen, "We got our interview."

She looked surprised and a bit wary. We both wondered what angle Campos was playing. The possibility that he was just doing his best to assist us in our investigation never occurred to us.

Bradley hadn't been home since the murders. He was still staying with his parents.

The Benton family had a knack for finding expensive neighborhoods in Long Beach. The congressman and his wife lived in one of the most exclusive areas of the city—Park Estates. It was a relatively small enclave hidden between the Recreation Park Golf Course and the Veterans Administration hospital on Bellflower. Driving past on one of the major streets around the community, you'd never actually know it was there. But once you went looking for it and started winding through the heart of the area, it felt like you'd taken a wrong turn and somehow wound up thirty miles north in Bel Air or Beverly Hills. It was one of the few places in the city where you could find an actual estate.

Which was exactly what the congressman had found about fifteen years ago, when he'd moved up the coast from Newport Beach to a location that was right in the geographic center of his district.

Before we left the squad, we looked up the residence on Google Earth. I'd already seen it from the street, but I wanted to see it from above to get a better feel for the place. It was quite a spread. It appeared that there were only two properties on the entire block. It had to be two acres. Maybe more. There were large expanses of green lawns, trees, garden areas, tennis and basketball courts, and a pool that looked to be about twice the square footage of my two-bedroom duplex.

"How much do you suppose you need to make to afford a place like that?" Jen asked.

"A United States congressional representative makes one hundred seventy-four thousand dollars a year," I said.

"How long have you been waiting for the chance to drop that number into a conversation?"

"Looked it up the first night."

"I figured." She took an obvious satisfaction in the moment.

"Not enough for that kind of spread, though. Where do you suppose the money comes from?"

"I don't know," she said, serious again after her moment of lightness. "But we should find out."

Patrick had put together a file on Bradley Benton III for us. As I had suspected he would, he'd gotten a lot further online than I had. He'd used LexisNexis and Google and half a dozen other search engines and databases to build a history of the congressman's son. I went over it with Jen as she drove us to the congressman's estate.

After spending most of his early education in private school, Bradley transferred to the public Newport Harbor High School, where he'd been a big success. He was on an academic decathlon team that made it to the national finals. After he graduated at the top of his class, he went to his father's alma mater, Stanford, and stayed there all the way through law school. He'd made a splash there, too. There was a list of accomplishments in the file that included things like editing the law review and inclusion on the dean's list and a student award from the American Bar Association. Either there weren't any blemishes at all in his academic record or he'd managed to erase them. I was betting on the second. After he graduated, he went to work for Sternow & Byrne. Patrick added a parenthetical here for us: *This is the same firm that represents his father.* So Julian Campos was probably more than just the family's attorney. That explained why he seemed to be as much a babysitter to Bradley as he was a legal representative.

The last entries in the file were bits and pieces from news reports that seemed to deal mostly with the congressman. Brad was mentioned here and there as a potential successor or even a candidate for another congressional district. The term *heir apparent* came up eight times, according to another note from Patrick.

It all added up to a tidy and spotless personal history.

"You think he could really be that spotless?" Jen asked when I'd finished running it down for her.

"Nobody's that clean."

When we stopped the unmarked department cruiser at the gate of the Bentons' estate and rolled down the driver's side window, we didn't even have to press a button on the speaker. A disembodied voice said, "Yes?"; and I answered by identifying myself and Jen and telling whoever was on the other end of the intercom that we had an appointment to see Bradley Benton III. The voice didn't say anything else, but the custom antiqued iron gate split up the center and the two halves floated inward. We curved along the driveway to the large house and parked behind a row of expensive cars.

"DMV says Bradley drives a Porsche," I said, eyeing the sleek black German car at the head of the line. "Maybe that Panera's his."

"That *what*?" Jen said.

"Panera. That's what they call that model."

"No, they call it the Panamera."

"That's what I said."

"You said Panera."

"Well, that's something, right? Panera? What is that?"

"It's that place we had lunch last week in Lakewood."

"Which one?"

"You called it 'Starbucks for bread.'"

"That chili was good."

As we walked toward the large front porch, I wondered what the style of the house was called. It was huge and looked vaguely Mediterranean, but it also had the distinct stamp of new construction, or at least of recent remodeling. There was a lot of stonework and ornate detailing, and it was painted half a dozen different shades of brown. The more I looked at it, the more I guessed it was a contemporary rendering of classic architectural details. No matter what it was in terms of style, though, I got the most important message that the building conveyed loudly and clearly to the kind of people who parked government cars in the driveway. The house might as well have had a YOU ARE BENEATH US sign planted in the lawn.

Before we could locate the bell, the dark wooden door swung open and Julian Campos appeared.

"Hello, Detectives," he said. "I trust you're well this morning."

"Yes, we are," Jen said, matching his smile watt for watt. "How are you?"

"I'm fine, thank you, Detective Tanaka." He let his smile fade and said, "I wish I could say the same for Mr. Benton. He is still struggling a great deal."

"I'm sorry to hear that," Jen said. "We'll make it as easy as we possibly can under the circumstances."

"I'm sure the family will appreciate that, Detective. Please," he said, "this way."

He led us through a larger foyer, past a formal dining room, and into a conspicuously informal great room with a long wall of windows and French doors that looked out into a yard that seemed to go on forever. I knew from the Google Earth aerial photos that there was a pool and a tennis court out there somewhere. We couldn't see either one.

Across the room, near the windows, three people sat on two large leather sofas. I assumed it was the congressman, his wife, and the elusive Bradley Benton III, but they were still about thirty feet away and the only light in the room was spilling in through the windows and backlighting the three figures, so I couldn't tell for sure.

As Campos led us closer, one of the men stood up and I recognized the congressman's bearing and posture. A few steps away, the angle of our view changed and I recognized Mrs. Benton. She was holding a younger man's hand in both of hers, and when she stood up, it looked almost as if she were lifting his weight, too.

The congressman nodded at Jen and me, but his wife didn't acknowledge us. She just stood next to her son.

He was tall. Six three or six four, with a swimmer's build. His clothes were impeccable—expensive jeans and a pale-yellow silk button-down shirt. But his shoulders slumped, and his poster-boy face was dull and worn. He looked liked he'd been on a days-long bender and we'd woken him somewhere in the middle of the first hour of sleeping it off.

"Mr. Benton," Jen said with genuine compassion, "we're very sorry for your loss."

Bradley raised his head and parted his lips, but no sound came out. He stood there for a few seconds, looking bereft, turned his face back to his mother, who returned to him a sad hint of a smile. They both sat back down on the sofa. Only then did he finally close his mouth.

Campos gestured to the empty sofa across from them, and Jen and I sat down.

I took out my notebook and Jen began.

"We'll make this as brief as we can," she said. "When was the last time you saw your wife and children?"

Bradley tried to speak but was barely able to get out a whispered "I" before his eyes began filling with tears and he raised a hand to his mouth. He put his other arm across his midsection and bent forward as if he'd been overcome by stomach cramps.

Then he began to moan.

There's a version of the pain scale with a chart designed specifically for children. It has a different cartoon face with its own unique expression for each number on the scale. The illustration over the zero looks like a smiley face. That over the ten resembles nothing so much as the face of the agonized little man in Munch's *The Scream*.

Nothing on that chart came anywhere close to the expression on Bradley's face.

Campos stood up. "I'm sorry, Detectives." He motioned for us to stand up and began leading us back out the same way we'd come in. "He's still not well enough to talk to you."

I took another look at Bradley before I followed. Either he was in genuine pain or he was an amazingly talented actor. I knew I wouldn't be able to stand there long enough to form an educated guess as to which was the truth, so I turned and caught up with Jen and Campos.

Back out on the porch, he said to us, "Unfortunately, that's how he's been since he found out about his wife and children."

I really wanted to mouth off to him, but Jen thanked him, put her hand on my elbow, and pulled me toward the cruiser before I had a chance to say anything we'd all regret later.

***

"So what was that?" Jen asked as the Bentons' gate rolled closed behind us.

"I don't know," I said.

"Still think he did it?"

"I don't know. I don't think he was faking that." We both looked out the windshield as we drove up through the winding streets and back out onto Bellflower Boulevard. "Maybe he did it, found out he didn't have the spine he thought he did."

"You want him to be the guy, don't you?"

"It's like you said. It would make our job easier." I think she sensed the lie. I needed the challenge. The last thing I wanted was for the case to be easier. And if Bradley's pain was real, easy wasn't going to be very likely at all.

***

That night, as I went over the case files and felt the sharpness of the pain snaking up my arm and into my neck, I wondered about my disingenuous answer to Jen's question that afternoon. I tried to be completely honest with myself. Of course I wanted to make the case. There was no question about that. But I also couldn't deny that the more complicated the case became, the more it seemed to occupy my attention and to ease my awareness of my pain.

So what did I want, really?

I tried to focus my attention back on my notes but couldn't do it. There wasn't anything on TV even vaguely interesting that I hadn't already seen. For a few minutes, I watched an episode of *House Hunters* that I had seen before but thought I could get through again because the hunt was in Portland, a city I've always been fond of, but that wasn't enough. I knew the couple was just going to pick the wrong house again and not even making snarky comments to the screen would change that.

The banjo case was still next to the couch. I opened it and took out the five-string. The weight still surprised me. With the fingers of my left hand hovering over the frets, I ran my right thumb across the strings. I liked the sound. But then I tried to hold down a few random notes high on the neck and strummed again. What I heard made me grimace. I put the instrument away, fearing my neighbors would think I was torturing some kind of small animal.

In the kitchen, I tried to decide between vodka and Vicodin. I couldn't make a decision, so I opened the cupboard over my oven and found a year-old bottle of Ambien. I'd given up on it when it didn't seem to have any appreciable effect on my insomnia. Just for the hell of it, I took two of them and went to bed.

A few hours later, I drifted off just long enough to dream that I had discovered new evidence in the case of the traffic accident that took my wife's life, proving that she had, in fact, committed suicide.

"Looks like most of his financials are joint accounts," I said.

"So we can track Bradley without raising any red flags," Patrick said. "Can't we do that anyway? We always have to look at the spouse, right?"

"We do. But this gives us a little bit of cover if it really is Bradley. Down the road, a sharp defense lawyer could argue that we focused exclusively on him when there were other viable suspects."

"But there are other viable suspects, right?"

"Right. We just need to keep turning over rocks."

"Starting with Bradley's."

"Yeah. Can you set up an alert so I'll get a text message whenever he uses a credit or debit card?"

"You're joking, right?"

"No." I left it at that because I wasn't sure if the joke he was referring to was that it was so easy to do or so hard. I should have known enough about Patrick's abilities by that point to realize it was the former.

A few hours later, as Jen and I were tossing ideas back and forth, Patrick came in with his giant MacBook Pro under his arm and sat down at his desk. "Hey, guys," he said. "Check these out." He flipped open the computer as we flanked him and looked over his shoulders.

"What is it?" I asked.

"ATM surveillance photos. From the Wells Fargo on PCH and Main in Seal Beach."

On the screen, he had pulled up a series of distorted fish-eye photos of a scruffy man in sunglasses and a Dodgers cap. "That look like anyone you know?"

"Taras Shevchuk?"

Pat pulled his mug shot and placed it side by side on the screen with a zoomed-in ATM photo. The two images looked like the same man.

"He has a checking account in his own name. He took out as much cash as he could two days in a row."

"When was this?" I asked.

"Yesterday afternoon at about three fifteen, and the day before half an hour earlier."

"How much was he able to get?" Jen asked.

"Both transactions combined, eight hundred bucks."

I didn't figure he'd be spending much of it on gondolas. Tiffany would be disappointed.

But why would Shevchuk be hitting the same ATM in Seal Beach the same time two days in row?

"He hasn't been seen at any of his regular hangouts for the last few days," I said to Jen and Pat, "but he's not running."

"He's hiding, though," Pat said.

"But something's keeping him local," Jen said.

"Nearly local. If he's staying someplace close to the ATM, he's across the Orange County line."

Jen raised her eyebrows. "That would turn the heat down a little."

"But why wouldn't he go farther?" I asked.

"Could it have something to do with the safe?"

Patrick said, "Did you ever find out what was in it?"

"No," I said. "We're still waiting on an answer from the Bentons' lawyer. That was on our list for our interview with Bradley, but we didn't even get close to it."

Pat absentmindedly tapped his fingers on his desk. In the lull in our conversation, the noise seemed particularly loud.

"Jen's right," I said. "It's got to be what's in the safe. Otherwise, he'd be a lot farther away. Must be something that's only valuable here."

"Information?" she asked.

"Could it be something political? Something on the congressman? Maybe on Bradley?"

"Hang on." Patrick's fingers stopped. "We know Turchenko's a dimwit. Even if Shevchuk is the brains, how sharp can he be?"

I thought it over. "True. Unless there's some other connection. Some kind of loyalty."

"Honor among thieves?" Jen sounded doubtful.

I didn't think we'd figure it out then, so I changed the subject. "Think it's worth sitting on the ATM for a few hours this afternoon?"

"I'm up for it." Pat grinned. "You never take me out anymore."

Two

ONE OF THE WELLS FARGO BRANCHES IN SEAL BEACH IS located in a shopping center anchored by a Pavilions supermarket and a CVS pharmacy. Jen and I sat in her 4Runner and watched the ATM while Patrick was on the edge of the lot keeping a lookout on the front door of the bank.

Jen likes to shop in rich-people grocery stores, so I couldn't really be blamed for giving her a hard time. "I can handle this if you want to go buy some soy milk and free-range chicken. Maybe a gluten-free scone."

"I'd love to. Want me to pick you up some Cool Ranch Cheetos?"

"If there were such a thing as Cool Ranch Cheetos, I would be unbelievably turned on right now."

People came and went. We'd arrived two hours before the time of Shevchuk's earliest withdrawal, and it was now almost half an hour after his latest. It was a long shot that he would show, but it was all we had on him. Still, I was wondering how long we should wait, and I figured Jen and Pat were, too.

I called Pat and watched him across the parking lot as he answered his phone.

"What's up?" he said.

"How long do you think we should give him?"

"A while yet. Might have been a coincidence that he hit the bank at such similar times."

"How's it going over there? Want to rotate? Come over here and sit with Jen?"

"Probably draw more attention than it's worth. Let's just sit tight for a while longer."

We hung up and went back to watching the cars come and go.

When we were just about ready to throw in the towel, a battered Dodge Neon pulled into the lot. It stood out among the newer and more expensive local cars. It might have been the oldest in the lot. The driver pulled around the corner and parked a few slots away from Pat.

My phone rang.

"Bingo," Pat said.

We watched Taras Shevchuk look over his shoulder, close the door of his car, and cross the parking lot to the ATM.

"I got him, too. Let him make the transaction so we get it recorded, then grab him," I said, reaching for the door handle.

Most rifle bullets travel at a velocity greater than the speed of sound. Because of this, despite what countless movies and television shows would have you believe, even with a sound suppressor, they still make a considerable amount of noise because the projectile actually creates a small sonic boom that, while it doesn't sound like what most people think a gunshot sounds like, it is still very distinctive and very loud.

We were both looking at Shevchuk when we heard the sharp shock of the ballistic crack, and half of his head exploded into a cloud of pink mist.

"Fuck!" Jen yelled.

On the other side of PCH, a Chevy SUV with tinted windows that was parked tail in next to an optometrist's office hit the accelerator too hard and screeched its tires.

"Across the street! White Tahoe!"

Jen and I both jumped back into her 4Runner. We were moving before I even slammed my door.

The SUV had pulled into traffic heading south. There was a raised, grass-covered median dividing the highway. We either had to try to drive over it or into oncoming traffic.

"What are—"

Before I could even get the words out Jen had hit the brakes and the front end of the Toyota hit the curb and bounced up onto the divider. The truck shuddered and screamed, but it kept moving, and as soon as all four tires had bounced down onto the southbound roadway, Jen gunned the engine.

A few blocks ahead, I could see the Tahoe weaving in and out of traffic. The driver would have to decide soon whether to turn onto a side street or onto Seal Beach Boulevard, the last chance before an unbroken mile-long stretch of the Pacific Coast Highway.

I was hoping he'd go straight.

The late-afternoon traffic wasn't heavy, but there was enough of it to slow us down. I was sure Pat would have already requested assistance, but just in case, I put in a 911 officers-in-pursuit call.

He turned left on Seal Beach Boulevard. That would take him north to the San Diego Freeway.

"Did you see? He's northbound on—"

"I got him," Jen said. She sounded almost as calm as she had when we were sitting in the parking lot.

I heard sirens in the distance, but I couldn't tell what direction they were coming from.

Jen hit the left turn hard, and I felt my weight press into the passenger door. As soon as we were pointed north, I looked for the Tahoe. The Seal Beach Naval Weapons Station was on our right, and there was no place to turn on that side of the street. He passed the first left and took another hard turn onto Bolsa, still several hundred yards in front of us.

As we passed an elementary school on our right, I saw the first flashing police lights coming toward us about half a mile ahead on the other side of the road.

We followed the Chevy onto Bolsa, and as soon as we made it around the corner, I realized the Tahoe was out of sight. There were three residential streets within view of the intersection on the right. He could have taken any one of them.

"Go for the second," I said. "Split the difference."

The street we turned on was called Sea Breeze. It was typical of Seal Beach—upper middle class and quiet. We slowed down and resigned ourselves to the fact that we had likely lost the vehicle we were pursuing.

I heard sirens behind us, but when I turned to look, I didn't see any lights.

"Right or left?" Jen asked as we approached the end of the block.

As she stopped, I leaned forward and looked both directions. "Right," I said. "Looks like more cross streets."

There was no sign of him.

Jen drove around the neighborhood. As we circled around and around, our expectation that we would come up dry grew with each corner.

Then we saw it.

On a short cul-de-sac called Coral Place, the white Tahoe was angled toward the left-side curb, its rear end extending out into the street, the passenger door wide open.

We parked about ten yards away. Jen turned on the 4Runner's hazard lights, and we drew our Glocks as we got out.

"I'll go," I said.

"Got you," Jen answered.

I couldn't see much through the tinted back windows of the SUV. There were two shapes where the driver and passenger's heads would be, but they were motionless, so I assumed they were the headrests.

As I closed in on the vehicle, sighting down the slide of my pistol, I had the feeling we were too late. That the shooter was gone and we'd missed our opportunity.

Ten feet behind the Tahoe, I moved to my left to check out the driver's side. I didn't see any movement, but the side-view mirror seemed to have an odd dark-red tint to it.

I circled wide around the passenger side and looked in the open door. When I did, I understood the odd shading on the mirror.

The driver was slumped dead over the steering wheel. The windshield and driver's side were sprayed with blood and brain matter from the bullet wound in the back of his head.

The adrenaline rush was coming on hard, so I forced myself to stand still and breathe deeply. My pulse began to slow, and I moved closer to the vehicle and looked behind the front seats to be sure the shooter wasn't waiting for us.

As soon as I was convinced that nothing was moving, I opened the rear door and looked inside.

Except for the suppressed M4 carbine abandoned on the backseat and the body of the driver, the big Chevy was empty.

I looked at Jen, shook my head, and saw the disappointment in her eyes.

Then the Seal Beach cruiser finally found us and screeched to a stop at the entrance to the dead end.

Jen and I held our hands high and wide.

The uniform was riding alone and rose out of the car with an uncertain look on his face and his hand on his weapon.

"I'm Detective Danny Beckett, Long Beach Police. This is Detective Jennifer Tanaka." We held our hands up as he said something we couldn't understand into the radio mic clipped to his shoulder.

A second or two later, we heard a garbled reply, and he seemed to relax. "Okay," he said. "Just sit tight. Backup's on the way." But he didn't move his right hand until two more squad cars rolled up behind him and we heard the guttural roar of a helicopter circling overhead.

Jen and I were still in the dead end with the shooter's Tahoe an hour later when Ruiz arrived. We'd been in an odd kind of limbo, the locals recognizing and verifying our police status but still a little hesitant to cede any control over a crime scene in their territory. Once our lieutenant talked to their lieutenant, though, they backed down. And, honestly, they seemed relieved. Two murders was about ten years' worth of homicide for them.

"The SUV's stolen," Ruiz said. "Owner's on vacation in Hawaii. Didn't know anything about it until we called him."

"This is heavy-duty shit." I gestured toward the open passenger door of the Chevy. "Professional. Weapon's a suppressed M4. The shooter even capped the driver. What do we do with this?"

"I don't know yet," he said. "I don't know."

"Any sign of the suspect?" Jen asked.

"Nope. Helicopters didn't see anything. And no luck with the canine unit."

It didn't seem like there was anything left for us to do there, so I said, "They find anything back at the bank?"

"Why don't you head back there and see."

Jen and I got in her 4Runner and retraced our route. She hadn't spoken in a while. Every time she turned the steering wheel, the front end squealed as if it were in pain.

In the Pavilions shopping center, the whole southeast corner of the parking lot was cordoned off by dozens of LBPD and Seal Beach uniforms and a seemingly infinite supply of bright-yellow crime scene tape. There were already two news vans at the scene. The closest empty parking space was a block north of PCH on Main Street. With our badges in our hands, we got out and went looking for Patrick.

Half a dozen cops stopped us for ID before we got anywhere near the Wells Fargo. The closer we got to the center of the mass of people, the more familiar faces we saw.

We ducked under the tape and found Patrick with a veteran patrol sergeant. They were leaning toward each other and raising their voices to be heard above the clamor of the crowd.

He turned to us and I realized the color of his face was a shade or two lighter than usual. I wondered whether it had been witnessing Shevchuk's murder or having to coordinate such a massive crime scene that was the cause. Probably a combination of the two.

"How you doing?" I asked.

He gave a confident nod, and I realized his paleness was the only sign of disquiet that was discernable.

"Fine. We got something."

He led us over to the Dodge that Shevchuk had driven into the lot and spoke to a crime-scene technician who was leaning into the rear door of the car. "Show them what you just showed me."

The technician pulled a paper evidence bag out of the box near his feet and held it open. He shone his light inside.

A plastic card in a paper slipcover was at the bottom.

"Is that a hotel key?" Jen asked.

"Motel," the tech said.

"The Seven Seventy-Seven Motor Lodge," Patrick added.

I felt a twinge of anticipation turning over in my gut. "How soon can you clear the scene?" I asked.

He shook his head. "Don't wait for me. Go."

———————— · ————————

Just over a mile south from the place where Taras Shevchuk made his last withdrawal is a stretch of the Pacific Coast Highway that runs through the picturesque little town of Sunset Beach. It's full of big houses and seafood places and surf shops and cheap motels, and surrounded by a number of channels where people moor their boats right next to their waterfront homes. Because of the water, PCH is the only way in or out, and it has left the community feeling like a little seaside getaway somewhere up the coast far away from the border between Los Angeles and Orange Counties. Appearances can be deceiving, though, and the small population there is an odd mixture of the wealthiest OC denizens and VW-van-driving-beach-bum culture of all of coastal Southern California. In Sunset Beach, it's not unusual to have a view of a million-dollar yacht moored on the private dock of a multimillion-dollar home from the window of your shithole motel.

And that's exactly what the 777 Motor Lodge was.

Years ago, I attempted to stay there one night when I had too much to drink while watching the ultra-kitsch hula show at Sam's Seafood, a retro tiki bar and restaurant, next door. Even though I was completely plastered, when I turned on the bathroom light and saw the cockroaches scurrying out of the sink, I wobbled back outside and called a cab.

As Jen drove south across the bridge over Anaheim Bay, I looked back at the LBPD squad car following us. "Did you see who's backing us up?"

"No," she said. "Why?"

"Remember Greg Adams?"

She shook her head, but I suspected she knew what I was talking about.

"From the Beth Williams case."

A year ago, Adams, a rookie, had been responding to his first homicide. He'd made the mistake of stepping in the victim's blood and leaving his own footprints at the scene. I'd insisted on bagging one of his shoes as evidence in the case. The watch commander made him finish out his shift doing paperwork at the station with only one shoe. To teach him a lesson. Some of the vets started calling him "Barefoot," which, in the manner of cop colloquialisms the world over, became streamlined and simplified.

"Think anybody's still calling him 'Foot'?" I asked.

"You should ask him," she said.

When we pulled into the parking lot, I let the question go and asked Greg and his partner to wait for us while we talked to the manager.

The 777 had probably been a decent place a very long time ago, but now it was everything and less than I'd remembered from my one and only drunken visit. I did notice that Sam's Seafood had become Don the Beachcomber, for whatever that was worth.

The office smelled like old sneakers and Thai food, and the manager was an aged East Asian man who nodded when we showed him Shevchuk's photo.

"He makes too much noise. People complain."

"We need you to let us into his room," Jen said.

The man looked us over with traces of suspicion in his eyes. Just when I thought he was about to challenge us, his expression changed, as if his misgivings were blown away by a sudden breeze.

"Okay." He took a plastic card out of his breast pocket, angled it in the light to get a better look, and put it back. "Upstairs. Second floor."

He stepped around the counter and led us outside and locked the office door. I motioned for Greg and his partner to follow us. We all fell in behind the manager and passed a few ground-floor doors on the way to the elevator. The little man pushed the button and looked back at me. He looked surprised to see four of us. I guessed that he hadn't noticed our uniform backup.

We all squeezed into the elevator. It was tight, but we made the best of it. Only had to go up one floor. I read the county inspector's tag posted next to the door. "It says on this that we can fit ten people in here."

No one else found that amusing.

The doors opened onto the second floor. The building was shaped like an L, and the elevator was in the inside corner. The manager led us down the long portion of the structure to the second room from the end. We divided up on both sides of the door. We all put our hands on our guns and unsnapped our holsters. No one stood in front of the window.

The manager watched us, and his hand shook as he pulled the card from his pocket.

"I'll do it," I said quietly as I reached out for the key card. He handed it to me, and I motioned for him to stand clear.

I drew my gun and took a position at the door. When Jen and Greg and his partner all gave me nods, I slipped the card into the slot and looked for the little green light. It didn't come on, so I tried again. No luck. I looked at the manager, and he was making a doorknob-twisting motion in the air with his hand.

I turned the handle and pushed the door open.

The room was dark.

"Lights," I said, and three flashlights clicked on over my shoulders and began scanning the room.

It looked clear, so I stepped inside and felt along the wall for a light switch. I found one, flipped it on, and a single floor lamp illuminated the dingy room.

I moved farther inside, my Glock extended in front of me, and scanned from left to right. Pointing the muzzle at the bathroom door, I closed the distance in half a dozen steps and looked through the door.

"Clear," I said.

Holstering my pistol, I began to look around the room. Shevchuk was not a tidy man. A duffel bag was open on the unmade bed, and half its contents were spilled out on the stained and rumpled bedspread.

The room smelled of stale body odor and dust. A smooth path was worn in the carpet from the door to the bathroom, and the furniture was nicked and chipped and scarred. The TV on the dresser was so old it had a knob on the front to change the channel.

I was still scanning the scene when Jen spoke. "Danny." She pointed to the table under the front window. On it was a wall safe that had been removed from its mountings. It was dented and covered in tool marks. There was a hammer and small pry bar next to it. Shevchuk had been trying to open it.

We gathered around the table and looked down at the beige-painted steel box and wondered if it was the reason that five people were dead.

PART THREE: DIAGNOSIS

—————— , ——————

On the plains of Jordan
I cut my bow from the wood
Of this tree of evil
Of this tree of good
　　—Bruce Springsteen, "Empty Sky"

Seven

I T WAS CLOSE TO ELEVEN AND FEELING EVEN LATER WHEN WE
made it back to the squad. The adrenaline was fading and an
aching tightness was settling into the left side of my body.

Patrick was sitting at his desk, staring at his monitor. The
overhead fluorescents were turned off and his face was lit with a
pale-blue glow.

"Hey," he said as we entered.

Jen dropped her bag on her desk. "How are you?" she said.

"I'm doing okay," he said. I didn't call him on it, but he didn't
seem well at all. Of course he was tired—days like that one don't
come along often, but I was betting that he was shaken up by
what he'd seen. Shevchuk's murder was a sight none of us would
get out of our heads any time soon. But I was fairly certain that
it was the first time Patrick had seen someone killed. Witnessing
the things that homicide investigators see on an almost daily
basis hardens our perspectives and gives us the ability to withstand a great deal of horror. But to witness a murder's aftermath
is a very different thing from witnessing the murder itself. Seeing
the moment of death, especially when it comes violently, leaves a
much more indelible impression.

I have seen four people die by gunfire. For me, it is practically
routine. Still, it's never easy. I didn't envy Pat his next few nights.

"Did you hear what we found at the motel?" I asked.

"The safe, right?" he said.

"Yeah." I hung my jacket over the back of my chair and sat down. "The techs say they'll have it open for us first thing in the morning."

"What do you suppose is inside?" He seemed to be weighing his words particularly carefully, as if he had a great personal stake in the answer to his question.

"I don't know." I looked at Jen, who had her elbow propped on the desk and was leaning her head on her hand. "Any ideas?"

"No," she said. "But I'll bet whatever's in there won't come close to explaining everything that happened today."

Neither Pat nor I were willing to take that wager.

When I got home that night, I sat down in my living room with a tall glass of Grey Goose and Tropicana No Pulp. I was physically exhausted, but the raw power of the day's events had me wired with a restless mental energy that I knew would keep me up for hours. I flipped through all the channels on the cable box twice and settled on a two-year-old *California's Gold* repeat on KCET. Huell Howser was in the desert somewhere talking to an old lady. He was very happy.

When I took another swallow, I saw the banjo case propped up at the end of sofa. Why would Harlan have given it to me? I began to wonder about it. I didn't know anything about musical instruments, least of all banjos. The feeling that there was more to his gift than simple convenience weighed on me. How much did it mean to him? How long had he played? I tried to think of a way of broaching the topic with him, but couldn't. Maybe, I thought, I could talk to his daughter. She'd know. I feared that the instrument was of more personal value to him than I could have realized when he gave it to me and that his medical condition had something to do with his actions. Was he letting go of his possessions because he was letting go of something else?

I knew the thoughts would keep bouncing around inside my head. The TV wasn't holding my interest.

Maybe a book? No. Not that night.

I slipped my arms back into my shoulder holster, put on my coat, locked the door behind me, and walked out into the midnight quiet of Belmont Heights.

———————— , ————————

I'd been in bed for about three hours, but I hadn't really slept. NPR's *Morning Edition* was playing on the clock radio, and at four a.m., Garrison Keillor's *The Writer's Almanac* came on. It was Toni Morrison's birthday. And Wallace Stegner's. The poem for the day was Robert Bly's "What Did We See Today?" It included the line "It's all right if we write the same poem over and over."

When the morning light began to glow against the window blind, the pain in my neck was sharp, so I ran the shower as hard and as hot as I could stand it. When I got out and wiped the condensation from the bathroom mirror, I could see the redness of my skin.

I got dressed and sat at the dining room table with my notes from the day before and hoped to lose myself again in the case.

———————— , ————————

We didn't get the call from the technician until after eleven that morning. While I was waiting for the word on the safe's contents, I called Julian Campos again. Even though our interview with Bradley hadn't worked, I thought he might have asked him the question about the safe. Surprisingly, he was available, and his assistant put me right through.

"How's it going, Julian?"

"Fine, Detective Beckett. And yourself?"

"I'm doing great. I was wondering if you might have had the opportunity to ask Mr. Benton about the safe?"

"I did, Detective. I did."

"And what did he say?"

"He said, 'What safe?'"

"He didn't know there was a safe in the bedroom closet?"

"No, in fact, he did not. My guess would be that if there was, as you claim, a safe in the bedroom closet, that it must have been in Sara's closet rather than in Mr. Benton's."

"He's claiming he had no knowledge of a safe."

"Yes, Detective. That is indeed what he is claiming."

"Interesting."

Campos was silent.

"We still need to talk to him."

"I'll let him know."

"Thanks, Jules. Have a good one."

"I wi—"

I hung up before he could finish.

Jen had been listening at her desk.

"Did you get that?" I asked her.

"He didn't know about it?" she said.

"That's the story."

"What kind of angle is that?"

"I don't know. Think it could be the truth?"

"Maybe. We've got nothing on him. He might as well be a ghost. How can we even guess if he's telling the truth?"

———————— , ————————

After Jen and I watched the DVD that had been the only thing in the safe, I could guess. And I was betting that Bradley denying any knowledge of the safe or its contents was the beginning of a carefully constructed legal strategy to avoid conviction for the murder of his wife and children.

The recording started innocuously enough. Three people were seated at one end of a large conference table. Two women, one young and one older, dressed in appropriate business attire, sat opposite a man with dark-gray hair in a dark-gray suit.

The man identified himself as John Willis, an attorney for Sternow & Byrne, gave the date and location, and then introduced the two women.

The younger woman, who had been identified as Heather Cassidy, had a weary weight hanging about her that seemed to tug downward on her facial features and curve her shoulders and spine forward in the manner of a much older woman. She did most of the talking.

Her attorney, Gladys Hernandez, established through a series of straightforward and simple questions that Heather had been employed by Bradley Benton III and his wife to work as a nanny for their young children during the summer of 2008. We watched another five minutes of the Q&A between the women; then the older woman asked, "Would you tell us what happened on August twenty-seventh, seventeen months ago?"

"It was pretty much just like any other day up until the end of it," Heather said. "We stayed home that day. But the kids had a lot to do in the house. They swam for a while. Then they played inside most of the afternoon. Bailey's friend Janine came over, and they watched videos. Jacob played with his Bakugan toys. He loves those. It was pretty much what we always did in the summer."

"What happened that evening?" Gladys asked.

"Well, Mrs. Benton was out for the day. With her friend in Irvine, I think. And she wasn't supposed to be back until late, so when Mr. Benton came home, I was supposed to be done for the day. He brought home food from P.F. Chang's for everybody. Said there was too much for him and the kids and that I should stay. He'd always been really nice to me, so I did. I was a history major, but I was thinking about switching to prelaw. So he asked me all kinds of questions about what I wanted to do and where I wanted to go to law school and all kinds of stuff like that. After the kids ate and went back to playing, we kept talking and he offered me a glass of wine. I didn't know if I should. I was only twenty and I was his kids' nanny, so I was worried what he'd think of me. He insisted, though, and went over to the wine cooler in the kitchen and poured two glasses. After I drank it, I started feeling tired. Later, I realized he must have put something in my drink. Roofies, maybe? It was way more than regular wine. I didn't feel right."

Gladys said, "What did you do?"

"I told him I didn't feel good. He said I should lie down in one of the guest rooms. So I did. I dozed off a little bit. But then he came into the room."

"Mr. Benton?" her lawyer asked.

"Yes."

"What did he do?"

"He came in and sat next to me. Then he talked to me. And then he started touching me. I think I told him no, but I was so sleepy and out of it. He started taking off my clothes. I remember thinking that I should try to stop him. I knew I should try. I think I did. But I couldn't. He tore the buttons off of my jeans when he pulled them down. I don't remember much after that."

"What's the next thing you do remember?" she asked.

"Waking up when it was dark. I was still feeling funny, but I was alone, so I found my pants and put them on, and my shoes. My bag was still in the dining room. He wasn't there, not anywhere that I saw him. I remember having to hold my jeans up with one hand while I ran outside. I knew I shouldn't drive, but I just wanted to get away."

"And then?"

"My apartment then was only about ten minutes away, so I went straight there. I wanted to take a shower and go to bed, but Crystal, my roommate, wouldn't let me. She made me go to the emergency room."

"You'll see in the records we copied to you the results of the rape kit, which provided viable samples of DNA and Ms. Cassidy's urine test, which confirmed the presence of Rohypnol."

Gladys Hernandez had a look of triumph in her face. Willis was a blank slate. And Heather looked so broken that no matter how much they paid her to drop the charges, it could never have come close to replacing what she had lost.

After we played the DVD for Lieutenant Ruiz and the rest of the squad, we batted theories back and forth like a beach ball.

"Maybe he really doesn't know about it," I said.

Marty said, "Could be she was thinking about using it in a divorce proceeding. Hold it over him, threaten to release it to the press."

"Maybe." I could see the thoughts progressing through Jen's mind as she spoke. "Or he could know all about it and is just thinking ahead to a possible legal defense strategy."

Ruiz went next. "Or the Cassidy girl could be fabricating the story. We have a report of the rape?"

"No," I said. "But the Bentons have plenty of juice. They could have had the record disappeared."

Marty spoke. "Yeah. But if Junior really is gearing up for a campaign, this would be a hell of a threat to hold over him."

Dave ate another donut. I thought we'd run out.

I asked, "Then why was Shevchuk killed? He had the safe. Was he refusing to deliver it?"

Jen said, "Or was it because he and Turchenko screwed up and killed the kids?"

"Back to one of the first questions—what was the objective?" Ruiz asked. "Killing Sara or taking the safe?"

"Both," I answered. "It's the only thing that makes sense. Punish the wife, get the evidence."

Dave displayed his usual sensitivity. "So you're saying Junior paid the dipshit twins to do the dirty work?"

"Him or someone close to him," I said.

"The congressman?" Marty asked.

"The hitter on Shevchuk was a pro," Jen said. "Maybe ex-military?"

Patrick hadn't spoken at all until he said, "If the congressman's involved, maybe he's not ex."

That stopped us.

"Fuck," I said.

"What?" Jen and Marty asked in unison.

"When's the last time a murder went down right in front of you?"

Everyone grumbled and shrugged. Then, one by one, the cartoon lightbulbs clicked on over their heads.

"Yeah," I said. "That's why we were all staking out the same location at the same time. Whoever did Shevchuk had access to the same bank records we did."

———————— , ————————

"If it's the feds, there's probably nothing we can do," Patrick said. We were all at our desks back in the squad. Ruiz had kicked us out of his office and closed the door.

Dave grunted. "You really think the sniper was GI?"

"He had a suppressed M4," I said. "One shot, no witnesses."

"A government spook is gonna kill his wheelman?"

"The driver dropped the ball," I said. "I wouldn't have made the SUV from the shot alone. The rifle shot gave me the direction, but it was the screech of the tires and the hurry to get out of the lot that confirmed the ID. Shooter probably figured that the only way he'd skate was to go it alone."

"He was probably right," Jen said. "The driver wasn't that good at his job."

"Maybe they're not as good as you think," Marty said.

I asked, "How do you mean?"

"They get a top-of-the-line triggerman, but an amateur behind the wheel."

"Limited resources?" I said.

Jen said, "Not that limited, if they can access bank records and maybe tap our phones and computers."

Ruiz opened his door and came out. "They're moving Turchenko into segregation."

Judging by everyone else's expressions, none of us had yet realized that if Shevchuk was killed because of his involvement in the Benton case, then his partner would likely be next on the list.

Every now and then, I like to be reminded that my boss knows what he is doing.

——————————— , ———————————

Jen, Patrick, and I went to the Rock Bottom Brewery for dinner. It was no one's favorite place, but it was close and busy and loud, the kind of place that might offer a distraction or two. We landed a table by the window facing Ocean Boulevard and ordered Titan Toothpicks, Ball Park Pretzels, edamame, and beers all around. We tried to chat, but with all that had happened crowding out thoughts of anything else, the conversation never went anywhere.

I mentioned Tim Grobaty's column from the *Press Telegram* that morning. He'd been impressed that Long Beach City College had made it onto Homer Simpson's Southern California must-see attractions, but upset that it had been placed behind such other highlights as the Watts Towers, the El Toro Y, and the Cerritos Auto Square. No one else had seen it. Pat mentioned a book he was reading called *36 Arguments for the Existence of God*. We didn't get too far beyond his explanation that it was a novel rather than something about philosophy or religion. But it was about those things. But it was a novel. Written by a philosopher. Something like that.

When the food came, Jen slid the soybeans in front of her and left the other crap to Pat and me. We dug in.

Four

ANSWERING THE BIG QUESTION WAS REALLY OUT OF OUR hands. How would the Shevchuk murder and that of the driver in Seal Beach be investigated? They were clearly linked to the Benton case, but what would really be the best way to investigate them? Of course, Jen and I wanted one investigation, treating the subsequent killings as part of the same case. The decision, though, on such a high-profile case was out of our hands. Especially with the congressman involved. The scenario had changed dramatically, and while we didn't know everything that was involved, we knew it was bigger than either a home invasion or a thrill kill that had gotten out of control. There was some kind of criminal conspiracy and the involvement of hard-core organized crime. Those would not go over well with the politicians at any level. We hadn't felt the pressure yet, but we knew it was coming. The brass would surely want to take Shevchuk and the driver out of our hands and to treat Sara, Bailey, and Jacob as an isolated set of victims. And even with all of the coverage, so far none of the news reports had connected the Seal Beach incident to the Bentons. We hoped to keep it that way as long as we could.

We'd gone back to Jen's apartment after dinner. She lived in a building on Fourth and Elm that had been renovated a few years earlier. It was nice enough, but the developers remodeled most of the character out of the building, and she didn't really feel completely comfortable there. For all of her talk about the financial advantages of a buyer's market, I believed that was the biggest reason why she was looking for a house. To find someplace that felt like home.

"How hard should we push back?" Jen asked.

"You know me," I said. "I'm the king of pushback. It doesn't usually do me much good."

She took a sip of herbal tea from a Smith & Wesson coffee cup and gave me a quizzical look.

"What?" I asked.

"Nothing. That just seemed like a surprisingly self-aware comment."

I couldn't decide if that was a compliment or an insult.

———————— , ————————

I've always worked too much. And I got even worse when my wife died. Work has always been a kind of refuge for me, and after Megan's accident, I dived headlong into it. My injury and subsequent leave left me facing something I had little experience with and little interest in—free time.

Even with surgeries and all the medical attention I required, I was left with a seemingly infinite amount of time. I grasped and groped for ways to fill the emptiness.

I embraced digital technology. Got a Kindle. Got a giant Vizio flat screen. Got an Xbox. Really learned how to use iTunes. Read more books than I had in years and joined Goodreads so I'd have someone to discuss Ross MacDonald and Neal Stephenson with. Realized Netflix made the wasteland much less vast and watched every episode of *Buffy the Vampire Slayer*, *The Wire*, and *Fringe*. Discovered a passion for video-game violence. An assault rifle with a chainsaw for a bayonet? Fuck yeah. Downloaded so much music that it would take more than a month of continuous play to listen to it all. Found myself more excited about mixes than I had been in seventh grade when I got a dual-cassette boom box for Christmas and made them for everyone I'd ever met. Jen listened to them all. Dave asked me if I was hitting on him.

And all of those things waited for me on the weekends. As much as I enjoyed them, and even got lost in them, they reminded me of the pain. One of the things I welcomed most about the Benton case was its size and scope. It was the first time since I'd been back that I'd been on a case big enough to justify working through the weekend.

I couldn't really bear the thought of taking a day off.

But there was one weekend tradition—a relatively recent development—that I was looking forward to.

Megan, who had very different literary tastes than I, once said, "It is a truth universally acknowledged in Long Beach that a hungry person in possession of an appetite for Mexican must be in want of Enrique's."

You might not guess from its location in a mini-mall on PCH, sandwiched in between a vitamin store and a Botox clinic, but Enrique's has always been a popular lunch and dinner spot. A few weeks earlier, they started serving breakfast as well. On my second visit, I asked if they could add carne asada to the potato, egg, and cheese breakfast burrito, and when they did, it turned out to be the greatest and most wonderful thing that ever happened in the entire universe. I'm not exaggerating.

I'd been there every time my schedule allowed since then and ordered the same thing every time. Michelle, Enrique's wife, told me on the fourth or fifth visit that they'd made a special button on the register for my order. It was the proudest day of my life.

If that weren't enough, there was never a crowd in the mornings. Dinner—at least between the hours of five and seven—always required at least a half an hour wait. Not breakfast. I figured that would change, though, when word spread.

Blissfully stuffed full of burrito and lemon-herb potatoes, I wobbled out of Enrique's and back into reality.

That afternoon, my BlackBerry vibrated. I had a new text. It was Patrick's automated reply—Bradley had, for the first time since the murders, used a credit card. I didn't know where, and I wasn't close enough to log in to Patrick's program and find the location. While I was still trying to figure out what to do, I received another text, this one actually from Patrick himself. It read, *Bradley's out. He spent $28.75 at Whole Foods on PCH.*

I wondered if there was a way I could make it there from my duplex by the time he got back in his Porsche and out of the parking lot. There wasn't.

Thanks, I wrote back. He'd probably be home by the time I could get there. *Too far.*

Next time, he wrote.

I noted that since I'd joked about proofreading my texts, Patrick hadn't used a single abbreviation. Had he always done that? I couldn't remember. Maybe he really was that adaptable.

———————— , ————————

In Ruiz's office Monday morning our suspicions were confirmed. "The deputy chief's making some noise about turning the Seal Beach crimes over to the FBI."

"On what grounds?" I asked.

"He's saying the weapon and the MO make it look like a Homeland Security issue."

"Funny how they never say that when MS Thirteen winds up with military hardware," I said.

"Do you know if it's coming from the congressman?" Jen asked.

"No," Ruiz said, "but I'm guessing that it is. Danny's right. There's not enough to justify federal jurisdiction without someone pushing hard for it."

"Who else would do that?" Jen asked.

"I don't know," I said. "It's pretty ugly. Maybe the department brass just wants to get it off their hands."

"Could be," Ruiz said. "We should know more later. Young and Goodman are coming in for another update. See if you can get anything out of them."

Patrick went over the Shevchuk murder with Goodman and Young, and then we walked them through the chase and everything that came later. It was the first time we'd seen them since I had taken Goodman to The Potholder. He nodded a lot and asked a question or two but didn't really say much of anything else. I wondered if my attempt at ingratiation had done any good. He was dressed more casually than we'd seen him previously, in khakis, a blue button-down, and a pair of brown New Balances. I recognized them because I had a pair of the same ones.

"Nice shoes," I said.

"Thanks."

"Think you guys might be able to help at all with the ID on the M4? The basic serial number check came back clean, but we're thinking maybe we might be able to trace it to the source." I wasn't actually hoping for any help, but I was hinting at an implication of a possible government connection in the rifle's history and watching to see if either agent picked up on it.

It seemed to go right past Young. He said, "We can put in a request with ATF, but I doubt they'll get back to us any quicker than they'll get back to you." That may or may not have been true, depending on how they put in the request and on other mitigating factors, such as whether or not they dropped the congressman's name.

Goodman, though, saw what I was implying and studied me as I studied Young. I thought about just laying our cards on the table and asking him about their intentions with the case. And maybe a few other things, too. How much are you telling the congressman? What's his intent? Is he looking to make things right or to cover them up? I suspected the two agents could shed a bit of light on the situation. But I seriously doubted they would willingly tell us anything.

When they'd packed up their briefcases and left, Jen and I sat down in Ruiz's office.

"You get anything off of them?" he asked.

"Not really," I said. "Goodman knows we're suspicious of their involvement, but he'd have to be pretty dense not to."

"Like Young," Jen said.

"No sense of where they're going to go with this?"

"Not really," I said. "You get anything from upstairs?"

"I'm meeting with DC Baxter and the chief of D's after lunch. We'll see what they have to say."

"Good luck," Jen said.

———————— · ————————

"Anything come back from the Shevchuk scene?" Jen asked Patrick.

"Nothing yet," he said.

"We don't know if the feds are going to try to grab it. We didn't get anything off the two feebs, either," I said. "And Ruiz hasn't heard from the brass yet. Where do we go next?"

"What do we have if we lose Shevchuk?" Jen asked.

"We can go at Turchenko again," I said. "With his partner dead, maybe he'll be willing to give something up."

"Assuming there is anything to give up," she said.

"The DVD," Patrick said. "Maybe we should try to figure out everywhere that Bradley's been sticking his dick."

"So where do we start?" Jen asked.

"Well, we could try the art professor and the nanny again, or we could start running down people from the video," I said.

Patrick said, "Let's do both. You guys start with people we know, and as soon as I get back from Shevchuk's autopsy, I'll get online and see what I can find on the cast of the epic deposition."

———————— , ————————

We made a call to the Bentons' most recent nanny, Joely Ryan, and set up an appointment to talk to her later that afternoon.

The CSULB website informed us that Catherine Catanio had lunchtime office hours, so we decided to drop in unannounced.

There was a student in her office asking about an assignment, so we loitered outside the door.

"It just seems like a lot of reading for one week," the young man said. "I thought it was art class."

"It's art *history*," Catherine said with a surprising amount of patience. "As I said on the first day of class, it's a lot more than just looking at pictures."

That shut the student up.

"Is there anything else?" Catherine asked.

"No," the student said.

Jen and I could hear the shuffling of a backpack being loaded and zipped shut. As he came out, we got our first look at him. He wore a blue oxford shirt tucked into his jeans, and his light-brown hair was neatly trimmed. I expected something a bit more slovenly from the conversation we'd overheard. Maybe he was a frat boy.

I stepped in front of the open door and tapped my knuckles lightly on the faded yellow paint.

"Professor Catanio?" I said.

She was surprised to see us, but the expression passed quickly from her face and was replaced with a gracious smile. "Hello, Detectives," she said. "Please come in."

"Sorry to stop by unannounced," Jen said.

"Oh, it's no problem. What can I do for you?"

"There have been a few developments in the case," Jen said. "And we were hoping you might be able to give us a bit more information."

"Of course," she said.

"We've come across some new evidence that confirms Bradley Benton's infidelity," I said. "And, honestly, goes quite a bit farther than that."

"Really?"

"Yes," Jen said. "Were you aware that he was accused of rape?"

The professor's eyes widened and her lips parted for a fraction of a second. But the surprise quickly turned into something else. Something very unpleasant. "No," she said. "But I can believe it. When was this?"

I glanced at Jen. She gave me a slight nod.

I told Catherine the date mentioned in the DVD from Sara's safe; she did a bit of silent mental calculation and said, very quietly, "Yes."

"Yes what?" Jen asked, only slightly louder.

"The timing's right."

"The timing for what?"

"For when Sara finally gave up on him. I knew roughly when it happened. Her attitude changed. She actually became less angry and hurt. I thought she'd somehow been able to make some kind of peace with his behavior. Maybe she had. Maybe. I think that's when she gave up the last of her hope that she could save their marriage. That's when she gave up on him."

"Did she ever tell you that?" Jen asked.

"No, she was very good at maintaining the front. But something changed in her. It was subtle. I doubt anyone else would have even noticed it."

"Do you think she might have been planning to leave him?"

"I didn't. But I've been thinking quite a bit about Sara and Bradley. Now, I have to say, I do think that's a possibility."

That didn't completely confirm our suspicions that Sara might have been using the DVD as leverage in a potential divorce proceeding, but it certainly supported them. And it strengthened my belief that Bradley may indeed have had a motive for killing his wife.

"We need to ask you something else," I said. "The rape accusation came from a former nanny. With what you told us before, we're starting to see a very distinct pattern in Bradley's behavior."

"I understand," she said.

"Do you know how many other nannies the Bentons have had?"

She counted in her head. "Four, I think."

"Did they fit the same profile? Were they all young? Attractive? College aged?" I asked.

"Yes," she said. She was sitting up straighter in her chair than she had before, and there was a level of tension in her posture that I hadn't seen before.

"We know he victimized at least one of them. Do you think he might have done the same to the others?"

She nodded, her anger now palpable in the small room.

———————— · ————————

In the car, Jen asked, "So what were you trying to do back there?"

"I wanted to get her riled up. See how much she had on Bradley."

"Did you really need to push so many of her buttons?"

"Maybe not. But I thought the vulnerable college student angle would get to her teacher instincts."

"It did," she said. "She was seething when we left."

"I'm confident she gave us everything she had," I said, trying to put a pleasant spin on it.

"Me too. Just hope she doesn't pop a cap in Bradley's ass."

"I'm not sure that would be such a bad thing."

"I wish you were joking," she said.

———————— · ————————

Joely lived with her parents in Costa Mesa, close to the South Coast Plaza. Fortunately, they were both still at work when we got there.

We parked on the street in front of the olive-green house, and she opened the door before we could ring the bell. She'd been waiting.

"Hello," she said as she led us into the kitchen. It looked like it had been remodeled. The house itself was a relatively typical Orange County midsixties three-bedroom tract home, but the granite countertops and veneered cabinets weren't original to that period. Her family wasn't rich, but they weren't poor, either.

"How are you holding up?" Jen asked.

"Okay, I guess." As soon as the two of us sat down at the table, she asked, "Can I get you guys something to drink?"

"No, thank you," Jen said. "We're fine."

I wondered if we should have asked for coffee so Joely would have something to focus on other than the questions we were going to ask her. She sat down across from us at the oval oak-topped table.

"This is your parents' house?" I asked.

"Yes," Joely said. "I lived in the dorms freshman year, but I didn't really like it, so I came back home."

"UCI, right?"

"Yes," she said.

"What are you majoring in?"

"Education."

"You want to be a teacher," I said. "What grade level?"

"I'm not sure yet. Elementary. Probably third or fourth?" She was easing up a bit and becoming more comfortable. That was good.

"No class today?"

"No. I have a two-day-a-week schedule this quarter. They're really long days, but it's better that way for work." She seemed as if she were going to continue but stopped as she remembered what had happened to Bailey and Jacob. "I guess I don't need to worry about that now, though."

"I'm sorry," Jen said to Joely, who was beginning to tear up.

There was a box of tissues on the counter on the other side of the room. I got up and brought it back to the table. Joely took one.

"Do you know who did it yet?" Joely asked.

"Not yet," I said.

Jen picked up the ball. "But that's why we're here. We just need to ask you a few more questions."

"Okay," she said, dabbing at the corners of her eyes with a Kleenex. As far as I could tell, she wasn't wearing any makeup, but she wiped at the tears as carefully as if she were.

"What we have to ask might make you uncomfortable," Jen said. "But please think about the questions and be as honest as you can, all right?"

"Yes," she said.

"In the time that you worked for the Bentons, was there anything at all unusual about Mr. Benton?"

"Unusual? In what way?"

"In any way," Jen said. "Anything that comes to mind."

"No. I can't think of anything at all."

"Was he a good boss?"

"Well, I really thought of Mrs. Benton as more of my boss. But he was always nice and everything. Why? Do you think he had something to do with—"

"Oh, no," Jen said. "Nothing like that. We're wondering if there might have been someone trying to get back at him for some reason."

"Okay. Because I can't imagine him doing anything like that."

"Would you say you liked Mr. Benton?"

143

"Well, I guess so. I didn't know him that well. He worked a lot, so I knew Mrs. Benton a lot better. She was awesome." A second wave of tears began forming.

"That's what everyone says about her," Jen said. "A lot of people feel like you do." Jen paused and let that thought take hold. "Just a few more questions," Jen said.

"Okay," Joely said.

"You said Mr. Benton never did anything that made you feel uncomfortable. Did you know that he had been accused of making advances toward one of the family's previous nannies?"

"No. I—" The astonishment in her expression told us everything we needed to know. "Really? I can't believe he'd ever do anything like that. He was always so nice."

Jen asked a few follow-up questions to take Joely's attention away from the bombshell and then wrapped up the interview.

As she opened the door for us, she asked, "When you find the people who did this, will it feel any better?"

Hearing the ache in her voice, I couldn't bear to tell her the truth. "Yes," I lied. "Yes, it will."

Five

"WELL, ACCORDING TO THE POSTMORTEM," PATRICK said, "Shevchuk died from a bullet wound to the head."

"Anything turn up we didn't expect?"

"Nope." He sat down at his desk and reached for his mouse. "Any news on the driver?"

"Jen's at his autopsy right now. I'm surprised you didn't pass her in the hall. We didn't get an ID off the prints. Maybe they'll find something on the table that will help."

Unlike me, Patrick can hold a completely coherent conversation while working on the computer. I am never sure how he does it.

He said, "I hope so. If it doesn't, where do we go next?"

"Who handled the canvass of the shopping center across the street from Pavilions?"

"Marty, I think, and some uniforms."

"Did he say anything about it?"

"I haven't had a chance to talk to him, but if he'd have found anything, he'd have let us know, right?"

"Anything big, yeah. Maybe he found something small."

Patrick said he'd seen him on the way in, so I went looking and found him downstairs hitting on a uniform patrol sergeant named Gretchen Murphy, who seemed happy for the distraction from the report she was working on.

"Marty," I said, "you got a minute?"

He looked at Gretchen with a put-upon expression and said, "Guess they can't handle things upstairs without me. Excuse me for a minute?"

She rolled her eyes. "Sure thing, Pops."

Marty winced and sucked air in through his clenched teeth. "Ouch."

Gretchen grinned and nodded at me. I returned her smile and followed Marty into the hall. "Really?" I said. "Gretchen Murphy? Isn't she about your daughter's age?"

"A little older, I think," he said matter-of-factly. His third marriage had ended more than a year ago, and he had decided that he only wanted to be involved with women who were on the job, certain that it had been his wife's lack of understanding of the difficulties involved in police work that had been their undoing. I didn't pretend to know better. My wife and I had been having problems of our own when she'd died in a car accident. Unlike Marty, though, I hadn't been involved with anyone in what seemed like a very long time.

"Did you get anything on the Seal Beach canvass?" I asked.

"Nothing, really. The receptionist in the optometrist's office saw a guy getting into the backseat of the SUV. White, average height, dark hair."

"Getting in? Did she see where he came from?"

"No," Marty said. "I asked her if he might have just gotten out of the front and into the back, and she just said 'maybe.'"

"And that was it?"

"Yeah," he said. "That's it."

———————— , ————————

"So far, so good," Ruiz said. He'd met with the department brass and tried to get some idea of whether or not they'd let us hold on to the Seal Beach murders.

"They're not trying to hand it off to the feds?"

"Not so far, but the wind can change pretty quick. And the feds haven't come knocking yet."

"But for now, it's ours, right?"

"For now."

Jen found us in the lieutenant's office. "Nothing new on the driver except a tattoo. The coroner thought it might be military."

"Well," Ruiz said, "at least it's something."

"How are we on overtime?" I asked.

"Let's keep it tight for now, all right?" he said.

Outside in the squad room, Jen said to me, "You're not going to call it a day yet, are you?"

"I figured I'd go through all the statement cards on the canvass from Seal Beach. And I imagine somebody's going to need to be Googling an assload of military tats before too long."

———————— · ————————

We got takeout from Domenico's on Second Street and ate in my front room while we worked. Jen had minestrone and a salad, and I knocked off most of a medium ground-pepperoni pizza. The restaurant is seriously old school and has been around forever. It is the only place that I have ever found a pizza with ground pepperoni. You could get it sliced, too, if you wanted to be lame.

The cards and notes from the canvass didn't take me as long as I'd thought they would, so we were both on our laptops and searching through image after image looking for a match of the tattoo that had been inked on the SUV driver's right shoulder. It was a pair of green footprints that reminded me of all those fake bigfoot tracks I'd seen when I was a kid.

"Why do you suppose the coroner thought this was military?" I said.

"I don't know. Think he's right?" she asked.

"He usually is."

"Maybe we should find someone military to talk to about it."

"Let's try something real quick." I typed "green footprints tattoo" into the search box on Google. "Well, shit."

"What?"

"Might be easier than we thought," I said. "There's a website here. Looks like the tat goes with the Pararescue division of the air force."

"What's that?"

"Some kind of special ops unit."

"The air force has special ops?"

"Yep. And if we can believe pararescue dot com, the PJs are pretty badass, too."

"PJs?"

"Pararescue jumpers," I said, reading off the computer screen.

"I guess they must be badass if they call themselves PJs," she said.

We poked around the Internet for another half hour or so, looking for more on the green footprints and the special air force unit.

When we felt like we had found enough, Jen closed her MacBook, went into the living room, and leaned back on the couch. "Not as late as I thought we'd be," she said. I had to look at the cable TV box to see the time: 8:38.

She noticed the case leaning up against the arm of the sofa. "What's that?"

"Harlan Gibbs gave me a banjo."

"What?" she said.

"Yeah. I told him my physical therapist said I should start playing the guitar, and the next thing I knew, he was handing me a banjo."

"When did your therapist tell you that?"

"She's been telling me for the last few appointments."

"Why didn't you mention it?"

"Because I didn't want to actually get one. I figured if you knew about it, you'd make me do it."

"Since when have I ever been able to *make* you do anything?"

I didn't know what to say, so I went with, "You know what I mean."

She obviously didn't, but she didn't push the point. "Why are you telling me now?"

"Because I'm worried about Harlan."

"You find out any more about his cancer?"

"No."

"Why does the banjo make you worry?"

"He gave it to me like it was no big deal, like he just had it lying around."

"You don't think he did?"

"Hang on," I said. I undid the clasps on the case, took the instrument out, and handed it to her.

"I didn't know banjos were this heavy," she said.

"Neither did I." I let her handle it, make the strings twang. "You know anything about music?"

"Not really," she said. "Piano lessons when I was twelve. That's about it."

"That seems like a good one, doesn't it?"

She rubbed her finger over the wood and metal, turned it over in her hands. "It does." She examined the frets and the neck. "Looks like it's been played a lot," she said. "But well cared for."

"That's exactly what I thought."

"This seems like the kind of thing that would mean a lot to somebody," she said.

"And I think it might be worth a lot of money, too."

"Is he giving up?" she asked. I hadn't expected her to be so direct, but I was glad she was. The conversation made me think I had pegged Harlan's behavior correctly.

"I think he might be, and I'm not sure what to do about it."

"How can I help?"

"What did you do for me when I gave up?" I asked.

Her expression warmed. "I just ignored it and pretended like you didn't. You came around. He will, too."

———————— ˌ ————————

After Jen left, I sat on the couch and strummed the banjo softly, which was not as easy to do as it sounds. I tried to get a slow, even rhythm going, but found myself speeding up without meaning to. Each time I caught myself, I slowed down again. Then I'd find myself thinking about Harlan or Sara and the kids and the tempo would pick up. After a while, though, I started getting better at maintaining the cadence. It took more focus than I would have thought.

I put the banjo away and went back into the dining room to go over my notes one more time. After I opened my computer and set iTunes on shuffle, the first song that came up was Springsteen's "Atlantic City." Not the '82 original, but the version from *Live in Dublin* with the Sessions Band. And fuck me if the intro wasn't a solo banjo that sounded like the coolest thing since The Big Man's saxophone.

Three

THE NEXT MORNING, WE WERE TALKING TO MARTY AND DAVE about the green footprints.

"I've heard of Pararescue," Dave said. "Supposed to be pretty tough. Go behind enemy lines and get people out. Pilots, mostly, I suppose."

"So they're tough, huh?" I asked.

"Well, it's the air force, so they're probably not like SEALs or Green Berets. But they've got a reputation."

"You know any of them?" Jen asked.

"Me? Hell, no. I was in the merchant marines. I don't know much about that stuff."

"I know a retired air force guy," Marty said. "Let me give him a call. See what I can find out."

———————————

I mentioned what I'd noticed about the news coverage to the lieutenant.

"Danny's right. The press doesn't seem to have connected Shevchuk or the SUV killing to the Benton murders," Ruiz told the rest of the squad.

"That's good," Marty said. "How do we keep it that way?"

"Patrick's already the lead on Shevchuk, and I want you to take point on the driver," Ruiz told him. "We'll keep them as separate as we can on paper. Maybe we'll be able to keep a lid on it for a while."

Marty Locklin had been on the Homicide Detail for almost twenty years, and he'd been a cop for more than thirty. He was long past the point of worrying about how a big case might help his career or even his ego. His preference was for what actually comprised most of our daily work—the routine. This case had a lot more flash than he cared for. But he was a pro, so he stepped up, and he didn't complain. He just looked at Jen and me to make sure we didn't feel like he'd be taking anything away from us, and when we both gave small nods of approval, he said, "Sure thing, Boss."

Jen had lunch plans, so I used the time for something else. I'd been driving past a place on Seventh Street called World of Strings for as long as I could remember. There was an empty spot a few doors down. I parked, got Harlan's banjo out of the trunk, and took it inside. The name of the store was appropriate. I'd never seen so many stringed instruments in one place. There were guitars, violins, basses, mandolins, and just about everything in between. They even had a few harps against the far wall. The place smelled like dust and furniture polish.

The guy at the counter was youngish—midtwenties—and had a flannel shirt and a long and shaggy hairstyle that looked like 1993. I wondered if he was old enough to remember Kurt Cobain. He smiled distractedly and asked if he could help me.

I put the banjo case in front of him and said, "I hope so." I undid the clasps and held the banjo out to him. "A friend of mine gave this to me, and I'm wondering how much it's worth."

His expression fell and I could sense his disapproval. "There's a lot more to an instrument than how much you can get for it."

"It's not like that," I said. "My friend is sick, and I'm worried he's being more generous than he should. I have a feeling that it might be worth a lot."

He considered me and must have decided I was on the level. "Banjos aren't really my thing, but let me take a look." He sat down on a tall stool and rested it on his leg. He strummed and picked a bit, then held it up and examined it from top to bottom. "It's a good instrument. Deerings usually are, I think. Well made, and it's got a real sweet tone. If you look here, though, I'm not sure about this." He held out the base and pointed at a ring around the drum head. "See this? It looks like its discolored and maybe even corroded a little bit. I'm not sure about that."

"Can you give me any idea at all? At least a few hundred dollars, right?"

"Oh, way more than that, I'm sure. More than a thousand, minimum. See the woodwork here? This is good stuff."

"Any idea how I could find out more about it?"

"You could bring it back when Greg is here later. Or you could leave it and I'll ask him to take a look for you."

"Okay," I said as he handed it back to me. "Thanks. I appreciate your help."

When I was halfway to the door, he stopped me. "Hey," he said. "You know what? Why don't you just call Deering?"

"That's a good idea. Thanks." I wondered why I hadn't thought of that myself. Sometimes I wish I were like a detective or something.

———————— , ————————

My BlackBerry went off. It was another automated text from Patrick's monitoring program. Bradley was using his card again.

I speed-dialed Patrick.

"Hey, Danny," he said. "What's up?"

"Just got another text about Bradley's card. Can you check it?"

"Hang on."

He came back a few seconds later.

"AMC Marina Pacifica. About ten minutes ago."

"He's at the movies?"

"Looks like it."

"Perfect."

———————— , ————————

His Panamera Turbo S was easy to spot. It was the only $170,000 car with a cognac metallic finish in the whole lot. I parked a few spaces up the row from it, and as I walked past, I pretended to tie my shoe while I slipped a GPS tracking unit housed in a magnetic case under the rear fender.

Then I headed down to the box office and tried to guess what movie he was seeing. Based on the start times, it was most likely either *Cedar Rapids* or *The Eagle*. I figured Bradley for a Channing Tatum guy. I couldn't imagine an Ed Helms fan driving that car of his. It was chock full of apparent aesthetic value.

Rather than take a chance on being spotted coming in late to one of the movies, I badged the employee behind the window selling tickets and asked her the end times of each of the movies. The first one didn't get out for an hour, so I wandered upstairs to loiter in Barnes & Noble. I dodged the guy in front trying to sell me a Nook and found a seat in one of the comfy chairs back by the magazines. An article in *Combat Handguns* gave a glowing review to a 1911 .45 made by a company called Nighthawk Custom. I gagged at the price. Who would pay $4,000 for a pistol?

A guy like Bradley.

I went back outside twenty minutes early and waited for him. He surprised me by coming out with the crowd from the comedy.

If the film had done anything to lighten his mood, though, it wasn't apparent. He moved slowly, and his shoulders were slumped forward. His hair was unstyled, and he wore jeans and a sweatshirt. The *Stanford* across his chest was the only recognizable thing about him.

He came up the stairs toward the parking lot, and I headed him off.

"Hello, Mr. Benton," I said, surprising him.

He looked taken aback for just a moment, as if he had been caught doing something he should not have been doing. Almost as quickly, though, his face fell again into the same sad emptiness it had held before I spoke. He didn't place me immediately.

"I'm Detective Beckett," I said. "How are you?"

In any normal circumstances, it would have been a stupid and thoughtless question to ask—his wife and children had been murdered. How could any answer adequately address that fact? But I asked it intentionally, so it was just callous and mean.

"I...uh..." He didn't know how to answer. I had been hoping he'd have a practiced response. A politician's response. One that would prove to me his insensitivity and coldness. One that would allow me to believe he'd been responsible for the deaths of Sara and Bailey and Jacob.

"It's okay," I said. "You don't have to answer."

I led him over to the tables outside the Starbucks, and we sat down. He looked a lot more like a shell-shocked war casualty than someone who'd just stepped out of a comedy that was pulling 86 percent on Rotten Tomatoes.

"You just see a movie?"

"Yeah."

"Good," I said. "Which one?"

He couldn't answer. He didn't remember.

"It's okay. I understand. I lost my wife violently a few years ago."

I think that was the first time he really looked at me. "Yeah," he said.

We sat there for a minute or two in our grief. I waited for him to talk.

"I thought…I thought if I got out for just a little while…that maybe I…"

"I know," I said. "I know. It's going to take a long time."

He nodded at me, and the pain in his eyes was so palpable and despairing that it was hard to believe he was a rapist.

When I called the Deering factory, which turned out to be located just outside San Diego, I talked to a guy named Barry, whose name I recognized from the company's website. It had identified him as their worldwide sales manager. I told him about the situation, and he asked me a few questions about the banjo. When I described the part with the metal that seemed discolored, he stopped me with an excited "Oh!"

"Oh?" I said.

"You've got a Saratoga Star with Jens Kruger tone ring."

"I do?"

"Yes." He told me a detailed story about a bell foundry in Switzerland and how they made a special part for that particular banjo. There was a keen enthusiasm in his voice that actually got me a little bit excited, even though I had trouble following much of what he was saying. Barry seemed to have a surprisingly thorough knowledge of metallurgy. He finished with, "It's a very subjective thing, but I think that model of banjo has a better tone than just about anything else out there."

"Really?"

"Oh, yeah. Tony Trischka and Bela Fleck have both played them."

I'd actually heard of Bela Fleck, so I didn't feel quite as lost as I had through most of our conversation. "It must be very valuable, then," I said.

"Well, depending on its age and whether or not there were any custom features added, it's probably worth somewhere between seven and eight thousand dollars."

I was silent long enough for him to think we'd lost the connection. "Hello?" he said.

"Wow, that's a lot more than I expected."

"It is an excellent banjo."

"Thank you, Barry. I really appreciate the help."

"Happy to. Do me a favor, would you?"

"Sure. What?"

"Let me know what you decide to do with it."

"I will."

And I really will, I thought, if I can ever figure it out.

We assumed Turchenko had heard the news about Shevchuk, but we wanted to see if we might be able to leverage some kind of information out of him. Bob Kincaid, the DDA handling the case, had an unusual idea. Because the Ukrainian had invoked his right to legal representation, we weren't allowed to question him without his attorney present. We could, however, make a death notification.

The interview room in the administrative segregation unit of the county jail was even smaller than the one we used back at the station. Looked about eight by eight or so. Jen sat at the table, and I stood just behind and to her left.

One of the two deputies who had led Turchenko down the hall waited outside, and the other prodded him into the chair across the table from Jen. He wore the ubiquitous orange jumpsuit and had his hands cuffed to a leather belt around his waist.

"Hello, Mr. Turchenko," she said. "Do you remember me? I'm Detective Tanaka."

"Without lawyer," he grumbled, "I am not supposed to talk."

"That's okay, Mr. Turchenko," she said. "You don't have to say anything. We won't be questioning you."

"Then what?" There was a dull groan in his voice, and I remembered the first time I had seen him, with milk running down his chin but thinking about going for his gun. The danger seemed suppressed. But not the oafishness.

"I'm afraid we have some bad news," Jen said. "Your friend, Taras Shevchuk, has been killed."

He already knew; that much was clear from his expression. But he was clearly confused. I figured he was struggling with what to make of the fact that we were bothering to tell him anything at all.

"I know," he said.

"Your friend was murdered," I said with as much sympathy as I could fake.

"Don't worry, though," Jen said. "We have it on good authority that you'll be able to stay here in ad-seg. Whoever killed your friend probably won't be able to get to you."

He raised his head and lost a bit of the slump in his shoulders. "Probably?"

"You shouldn't worry, Mr. Turchenko," Jen said, leaning forward. "I'm sure you're very safe here."

It actually was unlikely that anyone would be able to get to him where he was. But we were betting on the fact that he wouldn't believe it.

"Is there anyone else you'd like to tell us about, Mr. Shevchuk?" Jen asked.

"Anton Tropov?" I asked, as if the idea had just occurred to me. Turchenko's eyes widened at the name, and he lost even more of the slouch.

"You might want to talk to your lawyer about him, Mr. Turchenko," Jen said.

"Yeah," I said, "you should. Unless, of course, he's Tropov's lawyer, too."

He looked confused.

I gave him the best fake look of surprise I could muster. "He's not, is he? Your lawyer doesn't represent Anton, too, does he?"

We watched him for a few moments, and we could almost hear the screws turning inside his skull, and then the realization that we were reading his behavior dawned on him and his shoulders re-hunched and his eyes returned to the slits they had been when he came in.

"No," he said. "No one else to tell about. Can I go now?"

"Of course," Jen said. "Good luck."

He glanced back at her once and then trudged back the way he had come with the two deputies at his heels.

"How do you think that went?" I asked.

"I almost feel bad taking advantage of someone that dim."

"Really?"

"No," she said, "not really."

It was a bit after seven when I stepped up onto Harlan's front porch. He saw me through the front window and motioned for me to come in. Before the screen door even closed behind me, I said, in what was probably the loudest voice he had ever heard me use, "Why the fuck did you give me an eight-thousand-dollar banjo?"

When I saw the expression on his face, I regretted my tone. When I saw the woman who came into the living room from the kitchen, I regretted it even more.

"Danny," Harlan said, "I'd like you to meet my daughter, Cynthia." The alarm I'd seen in his face had given way to a bemused smirk as he saw me squirm, trying to cover my embarrassment.

"Hello, I…uh…" I realized I'd misspoken, but she spoke before I could correct my mistake.

"Hi," she said. "Dad's told me a lot about you."

"Yes," I said. "Me too."

"He's right," Harlan said. "I tell Danny a lot about himself. He just never listens."

They both thought that was very funny. She was tall, like Harlan, with broad shoulders and hips, and a smile that seemed comfortable on her face.

"We just finished eating," she said. "Can I get you a plate?"

"No," I said. "I'm fine. Thank you." I wasn't sure why I said that. I hadn't eaten, and my stomach had been growling in the car on the way there.

The three of us chatted a bit about things that didn't really matter, and when we reached a natural lull in the conversation, Cynthia said, "Why don't I go clean up the kitchen and give you guys a chance to talk?"

"Thanks," Harlan said.

"So?"

"So what?"

"Why did you give me the banjo?"

"I told you why. For your physical therapy."

When I tried to stare him down, he said, "It'll be even better than a guitar. For your left hand. You have to do more hammer-ons and pull-offs and such."

"I think you're full of shit."

"You know what I did to the last man who said that to me?"

"I don't know. Dragged him through the town square behind your horse?"

He didn't quite laugh at that, but I could see that he came close.

"In all seriousness, Danny, I gave it to you because I thought it would do you some good. It's different having a really good musical instrument like that Deering. You can't just blow it off like you would some crappy hundred-and-twenty-dollar guitar. It's serious having something that valuable, and you have to take it seriously. I want your hand to get better. I thought it would help. Besides, I have two more even better than that one."

"Even better than the Jens Kruger tone ring?"

He did laugh a bit then. "Spent some time on Google, did you?"

"Even talked to a guy at the factory."

"Wow."

We were quiet for a few moments, and then I came right out and asked him the question that had been on my mind since I'd first seen the Deering.

"What if I don't want to play the banjo?"

"What if I don't want stomach cancer?"

Fortunately, I didn't have to reply to that because Cynthia came back into the living room with a plate in each hand and said, "Who wants pie?"

———————— · ————————

An hour and a half later, I had just left and was putting the key in the lock on my Camry's door when I heard Harlan's screen door close and turned to see Cynthia walking toward me with an aluminum foil–covered plate.

"Hey," she said. "I brought you a piece of pie."

"Thanks," I said.

"I don't think my dad believes that I just came out here to give you dessert."

"Did you?"

"No. I came to ask you about the banjo. Which one did he give you?"

"It's a Deering Saratoga Star."

"That's what I was afraid of."

"Why? He said he had two others that are even better."

"He has others that are more valuable, but that one's his favorite," she said. "He always said it had the best sound of any banjo he'd ever played."

Nine

I DON'T KNOW WHAT WAS WORSE THAT NIGHT—THE WORRY OR the pain. I'd trimmed an hour off the prescribed interval between Vicodin doses, and at two thirty in the morning, I was sitting in the living room watching *Shake 'Em Down* for the sixth or seventh time. Too bad the movie's star, Jack Palms, turned out to be a junkie asshole wife beater. He might have filled that big gap between Bruce Willis and Jason Statham with a few more decent action flicks if he hadn't had to go to prison. I'd seen the movie too many times for it to distract me, though, and I couldn't stop my attention from ping-ponging back and forth between Harlan and the Benton victims. And the viciously constricting tension in my neck and shoulder was constant.

In the bathroom, I turned the shower on to hot and let the water blast me lobster red. When the water heater exhausted its supply, I toweled off and reluctantly put myself to bed, my skin numb and stinging from the heat just enough to pull my focus away from the pain and allow me to settle into a shallow and fitful sleep.

———————————

The next morning, Marty came in a few minutes after Jen and me with a big pink box, and I found the only cruller in the batch.

"Good news," he said.

"Yeah?" I replied, my mouth full of coffee and cruller.

"Driver had two cell phones," Marty said. "A prepaid throw-away and an iPhone."

"Get an ID?" Jen asked.

"Not unless he's a fifty-two-year-old woman from Simi Valley. But there's an assload of data there. The techs are downloading everything and running it through that new Lantern software to see how far back we can trace the locations."

"Maybe we'll catch a break," I said.

Jen peeled the foil top off a Yoplait and asked, "Any other smartphones we can cross-reference?"

I'd been through the files enough times to know the answer without looking. "Only Sara Benton's," I said. "But let's check the call logs against everything else we have to see what might connect. And let's check with Patrick, too. See if he's got anything he picked out of the data."

An hour later, Marty came back from tech services with what looked like a ream of paper in his hands.

"They printed it all out. Two and half months' worth of location data." He dropped the pile on his desk with a thud and fished around in his shirt pocket. "I had to ask them for this." He held up a black plastic thumb drive.

"You know how the techs are," Jen said. "They think everybody over forty is still living in the dark ages."

"Yeah?" he said. "What do you think?"

"I think it's cute when you type with two fingers."

Marty seemed satisfied with that. "Want copies?" he said.

"Yeah," I said. "Why don't we all start working on it?"

We agreed and divided the spreadsheets by date, with a section each for Dave and Patrick as well.

Smartphones record their locations by triangulating with cell towers and Wi-Fi hotspots and occasionally pinging off satellites, all in the form of latitude and longitude coordinates. The techs were able to download this data from the SUV driver's iPhone and translate it into a series of street addresses laid out in spreadsheet form that we could check against all the addresses we had that were related with the case. If we came up dry in that regard and couldn't make any connections, we'd start Googling the addresses one by one and hope we found a needle in the haystack.

"I'll cross-reference all the addresses we have in the murder book," I said. "Let's see if we get lucky with anything before we start checking the locations one by one."

Marty and Jen both seemed relieved that I'd volunteered for what amounted to the glorified data-entry task. The truth was, even though I didn't relish the idea of spending the morning in front of a spreadsheet, the new information kindled the excitement and the connection I felt to the case. As long I believed there might really be a needle in that haystack, I didn't mind going through it straw by straw.

I ate lunch at my desk and was just finishing up a Modica's meatball sandwich when Jen came back into the squad.

"Just got off the phone with Kincaid," she said.

"What's up?"

"Turchenko wants a meet."

"Think he'll roll on Tropov?"

"What else could it be?"

"Did he get a new lawyer?"

"I forgot to ask," Jen said.

"If Shevchuk was killed to keep him from talking and they were both working for Anton Tropov, how do you figure he'll play it if he gets word that Turchenko is going to roll?"

"That's why Ruiz got him transferred to ad-seg. Tough to hit him there."

"So we're figuring Tropov's either got to shut him up or skip."

"Yeah." She looked at me and saw the idea take root. "What are you thinking?"

"Why would Tropov want Sara Benton killed?"

"I don't know."

"What if he's not the shot caller?"

"A contractor?"

"Yeah," I said. "What if?"

"Then he could be the next target."

―――――――――― , ――――――――――

Whenever Bob Kincaid and Jen are in the same room, I always feel like a supporting player. The three of us were in an interview room waiting for the guards to escort Turchenko in for his visit. We had already filled him in on everything we needed to, so they chatted.

"Any leads on houses?" he asked.

"Saw a nice Craftsman last weekend in Belmont Heights."

She didn't mention that I'd found it and pointed it out to her.

"Yeah?" he said. "Is it the one?"

"I don't know."

"Then it's not. You'll know when it is."

"How?"

"Trust me," he said, "you'll just know."

"I'm not sure I have your confidence."

"Don't settle. It's a buyer's market."

She was about to say something else when the door opened and Turchenko was led in and told to sit by a single hulking guard. Usually there are two escorts. Maybe this one was big enough to be counted twice.

The guard looked at Jen, then at Turchenko's handcuffs. She nodded, and he removed them. The bracelets dangled from the strap around Turchenko's waist.

After Turchenko was seated, the guard leaned out the door toward the public waiting room and motioned to someone outside. A man we hadn't seen before entered. The new guy wore a nicer suit than I did and had a shiny gold watch on his wrist that would have looked too big even on the guard.

"You wanted to see us?" Kincaid said to the Ukrainian.

The new suit talked before Turchenko had a chance to reply.

"Hello. You must be DDA Kincaid and Detectives"—he opened a leather portfolio and pretended to check his notes—"Tanaka and Beckett."

We nodded.

"I'm Robert Pfister. Mr. Turchenko's new counsel. He's agreed to meet with you on my advice."

"How do you spell that?" I asked, holding up my pen and notebook as if I were about to write it down. "F? P-h?"

"P-f-i-s-t-e-r."

He hid his irritation well, but it was there. I pretended to write it in my notebook and didn't press him any further.

"What did you want to talk about?" Kincaid said, directing the question at Turchenko.

He might have been dim, but he knew enough to let his lawyer speak for him.

"There's a possibility my client may have some information that could be of use to you."

Six

"I NEVER WANT THIS," TURCHENKO BEGAN. "TARAS, TOO. THIS is not why we came to America. Not to kill children."

They both had criminal records that had followed them from the Ukraine. But there was so much going on politically and societally in the late nineties that we had to wonder how much they got away with that nobody ever noticed. Still, judging from everything we were able to dig up, they were petty criminals who upped their game to the big leagues when they immigrated to the States.

"Tropov," he said, "is my cousin. He promised much work for us. Good work on the docks. Longshoreman. Legitimate." There was a heavy sadness in his voice, and his regret seemed to thicken the air in the small room. "That's what it seemed like at first. Loading trucks. Driving van. Delivery. Things like that."

"But..." Kincaid let the single word sit there.

"Yes, there is 'but' always." Turchenko looked at the three of us. Whether he realized that winning our sympathies was not only impossible but pointless as well, or whether he just got tired of speaking, I don't know. He gave up on the story of his tragic fall from grace at the hands of the dark side of the American Dream and got right to the point.

"Tropov hired us to kill the wife."

"Which Tropov?" I asked.

"Anton."

"Just Anton? What about his cousin, Yevgeny?" At the mention of the other Tropov's name, Turchenko's eyes widened. I couldn't be sure it was fear, but it might have been. He was certainly surprised by the fact that someone might think him associated with Yevgeny.

"No, no. Anton only."

Kincaid asked, "You were hired to kill only Sara Benton?"

"Yes."

"Then why kill the children?"

"They saw Taras," Turchenko said, staring down at the dull metal surface of the table. "His face." He raised his hands in a gesture of helplessness, as if we were sure to understand that they just had to kill Bailey and Jacob after the children had seen their faces. They just had to. I mean, what else could anyone do in that situation? We'd all do the same, right?

I had to hand it to Kincaid. He played the moment perfectly enough that even Pfister seemed surprised. The DDA nodded so sympathetically that, for a moment, I thought he might actually be sincere. "Of course," he said so quietly that it was almost inaudible. "What else could you do?"

They looked at each other, Turchenko and Kincaid, and it wouldn't have surprised me if they'd gone on to share a good cry. They didn't, but I knew we'd just had a major break.

———————— , ————————

Turchenko not only rolled on Tropov but pled out. He agreed to life with the possibility of parole instead of life without, and Kincaid promised him that, for his protection, he'd be segregated from the general prison population for as long as he was incarcerated.

After the guard re-cuffed him and escorted him out of the room, Kincaid looked at Jen and said, "I hope the judge will go for that."

"Me too," she replied.

It would have to be officially approved by the DA and a judge, and the LBPD brass would have a say as well. The feds, too. It could be vetoed by any of them. The downside of the deal would be that the case was close to a slam dunk. It would be hard to imagine a situation in which he wouldn't go down for life. The death penalty was even a strong possibility. But the big sacrifice the higher-ups would be making was a closed case. For Jen and me, and even for Kincaid, following the trail to whoever ultimately decided to kill Sara Benton was of the utmost importance. From a political standpoint, it was a better bet to stick a needle in the arm of the big scary foreigner and call it a triumph of the justice system.

But that wouldn't get us Tropov. And whoever pulled his strings.

"What do you think the odds are?" I asked.

"Hard to say." Kincaid fastened the latches on his briefcase. "I think my boss will be happy with the plea. There are a lot of other fingers in the pie, though…"

We stood by the door and waited for the guard to escort us out.

"When was the last time you ate an actual vegetable?" Jen asked me after we picked up takeout from Carnitas Michoacan across the street and down the block from the station. The place was no Enrique's, not even close. But what the food lacked in quality it made up for in convenience.

"There's corn in the tortillas," I said. "And I'm gonna have at least a tablespoon of salsa."

"Oh," she said, "my bad."

"What do you think about Tropov?" I said as we stood on the corner of Broadway and Cedar waiting for the light to change. We'd parked in the department garage and walked over before heading upstairs.

"I can't see him having an angle. There's no connection between him and the Bentons at all."

"My thoughts exactly. I'm betting he's just a contractor in this, piecing the work off to Shevchuk and Turchenko. What else fits?"

"Well, Bob's already on the warrant for Tropov, so we'll pick him up and sort it out later."

"Yeah," I said.

There must have been something unfinished in the way I spoke, because when I didn't continue, Jen said, "What?"

"If Tropov's the contractor, did he have Shevchuk killed, or was it whoever he was working for?"

"I don't know. But we better get to figuring it out."

"How do we do that?"

"That's your job," she said. "I'm just here to nag people about balanced diets."

Upstairs, we filled in Ruiz and the rest of the squad while we ate our lunch and waited on Kincaid for the arrest warrant for Tropov.

The lieutenant shared our concerns about closing the case. "But we still have Shevchuk and the Seal Beach SUV cases. Even if they reject the plea and decide to pin the whole thing on Turchenko," he said, the Texas creeping back into his voice, "we've still got irons in the fire."

He looked at Marty. "Anything new on the SUV?"

"Found out more about the green footprint tattoo," Marty said, tipping back a venti Starbucks cup.

I wasn't sure if he'd eaten and felt a momentary twinge of guilt at the fact that we didn't ask anyone if they wanted us to bring any food back for them. I stifled a burp, though, and the feeling passed.

Marty went on. He wasn't sure how much Patrick and Dave knew about the tat, so he covered the connection with air force Pararescue and a bit of the history we'd found on the web. "Funny thing, though—if you're a real PJ, you only ever get the footprints on your ass. But not everybody knows that. The word from my guy is that they see anybody with the footprints anyplace other than a butt cheek, they take them out in the alley and kick the shit out of them."

"Or maybe make them pull the getaway car over and blow their brains all over the windshield?" Dave asked.

"Maybe," I said. "Could be that the tat was only part of it. We know the driver fucked up. The shooter knew, too. He should have been able to lie down in the backseat with his rifle across his chest as they calmly pulled out of the parking lot. But the driver blew it. Even after that, he should have been able to lose us. If he'd researched the route or had any tactical driving skills, we wouldn't have been able to stay on them. The shooter knew all this, too. And he'd already seen the footprints on the driver's arm. That's three strikes."

"Does that mean the shooter's Pararescue?" Jen asked.

"Either him or someone close to him," Dave said. "He's got the training. Don't forget the way he disappeared into the wilds of Seal Beach even with two helicopters, three dozen uniforms, and a couple of canine units looking for him."

For me, that was the most compelling piece of information. Special forces evasion training helped that make sense.

"So," Marty asked, "how do we start working the PJ angle?"

"With the congressman," I said. "The bio on his webpage mentions his having served in the air force."

"Does it say anything about his unit?" Marty asked.

"No. And there's only one brief mention. Something about a period of service between college and law school."

Jen asked, "What kind of politician only gives their military service a passing mention in their official bio?"

"He didn't have an Other Than Honorable discharge, did he?" Patrick said.

"No. If it was anything like that, it wouldn't be there at all," Ruiz said.

"It's someone who's proud of what he did in the service," I said, "but isn't allowed to talk about it."

———————— , ————————

While we continued to wait for the arrest warrant on Tropov, we reorganized our priorities. We wanted to talk to the congressman about air force Pararescue, but first we had to check out his actual service record and look for any other possible connections between him and any other Person of Interest on the case and the PJs. We needed to be sure we'd found all the angles before we questioned him. None of us had finished cross-referencing our location data from the green-footprinted SUV driver yet, either. And we still hadn't explored the DVD we had recovered from the safe. We needed to find and interview everyone involved. Especially the girl Bradley had raped. And we still needed to look for more of Bradley's victims. None of us who'd seen the deposition believed that the sexual assault being detailed was his first. And those were just the afternoon's priorities.

So the first thing I did when I sat down at my desk was check CalBungalow.com to see if there were any new listings Jen might be interested in. There was a terrific Spanish Revival bungalow in California Heights that was brand-new. It was a little bigger and slightly over her budget, but I couldn't recall working a case with her anywhere too close to the neighborhood. It looked like a good possibility to me. I e-mailed the link to her. She had three or four already in her inbox that she hadn't yet commented on.

Marty and Dave were out of the office, and Jen had gone downstairs.

Patrick and I were the only ones in the squad room, and he had been clacking away at his keyboard. He looked over at me and asked, "How far have you gotten with those location logs from the driver's iPhone?"

"Not far," I said. "Why?"

"Because I've got the database here sorting it for us. Give me a couple of hours, and I think I'll get what we need out of the files."

"Sweet." I wasn't sure if he really had the impression that I was going to dive into the data, but I didn't do anything to disabuse him of the notion.

I opened my browser's bookmarks and clicked on the congressman's website again and found the passing reference to his USAF service. It was just as I had remembered—a brief, single mention: "After graduating from UCLA, Congressman Benton enlisted in the United States Air Force before returning to law school at Stanford." That was it. The more I thought about it, the more I believed our theory fit and that he might indeed have been a Pararescue jumper during his enlistment. We'd find out soon enough.

"Hey," I said to Patrick. "Did we ever finish the background on Roger Kroll?"

"Good question," he said. We both started searching our notes and files. "It doesn't look like it. Why? You have something on your mind?"

"Did he do any military service?"

"I don't know." His fingers started clacking on the keys again.

Before he looked up again, Jen came back into the room. "Just got the call from Bob. We're good to go on the arrest. They want to take a SWAT dangerous-warrant team."

"You call it in?" I asked. "They good to go?"

She nodded. "Ruiz, too. We're meeting them a few blocks over from Tropov's warehouse. Going in hard."

"You want to come?" I said to Patrick.

He hesitated just long enough for it to be noticeable, then stood up and said, "Yeah," with an enthusiasm none of us bought. The ATM shooting still had him rattled.

Jen looked at me, and I tried to indicate that I thought it was a good thing that he was ready to step back up to the plate. I don't think she got it, though, because all I saw was a question in her eyes. Then Patrick caught us trying to figure out each other's expressions, and I tried to break the awkwardness by tossing the keys to the unmarked cruiser we'd checked out that morning and saying, "You drive."

It didn't work, and the weird uneasiness followed us all the way down in the elevator and into the garage.

Patrick finally lightened the mood by saying, "If this one gets his head blown off, too, I'm going back to Computer Crimes."

―――――――――― . ――――――――――

"What do you mean he's not in there?" I asked the SWAT sergeant on the scene. His name was Phillips. We knew each other but hadn't worked together.

"There's someone inside." He plopped a Panasonic Toughbook down on the hood of his Police Interceptor, flipped the screen up, and hit a button on the keyboard. "It's just not him." He spun the notebook computer toward us. "It's this guy."

Someone had snapped a photo of a man sitting behind Anton's desk. They must have used a telephoto lens, because it looked like a close-up. And I could easily recognize the face.

"You know him?" Phillips asked.

"Yeah," I said.

"Well?"

Jen answered for me. "That's Anton's cousin. Yevgeny Tropov."

"What do you want us to do?"

"Can we sit on him for a while?"

"For a couple of hours," Phillips said. "After that, we'll need to get a surveillance authorized. You want us to stay on him or on the warehouse?"

I looked at Jen. "What do you suppose Anton knows?"

"At the very least, he knows Turchenko's got a new lawyer," she said.

"And if he knows that, he must know there's a good chance he flipped."

"Stay on Yevgeny," I said. "We'll go back to the station and try to get a full surveillance authorization. You call us if he moves, and we'll call you as soon as we get authorization for a new operation."

"You got it," he said.

"So you think Anton's in the wind and we need to tail his cousin?" Ruiz asked.

"Yes," Jen said.

"What are you asking for?"

"Everything," I said. "Wire and cell taps. GPS smartphone tracking. Twenty-four seven eyes-on surveillance."

"If I can't get the captain to go for a full team, you think it's important enough to sit on him yourself?"

Jen and I had talked about that on the ride back to the station. The decision hinged on what strategy we thought was most likely to get us to Anton. Would we be better off staking out Yevgeny and hoping he'd lead us to his cousin, or would the chances be better if we pursued other strategies? As long as we were staking out a suspect, we'd be pretty much useless in any other capacity.

"Probably not. If Anton is hiding, then he's enough of a pro to know we'll be looking at Yevgeny, and it's not likely they'll meet," I said.

"I think we'll get the taps, but probably not the team," Ruiz said. "Let me make the calls."

———————— · ————————

He was right. When Phillips checked in a few hours later, I told him to wrap it up. The GPS tracking had been authorized and we'd be able to monitor Yevgeny's movements through his smartphone, assuming the Android in his name at Verizon was actually the one he was carrying. I suspected he'd be sharp enough to dump it somewhere and carry a throwaway. Or maybe even to plant it on a decoy. I thought maybe I'd try sitting on his house for a while on my way home.

Jen and I were back at our desks. Marty and Dave were still out. Ruiz told us they were working leads on another case. No new murders had come in since the Bentons'. That was good, but the squad still had half a dozen active open cases. We couldn't put them on the back burner for very long. No matter how high profile our current case was, the other victims were every bit as dead as Sara and the children. And they deserved every bit as much effort no matter how much wealth and influence they didn't have.

"Here we go," Patrick said softly. I couldn't tell if he was speaking to us or to himself.

"Sorry?" I said.

"I think we might have something," he said.

"What?" Jen asked.

"I entered every address that came up anywhere in our records on the Bentons and had the database cross-reference it with every address in the location logs from the driver's phone."

We waited for him to go on. He didn't.

"And?" I said.

"And the only match was an address at Olympic and Avenue of the Stars in Century City. He was there for about three hours last week."

"Is that location supposed to mean something to us?" I was trying to keep the frustration out of my voice and not doing a very good job.

He picked up on it and got right to the point. "Sternow and Byrne," he said. "That's their building."

"There was an article in the *LA Times* several months ago. I think it got a little TV play, too," I said.

Patrick, Jen, and I had managed to corner Ruiz on his way out of the office. He had been ready to go—sleeves rolled back down, suit coat on again, briefcase in hand. But when he saw the three of us, he took off his jacket, let out a barely audible sigh, and sat back down behind his desk.

"Do you have a link to the article online?" he asked.

"Not yet. I will, though, and I'll get it to you ASAP," I said.

"Give me the gist of it."

"Sternow and Byrne were huge and getting even bigger. They bought one of the smaller private military firms that had been operating in Iraq and Afghanistan. Said they were going to turn it into a security, investigation, and protection arm that would work with clients worldwide. The international angle was a big part of how they were justifying the whole deal."

"How much did they pay?"

"Nobody knows. The PMF was privately owned, and apparently the sale actually took place out of the country. Didn't have to report anything."

"Danny," Ruiz asked, "what do you want to do with this?"

"First, we have the driver at their headquarters. Maybe he's ex-military and trying to impress people with the green footprints. Or maybe with something else, but he was there. Also, there have to be government connections. Is the congressman tied to them in any way other than by his personal attorney? Are

there any business connections? Any congressional wheels getting greased with the PMF purchase? We need everything from
their employment records on up."

"If they're doing government work, everything that might
help us will probably be classified," Jen said.

Patrick nodded in agreement. "We'll send up red flags if we
start making any formal requests. Let's see what I can dig up
before we do anything that might tip them off."

"Good," Ruiz said. "Find out everything we can before we go
forward on this."

"What about the feds?" I turned to Patrick. "Are they monitoring our investigation?"

"Probably," he said.

"Anything we can do about that?" I asked.

"No. But I can poke without them knowing about it."

"How?" Ruiz asked.

"I can use my personal machine, make sure nobody's watching."

Ruiz thought it through. "Do it," he said to Patrick. "You two
start thinking about the connections. What does it mean if the
driver's connected to Sternow and Byrne? Does that come back
to the congressman? To Bradley? Check out every other building within half a mile of the Century City address. Be sure he
couldn't have been anyplace else. And follow through on the
congressman. Find out if he actually was Pararescue. See if you
can link him to anyone in the company besides Campos."

"OT?" Jen asked.

"Whatever you need," Ruiz said.

———————— · ————————

Patrick said it would be better if he didn't use any city connections, so he headed home and told us he'd check in a few hours
later or as soon as he found anything relevant.

"Should we get food?" Jen asked.

"Sure," I said.

"What do you feel like?"

"Whatever sounds good to you."

She gave me an odd look. "You always have an opinion about food. What's wrong?"

"Nothing," I said. "Just anxious to get to work."

Needles of pain stabbed my shoulder and neck.

"You're lying," she said.

"Why would you say that?"

"You don't want to leave."

"We're working the case."

"No, it's more than that."

"I don't know what you mean."

Her eyes drilled into me. Just when I thought I couldn't hold her gaze for another second, she spoke.

"Fuck you," she said.

Then she turned around and left.

———————— · ————————

I sat there stewing for an hour and made half a dozen attempts to get my head back into the case. Every time I tried, though, the pain in my arm or shoulder would flare, and I'd get pissed off either at Jen or at myself. The longer I kept at it, though, the more I blamed myself.

And the more the pain burned in my arm and shoulder.

I looked at photos of Bailey and Jacob. Watched a few videos. Opened Sara's Facebook page.

Nothing pulled me in.

Jen knew me better than anyone. Better than I knew myself. She'd been watching me and watching my pain. She'd figured out what was going on almost as quickly as I had. By the time she understood out how to read my pain and place it on the scale, she knew what the work was doing for me. She'd even hinted at it and waited for me to talk about it.

But I wouldn't. Fear stopped me. I worried it might change things. If I acknowledged what was going on, somehow the effect might dissipate and disappear.

I should have talked to her. She deserved it.

When she answered her cell, I said, "I'm sorry."

"You are? Since when?"

"I was born sorry." I imagined I could sense the tension ease. "Where are you?" I asked.

———————— , ————————

Twenty minutes later, I met her at Berlin, a coffeehouse across the street and a block down from her building on Fourth Street. It was attached to Fingerprints, a new and used music store that had moved to the East Village from Belmont Shore and expanded. They had a reputation for bringing big-name musicians to play at in-store events. I'd never been to one, but the few people I knew who were cool enough for things like that said lots of good things about them. Apparently, Foo Fighters had recently made a big splash.

The café had large sliding doors that, when opened, gave the impression that the place didn't have a front wall. They filled the space between the sidewalk and counter with a large communal table. The sight of it made me grimace. I've always believed communal tables should be banned on Eighth Amendment grounds.

Of course, Jen was sitting right in the middle of it, watching me walk up.

"You sat there on purpose, didn't you?" I didn't worry about the people at the ends of the giant slab hearing me.

"Yeah," she said. "Get over it. I got you a coffee." I couldn't decide whether to sit across the table from her or to go around to the other side and sit next to her. The table was big enough to make either choice awkward, so I reached over, picked up my coffee, and took it through the café and into a back corner of the store that was filled with used books and comfortable furniture. I sat on an oversized leather couch and hoped she'd follow me.

When she didn't, I sent her a text message. One word: *Please.*

I tried a sip of my coffee. She'd gotten me a mocha. It burned my tongue.

While I was wondering if some ice water would do me any good, she sat down next to me.

"You ever going to talk to me about it?" she said.

"I think you know everything there is to know."

"Work is the only thing that lessens the pain?"

"Some other things help a little."

"But not like the job."

"No."

I wondered how far she'd go. If she'd actually give voice to the thought that had been haunting me for weeks.

Looking at her, I didn't know what to do with all the sadness and compassion I saw. She knew, but she couldn't say it out loud, either:

The only thing that could truly ease my pain was death.

Eight

I F IT WAS THE TRUTH THAT I'D TOLD JEN, IT DIDN'T SET ME FREE. It left me feeling awkward and exposed. My natural inclination was to withdraw, but I knew I should resist it if I could.

When I'd last spoken to Harlan, he'd invited me over that evening. I'd said I might stop by if it wasn't too late when we wrapped things up. It wasn't unusual for Harlan and me to stay up well past midnight, so I stopped at the Ralphs on Fourth Street and picked up a six-pack of Samuel Adams and drove the short distance to his house. He usually left the porch light on all night. But when I got close enough to the door to knock, I realized none of the inside lights were on. It wasn't long past ten, but he'd been particularly tired the last few days, so I crept off across the front yard as quietly as I could and went home.

I'd been looking forward to a beer with Harlan since I'd left Berlin, but as soon as I put the bottles down on the kitchen counter, I felt a sudden thirst for Grey Goose and OJ. The burning in my shoulder had started near the elbow and radiated up and into my neck. Vodka, I wondered, or Vicodin?

In the few seconds I allowed myself to make the decision, I realized that I was likely in for a very long night alone with my pain and my guilt, and that was unlikely to change no matter how I decided to begin it. So I walked through the dining room and out the front door into the damp chill of the Long Beach night.

With no plan or direction in mind, I walked over to Park Avenue and angled off onto Appian Way as I passed Colorado Lagoon. I thought about the case as I walked, and as I did so, the pain receded farther and farther into the periphery of my consciousness. I ran through the details. Every fact I could come up with. When one didn't lead to another, I forced my attention back on Sara and the children. I focused on the memory of the three of them on their autopsy tables, and then I tried to remember each of the video clips I'd seen of them. After watching them so many times, it seemed I could recall them at will—Bailey on the merry-go-round, Jacob sleeping in the sunlight next to the window, and all the others.

I was getting better at it. Every time something pulled my attention away—a street to cross, a dog walker, an oncoming car—I registered the moment and then went back to my concentrated focus.

Before I knew it, I had walked all the way down Appian Way, looped around Naples Island, and was approaching the intersection of Second Street and The Toledo.

It was 11:45. I hadn't thought to check my watch before I'd left, but I'd been walking for well over an hour, and it would be another half an hour before I made it home.

Halfway along the Second Street business district in Belmont Shore, I decided to detour into the Shorehouse, a 24/7 café that, at least after the other restaurants along street closed for the evening, catered largely to the bar patrons who frequented the fifteen-block stretch. It was too early for the drunks to be out in force, so I settled down in a booth that looked out on the sidewalk, and studied the menu. It hadn't occurred to me until I sat down that I had never eaten dinner. After carefully considering half a dozen dishes, I gave up and ordered the same thing I had just about every time I ate there: an omelet with carne asada, jack cheese, and sour cream. I took my time eating it and then drinking a cup of decaf and three refills before getting up and heading home.

During that last portion of the walk, it occurred to me how easy it was becoming for me to shift my focus to the Bentons and the details of their murders, and I couldn't stop thinking about the implications of my actions.

Yes, concentrating my attention on the case helped me. It eased my pain. From a certain point of view, I could even make the argument that focusing relentlessly, even obsessively, on the murders would actually be a net benefit. The more time and attention and effort I put into the case, after all, the more likely we'd be to close it. Even as I thought that, though, I knew it wasn't as simple as I wanted it to be. And I couldn't even convince myself that what I was thinking about was just hard work.

It was something more than that. What it was, exactly, I wasn't yet certain. And I knew that as beneficial as it might be as a way of dealing with my chronic pain, it wouldn't be only that. Nietzsche even had that famous cliché about it. I was sure the abyss was gazing into me as I walked up Second Street.

I knew there would be a cost. But what would it be?

This time, after the saw has finished its work and my severed arm has thumped to the floor and released me from my pain, I see two small figures in the shadows. They drift toward me. Before I can even see them clearly, I know who they are. They come closer still, the harsh light illuminating their frightened faces, and they stand before me—Bailey and Jacob, blood languorously dripping from their bullet wounds. They look at me, sadness and longing in their expressions, and I know what they want.

They want me to use the saw on them.

I can't, I tell them. Where would I cut?

PART FOUR: TREATMENT

————————, ————————

And judgment is just like a cup that we share
I'll jump over the wall and I'll wait for you there
    —*Iron & Wine*, "Rabbit Will Run"

Four

THE CONGRESSMAN'S OFFICE WAS ON THE TOP FLOOR OF A three-story mixed-use building at the corner of PCH and Main in Huntington Beach. It was directly across from the pier and had an unobstructed view that stretched from Newport to the south, to Long Beach Harbor to the north. It must have been one of the most expensive pieces of real estate in the city. So Jen and I were surprised to find Jack's Surfboards, La Rocco's Pizzeria, and a Jamba Juice on the first floor. The congressman really didn't seem like the kind of guy whose office would be over a place that had a Mr. Zog's Original Sex Wax display in the window, but indeed it was.

The office itself surprised us, too. It was smaller than I'd expected and looked more like a dermatologist's workplace than a politician's.

"Not as upscale as I would have imagined," I said to Jen as we entered.

She wrinkled her eyebrows at me, and I realized that she was worried that the assistant at the reception desk opposite the door had heard me. The young woman was finishing up a call, so I didn't share Jen's concerns. But she was right. I had been careless.

There was a brass-colored nameplate on the desk that read, MELANIE LEVINE. She looked like a college student, and I wondered if she was an intern or actually on the payroll.

"Hello," she said. "Welcome to Congressman Benton's office. Are you the officers from Long Beach?"

"Detectives," I said. "Yes, we are."

She stood up and said, "Right this way."

We followed her down a short hallway past two or three doors on each side. One of the doors was opened a few inches, and I caught a glimpse of Roger Kroll hunched over a desk. It occurred to me that he had left the door exactly as it was so we'd see him working. I don't know why or to what end, but I couldn't shake the feeling that he was involved in everything the congressman did, especially when he was trying to look like he wasn't.

Melanie led us into the office at the end of the hall. The congressman was standing next to his desk waiting for us.

"Hello, Detective Tanaka," he said, shaking Jen's hand.

He motioned to a comfortable-looking sofa against the far wall, then turned to me. "Detective Beckett." His grip was firm and practiced, and I couldn't help thinking that he really knew how to shake someone's hand.

I sat next to Jen as he pulled one of the chairs from in front of his desk over to face us across a coffee table. While he was rearranging the furniture, I studied the office. Everything was immaculate, but nothing was too ostentatious. Each element of the decor had been carefully calculated to seem tasteful and well-appointed without seeming too expensive or indulgent. The only people whose opinion he was trying to influence with the furnishings were his constituents. This was a very nice office. But it didn't look like a wealthy man worked here.

No.

It looked like the high end of middle class. The kind of place a good, honest working man could aspire to. Only the ten-million-dollar view out over the large balcony belied that impression.

He sat down and shot us a smile tinged with grief. "Can I get you anything? Coffee?"

"No, sir," I said. "Thank you."

"What can I do for you, Detectives?"

He didn't ask about the investigation. Family always asks about the investigation. They want to know about progress, if we have leads, suspects, solutions. They always ask. The congressman didn't. Because he already knew everything that there was to know. Or he thought he did.

"We just need to ask you a few questions," Jen said. "And then we'll let you get back to work."

"I'm never too busy to help, Detective. Never."

"Thank you," she said. "There's been a development in the investigation, and we need to ask you about your military service. You were in the air force, correct?"

"Yes," he said, "I was." He wasn't surprised or even curious. Jen and I had discussed our interview strategy on the drive south to Huntington. We needed to feel him out. If he didn't know about the Pararescue connection, we didn't want to tip him off. But if he hadn't known where we were going, the question about his time in the USAF would have seemed random and been unexpected, and we would have seen that.

"There's not much in your public bio about the specifics of your service," Jen said. "Forgive me for saying so, sir, but that seems unusual for someone in your line of work."

He smiled for us. "You're right. What kind of self-respecting politician wouldn't trumpet his veteran status from the rooftops?"

"Yes," I said, "that is what we were wondering. You were special ops, weren't you? That's why you don't talk about it."

He smiled again. "I knew you two were sharp as soon as I met you. You're right, Detective Beckett. I was in air force Pararescue."

"And what you did was classified?" I asked.

"Some of it was, yes." He looked down at the table and didn't speak for a moment. I guessed that he wanted us to think he was coming to some sort of a decision, to give the impression that he was letting us in on something secret and special. "It's not just that, though."

"What is it, sir?" I asked.

Jen answered for him. "Honor," she said. "It's just not right to talk about some things. To use them for personal gain."

This time I actually bought his smile. "That's absolutely right, Detective Tanaka. If I used my service for political ends, I could never live with myself." I bought that, too. What was the old joke? The secret of success is sincerity. Once you can fake that, you've got it made.

"I'm sure you're wondering why we're asking about this," she said. We'd been betting she'd hook him with the honor line, and she did. Unless things took an unexpected turn, she'd be asking all the questions from here on out. "Agents Young and Goodman briefed you on the two incidents in Seal Beach?" We hadn't copied them yet on the autopsy report, so the congressman shouldn't have known any of the details.

"Yes, they did."

"Well," she said, "the driver of the SUV had a distinguishing mark that we felt you should be aware of."

"What was that?"

"Two green footprints tattooed on his right arm."

Turned out he could fake not only sincerity but righteous indignation as well. He took a few deep breaths as if he were trying to calm himself down. "I'm sure you understand why I'm so upset," he said.

"Yes," Jen said, leaning forward. "Not only did he disrespect the PJs by faking his own service, but he dragged them into a multiple-murder investigation."

He looked her squarely in the eye and said, "I'm glad you're the one who's going to find out who killed Sara and the children. You really do understand."

That one we didn't expect. But he seemed to be genuinely taken with Jen, and they seemed to have formed some kind of connection. I was already trying to think of ways we might exploit it.

"So what do you make of it?" Ruiz asked.

"He knew about the tattoo," I said. "So he's getting information somehow."

"We have a leak?"

"I doubt it," Patrick said. "Probably looking in our computer files. The case-management system would be pretty easy to hack. Maybe listening to our phone conversations as well. Do you remember if you texted or e-mailed anything about the tattoo?"

"I sent myself a link to the website I found the footprints on," I said. "So I could access it here without having to search for it again."

"That's probably where they got that, then. E-mails and texts are the easiest to track. Don't even need eyes—just set up a list of search terms to flag and the computer will do all the work for you. They can do the same thing with your hard drive, but that gets a little more complicated."

While the idea of the FBI or some other branch of Homeland Security prying into our case files didn't sit well with any of us, we knew we were powerless to do anything about it.

"Did you get any kind of a read off of him?"

"He's slick," Jen said.

"We knew that already," Ruiz said.

"Yeah," I said. "Jen built up a good rapport with him. And I bought that line he gave to Jen, about her understanding. He knows every detail of our case, but I don't think he knows anything else."

Ruiz examined me.

"What?" I said.

"Coming from you, that's a surprise."

"Why?"

"I figured you'd have some kind of 'all politicians are sociopaths and can therefore lie undetectably' argument all ready to go."

"Actually, you're right," I said. "Can I change my answer?"

When Jen and I sat down at our desks, I said, "I don't like knowing they're watching us."

"It's nothing new. Not since the Patriot Act."

"I know. But I've never really felt like they were paying attention before. That's what makes the difference. Every other case is just a trickle in a massive flow of data. Knowing they're picking out details now makes me self-conscious."

"It shouldn't."

"Why?"

"Because they don't think we know."

I saw where she was going, but I let her finish.

"And we can put anything we want in the files."

One corner of her mouth turned up, and she leaned back in her chair.

"It's not much," I said.

"No, it's not. But it's something."

That afternoon, Jen had to meet with a DDA about a trial she'd be testifying on a few days later. I don't dislike court appearances as much as many detectives do, but one of things I was really appreciating about my return to active duty was the fact that I didn't have a backlog of cases lined up that would require my testimony. Nor did I have any old open investigations that required my attention. I was the only detective on the Homicide squad with only one case to work.

All I had were Sara, Bailey, and Jacob. And I took some satisfaction in the knowledge that they had me, too.

Patrick came in early the next morning. I'd had the squad room to myself for nearly an hour.

"You asked about Kroll?"

"Yeah," I said. "Got something?"

"He was Pararescue, too."

"That can't be coincidence."

"No, it can't. I don't have much else yet. Where do we go next?" he asked. "Phone records?"

"The connection's too thin for a warrant. And we'd tip off the congressman." Something clicked in my head, and I asked, "You didn't find that out on your computer here, did you?"

"No," he said. "It was secure. Nothing's going to get back to anybody."

"How would you feel about doing a little more off-the-radar digging?"

"As much I love working here with the best technology 2003 has to offer, I think I'd enjoy getting out of the office. Where do you want me to start?"

"With Kroll. Get everything you can. Then let's start digging into Sternow and Byrne. If we're going off the record, we should get as deep into their shit as we can."

Patrick turned his head and winced.

"What?"

"You've got to work on your metaphors."

———— · ————

"If you're really going to do this," Ruiz said, "be careful."

"We know," I said.

"Does Patrick?"

"I'll ask him," I said. "But I'm pretty sure he knows even better than me what we're doing."

In a routine investigation, we sometimes knowingly obtain information by means that would not be considered acceptable in a court of law. We do this because the value of the information promises to be high enough that it's worth the risk to the success of the investigation. In most cases, the only thing we really have to worry about is losing the ability to use what we gain at trial. Once we know something, we can often confirm it by other means or find other evidence that is just as effective.

With the feds, we were risking more. If we stumbled onto classified information, for example, or interfered in some other way with any ongoing FBI or Homeland Security business, we'd run not only the risk of departmental castigation, but also criminal prosecution for anything from obstruction of justice to espionage.

"You think they'd go that far?" Jen asked when I filled her in.

"I doubt it. If we do find anything we shouldn't, they'll keep it quiet. They'd lose too much face if word got out that a couple of local cops were able to get past their security."

"So, what you're saying is that we don't really need to worry about going to jail, just about losing our jobs."

"Exactly," I said. "You in?"

———————— , ————————

We stopped at Target and picked up three prepaid cell phones and six extra cards in case we used up the time included with the original purchase.

"This is just like Stringer Bell did it," I said.

Jen didn't respond.

I added, "On *The Wire*."

It wasn't just the bad joke. Something else was on her mind. She was thinking. I wondered if what we were doing was weighing on her.

"You don't have to do this," I said as we got in line at the only open register.

"What do you mean?"

"You can leave this to Patrick and me."

It was clear that she didn't want to talk about it where we were. So we were quiet while an overweight woman with a surprisingly mellow toddler loaded her groceries onto the moving belt. As I watched her lifting boxes of Raisin Bran and Shredded Wheat out of her red plastic shopping cart, I noted with some consternation that she was buying much healthier breakfast cereal than I ever did.

"Think there's any way we can expense this?" I asked Jen as I handed my credit card to the teenager in the red vest.

She didn't bother with a response.

In the car, she said, "I don't know."

"It's not too late to let us run with this."

"No, I said I was in, and I am."

"You're sure you're okay with it?"

"Yes," she said. "That's what's bothering me."

Six

PATRICK HAD ONCE MENTIONED OFFHANDEDLY THAT HE LIVED in a loft. I had visions of the downtown Long Beach buildings that had been converted from commercial spaces back in the midnineties before the redevelopment boom kicked into high gear and yuppified open-floor-plan condos sprang up in remodeled downtown buildings that promised "Loft-Style Living!"

It was the first time either Jen or I had been to his home, so we were both surprised that his address was located on Obispo Avenue along the east edge of Signal Hill in a row of hybrid industrial/office/warehouse spaces.

"Can this be it?" I asked Jen as we approached the glass door and saw our reflections in its mirrored surface.

Next to the door was a doorbell button beneath a small sign that said, UNIT A.

We pushed it and waited.

After what seemed like a long time, we heard the bolt slide back. Patrick pushed the door open toward us and said, "Hey, guys."

"This is an"— Jen paused, searching for the right word— "interesting place you've got here."

I was sure he picked up on the sarcasm, but he said, "Thanks," to her just the same.

Inside the door was what would have been a small reception area had the place been functioning as it had been designed to.

But it was empty, save for two bicycles leaning against opposite walls to the right and left. I looked behind me and saw that the view into the parking lot was unobstructed. We could see out, but no one outside could see in. I wondered if the mirror effect was due to paranoia on Patrick's part or simple happenstance. Maybe it had been like that when he moved in.

He led us down a short hallway, past another room on the left that had been turned into a makeshift kitchen and the bathroom on the right.

"Sorry it's a mess," he said, ushering us into the cavernous open space that took up the rest of the building. There were clusters of furniture spread around the place with empty ten-foot buffer zones between; these were the only indicators of the areas' intended uses. Sharing the space were two chairs and a sofa facing a huge flat-screen TV mounted on one wall, a king-size bed and a wardrobe and dresser tucked into an alcove around the corner from the hallway, an office area with several worktables and at least three computer monitors and stacks of other electronic equipment, and what looked like a barbeque and some patio furniture set up by the giant metal rolling door in the back corner. But even with the various furnishings grouped around the warehouse, it still felt vast and empty. It was impossible not to be conscious of the size of the place.

"Wow," Jen said, examining the surroundings, "I had no idea you were a closet hipster."

Patrick looked like a child who'd just been threatened with vegetables. "That's messed up."

I wasn't sure which side of the debate to take until I saw a distressed straw fedora fifteen feet away on a side table near the sofa. I walked over, picked it up, and flipped it up onto my head. "Exhibit A."

He looked so embarrassed I couldn't continue.

Still, though, I would have kept it on if it hadn't been at least two sizes too small.

He started to speak, but I cut him off. "When you're in a hole," I said with a smirk, "stop digging."

The joviality didn't last long. He looked at the Target bag in my hand and asked, "Those the throwaways?"

"Yeah."

We opened the packages, set up the phones, exchanged numbers, and gave them a trial run.

Once we confirmed that they were working properly, Jen flipped hers closed and put it in her pocket. "Now what?"

"Now we get back to work." Patrick rose from the armchair he'd been sitting in and headed toward his computers. We followed. As we got closer, it became clear that the array of equipment was even more extensive than I had realized. He had two large worktables set at a right angle to each other that formed an L-shape extending from the wall. There was a third identical table perpendicular to the wall a few feet away from the others—just far enough to allow Patrick to slip between them.

"This is where the magic happens," he said, sliding into what appeared to be a very expensive ergonomic desk chair.

Sometimes, I thought, *the line between hipster and nerd is a very narrow one.*

With his back to the wall, he started tapping keys on a keyboard attached to a twenty-seven-inch iMac. There were at least two other machines within his reach. A desktop PC and a MacBook. There was a printer, a stack of external hard drives, and a whole bunch of stuff I couldn't identify.

The urge to ask him to explain what he was doing was strong, but I fought it and inquired instead if he had any new information.

"Ran a full background on Kroll. Nothing too surprising. Confirmed that he was in the air force at the same time the congressman was. I'll have phone records and location logs soon. I've also been looking at Sternow and Byrne's computers. Their security won't be a problem."

The printer, a sleek black cube the size of a small microwave, buzzed to life and began spitting out pages. "That's the file I started on Kroll. I ran his assistant, too. Molly?"

"Good," I said. "Anything on her?"

"Nothing you wouldn't expect."

"And this is completely secure, right? There's no way it can get back to the congressman?"

Patrick eyed me as if I'd just insulted his mother.

"Okay," I said.

"What's next?" Jen asked.

"I told Ruiz we'd update him." Before Patrick and I separated, we agreed that Jen and I would power down our phones while we were still a few miles away from his place. We knew the congressman's contacts could use the same techniques we were using on the SUV driver on us and could potentially use our locations and phone records to put the three of us together at times and places that wouldn't ever be accounted for in the official case files. We'd also promised the lieutenant we wouldn't be out of contact for too long. "Why don't we take the files and head back to the station?" I said to Jen.

She nodded. "Call us if you need anything," she said to Patrick.

"I will. Listen for text messages, too."

As we headed for the door, music started playing behind us. I didn't recognize the tune.

"You know what that song is?" I asked Jen.

"I think it's the new Fleet Foxes."

"Really?" I said. It only then occurred to me that I hadn't been listening to very much new music since I'd come back to work. I wasn't sure if that was good or bad.

"Like it?"

"I do."

"I'll burn you a copy."

Jen drove, and as soon we were five minutes away, I turned my phone back on. There was a message waiting from Ruiz. It was curt, even for him. "Danny, get back to me."

I touched his name on the screen to call him back.

"Where are you?"

"Jen and I are on the way back. Why?"

"You'll see when you get here."

"You're Oliver Woods?" I said without even bothering to try to hide the disgust in my voice.

He was with the lieutenant in the interview room, and now so were Jen and I.

"What the fuck do you want?" I said.

"Detective Beckett," Ruiz said, calmly and quietly. Only Jen and I understood the full weight of the warning in his tone.

Woods focused on Jen and the lieutenant. "I have some video that might be helpful to the investigation," he said.

"Nobody would pay you for it, huh?" I said.

"It's not…I mean, it wasn't…The thing with Channel Four isn't what you think. They found the clip on my Facebook page. They were going to run it anyway, but they made me an offer. What was I supposed to do?"

"Say no?" Jen suggested.

"But they would have run it anyway. With what they paid me, I can almost pay off my student loans." He was younger than I'd expected him to be, and rounder, with prematurely thinning hair. There was just enough sincere doofus about him to smooth some of the hard edges off my anger.

"What is it that you have, Oliver?" Jen asked.

"Well, I didn't realize I had it until yesterday. I felt bad about all the play that the first video got, and I wanted to do something to help. I thought I might have a clip or two of Sara in some of my old stuff. But I've got shitloads of it, and I had to go through it all to find what I was looking for."

"And you found it?" I asked.

"Yeah."

"What is it?"

"Well, I've been doing videography for a long time, okay? And I've known Sara for a while, too. That's why I had that first clip. She was helping me with a project for a class."

"What about this other clip?" Jen asked. "Tell us about it."

"Okay, well it's a vérité kind of a thing. Some footage I got at a gallery opening for a grad-student exhibit. Shots of the crowd looking at the paintings and stuff."

"And stuff?"

"Well," he said, "I accidentally got a bit of a conversation between Sara and Professor Catanio."

"Accidentally?" I said.

"Yes. I thought they were talking about art and stuff, but it wasn't about that."

"What was it about?" Jen asked.

"Do you want to just watch it?"

We said we did, and he began fumbling with a backpack at his feet. After he unzipped the flap and pulled out a padded sleeve and unzipped that, too, he put a Sony Vaio notebook on the table and turned it on.

We let him stew in the silence as it powered up.

"Okay," he said. "I had a couple of hours from this, but I picked out the one bit that I thought might help." He clicked an icon on the desktop and a window opened. An animated hourglass hung in the middle of it for a few seconds; then the clip began.

The shot bounced around a bit and then stopped and zoomed in on Sara Benton and Catherine Catanio in a corner of what appeared to be a small art gallery. There weren't too many other people in that part of the room, and to my surprise, their conversation could be easily heard.

"Again?" Catherine said. Her voice was louder and more forceful than the others in the room, and while Catherine didn't seem to notice, Sara did. She looked around, as if to make sure no one else was listening.

Catherine spoke again. "You know what you said."

"I know," Sara said.

"Well?"

"I don't know." She bit at her lip and shook her head. "The kids...I can't afford the kind of lawyer I'll need to go up—" Sara paused while someone walked through the frame between the camera and the two women. When the dark figure had passed, Sara continued. "You know what kind of lawyers he has, his connections. What's going to happen with the kids?"

"With what you know," Catherine said, "he won't stand a chance. You've got the evidence on your side. You can end—"

Sara shook her head and raised her hand to quiet her friend. "Not here. Can we go someplace else?"

Catherine nodded, and the camera panned quickly to the left, focusing on a red-and-black abstract painting that looked like a bleeding wound.

"So you just stood there and shot that?" I asked Oliver. "I thought you said Sara was your friend."

"She was," he said, lifting his chin to a defiant angle.

"She must have been if she let you record that," Jen said. We were double-teaming him, pushing him off balance.

"Well, she—"

"How'd you get that footage?" I asked.

"She knew I was shooting the—"

"But she didn't know you were shooting her."

"No, but—"

"But you shot her anyway," I said.

"I—"

"You what?"

"She didn't know."

"She didn't know?"

"No." He hung his head. His sense of shame filled the small room.

Jen softened her tone. "How'd you do it?"

"There's a temporary wall in the middle of the room, paintings hanging on it. I shot around the corner of it. They didn't know."

I snorted with as much contempt as I could muster, and his shoulders slumped even more. What he brought us was genuinely useful. It was Sara adding even more confirmation to our suspicions about the state of the Bentons' relationship in her voice.

Her own voice.

But I wasn't going to let a douchebag like Oliver have the satisfaction of knowing that.

I left the room and let Jen and the lieutenant wrap things up.

———————— , ————————

"Remember what I said when we were at the crime scene? In the den, looking at the family pictures?"

"Yes," Jen said.

"So far, he's the only one with motive."

"Could be his father, too."

"Maybe. What do you want to do now?" I asked.

"See if we can find out who they were talking about in the video."

Catherine Catanio wasn't on campus that day, but when Jen called her, she agreed to come in to the squad and look at the video clip.

While we were waiting, I used my throwaway to call Patrick and see if he'd made any progress.

"I've got a source who can give us all of the congressman's cell phone records. Kroll's, too," Patrick said. "Do we want to go that far?"

"Think we'll get caught?"

"I don't think so. But I can't guarantee we won't."

"Let's do it," I said. "We've got some cover. If it goes bad, we've got enough ugly shit on Bradley to leak if it comes to that."

"Mutually assured destruction?" he said.

"If it's good enough for the Cold War—"

"You're forgetting something."

"I am? What?"

"For that to work, the other guys have to know about your missiles."

I thought for a moment about how good it would feel to phone in a few anonymous tips to the *Press Telegram*, the *LA Times*, maybe even Channel 4. "They'll know," I said. "They'll know soon enough."

"Really?" Patrick sounded puzzled.

"Well, no, not really. I just thought it would be fun to say that."

———————— , ————————

"That fucking creep," Catherine said as soon as we began playing Oliver's clip for her. "I can't believe he did that."

"Remember the other clips of Sara and the kids on the news?" I asked.

"Yes."

"Apparently, Oliver sold those to KNBC."

"Really?"

"At least one of them."

Jen said, "Thanks again for coming in. We just needed to show that to you and ask you a few questions about it."

"What can I help you with?" she asked.

"Well, in the video, you say 'not again,'" I said. "What exactly did you mean by that?"

"Sara had just told me that she found out Bradley had been involved with someone else."

"Did she tell you who?" Jen asked.

"No," Catherine said. "Just that it was someone he worked with."

"Is there anything else she might have said about it?" I asked. "Any details at all? Anything could be helpful."

"Nothing I can think of."

"Bradley's been working in Washington lately, hasn't he?"

"Yes," she said.

"Do you know if the woman he was involved with was here or back east?"

"Here, I think. Sara answered Bradley's cell phone one day when he was in the shower. A woman was on the other end. Sara said she knew from the awkwardness of the caller's voice what was going on."

"What makes you think she was local?"

"Sara said the caller's number was in the seven-one-four area code. 'That figures,' she said to me. 'That's why I remember.'" Catherine smiled sadly at the memory of the dig at the Orange County area code.

"Thank you. This is very helpful," I said.

"Let me know if there's anything else I can do," Catherine said.

"We will." Jen extended her hand.

Before she let go, Catherine said, "I want to help you nail that fuck to the wall."

After she was gone, I said to Jen, "Do you think that's some kind of an art thing?"

She smiled. "What do you make of the OC number?"

"I have an idea. Let me check my notes."

Three

MOLLY FIELDS LIVED IN HUNTINGTON BEACH, ABOUT THREE miles from the congressman's office. Her cell phone was a 714 number.

Patrick ran their phone records—illegally, of course—and found that, several months before the murders, Bradley had called Molly thirty-seven times over a three-week period. She'd called him only six times. The last call was nine days before Oliver had shot the video of Sara and Catherine at the art exhibit.

"That sounds like something," Jen said.

"It is."

"Where should we interview her?"

She had a good question. Did we want to be friendly or intimidating? Which would get us better results?

"Look at the numbers," I said. "Think she didn't want to talk to him? Maybe he was harassing her?"

"That's a possibility," Jen said. "But it could have just been a practical thing; he told her not to call him at home, when he was with Sara. Could be he just likes to be in charge, to control things."

We decided to bring her in. It would give us more options. She'd never be as relaxed as she would be at her home, but if Jen was right and she was enthusiastically involved with Bradley, we'd have a better shot with her in the interview room. We could pursue a harsher interview strategy if we needed to.

Jen thought I should make the call because I'd had the chance to build a bit of rapport with her.

"Hi, Molly," I said when she answered her cell. "This is Danny Beckett. How are you doing?"

"I'm well," she said. I could hear both surprise and curiosity in her voice. "How are you?"

Good, I thought. She was treating the call like a conversation and not an interrogation. "I'm good, thanks. How's the congressman holding up?"

"Better than I would have believed. I don't know how anyone could take that kind of loss."

"It's amazing what people are able to withstand," I said. "I never cease to be surprised."

"You must see a lot of it."

"I do. I do." I let the weight of that thought play for a moment and then went on. "Molly, I was hoping you might be able to help us out with something."

"Of course, Detective Beckett."

"Call me Danny, please." She was quiet, and I wondered if I'd gone too far with that familiarity.

But she broke the silence. "What can I do, Danny?"

"Do you think you could answer a few more questions for us?"

"Yes."

"Would you mind coming into the station? We'd like you to look at a few video clips and get your take on them."

"Video clips?" she said. Was it still curiosity in her voice, or something else?

"Yes," I said, trying to sound as mundane as possible. "Just a few public events. We wanted to get a staffer's opinion on a few things. We know how busy Mr. Kroll is." Technically, none of that was untrue. Only misleading. I wondered why I was hesitant to tell Molly outright lies. I think I wanted to trust her. To believe that she'd help us close the case.

"Oh, okay. When do you want me to come in?"

"The sooner we can get these questions cleared up, the better. What's your schedule like today?"

———————— , ————————

Virtually no one is at ease in a police interview room. Molly certainly wasn't. But we went out of our way to make her feel as comfortable as we could. We got her a fresh cup of coffee. Chatted with her, making small talk. Our aim was to create a sense of cognitive dissonance. For her to feel nothing but friend-liness and support from us, while at the same time letting her feel the distress and anxiety that the harsh fluorescent lighting and cold metal brought out in her.

After we tossed ten minutes' worth of questions to her about the congressman and his work and her work and their work and her relationship with the rest of the Benton family, I had a very strong sense of how she behaved in normal conversation and of how she sounded and acted when she told the truth. Then I asked, "How well do you know the congressman's son, Bradley?"

She hesitated for a brief instant and almost blinked. "Fairly well," she said, apparently not recognizing the hairline crack in her composure. "He works with his father a lot."

"Is it true he's going to be running for congress himself?"

"We're not supposed to say anything about it, but I guess at this point, there's nothing to hide, right?"

I held her eyes and gave her a sad half smile. "Right."

"Yes. He was going to run for the thirty-seventh district next year."

"Was?"

"Well, I don't know for sure. I guess it's way too early to know for sure."

"You said that when we spoke before. Has anything changed?"

"Not that I know of. But Bradley now…" She didn't finish the thought, and it was a few seconds before she went on. "With what happened to Sara and the kids…"

"Of course. Did you like Sara?"

The half blink again.

"Yes," she said. "Everybody did. She was the nicest person in the whole family." She cast her eyes down. I couldn't tell if the action was caused by grief or guilt or something else.

"Did you know her well?"

"I guess so."

"How often did you talk to her?"

"Every two or three weeks. She'd bring the kids to see their grandpa, or at an event or something. The family's very friendly with the staff."

Jen and I had talked about how to present the video, about whether to confront her first and then show it to her or to show her the clip first and hit her with the accusation. We'd decided to play it by ear.

"Would you take a look at something?" I asked.

"Sure," she said.

I flipped open the MacBook on the table and played Oliver's recording.

I watched Molly watch the screen.

As Sara and Catherine spoke, the color slowly faded from Molly's face. By the end of the clip, her eyes were wet.

I offered her a tissue and said, "Tell me about Bradley."

She did.

———————— · ————————

"He didn't rape her?" the lieutenant asked.

"No, but she has a slam dunk sexual harassment lawsuit," Jen said.

"She slept with him once because she was afraid of losing her job, then he wouldn't leave her alone?"

"That's right," I said. "She was about to quit working for the congressman when Sara found out."

"But there weren't any repercussions from that?"

"Not according to Molly," I said. "She kept waiting for something to happen, but it never did."

Jen said, "She thought Sara protected her."

"Really?" Ruiz asked.

We both nodded.

"Anything really new, or does it just reinforce what we already know?" he asked.

"Nothing completely fresh," I said, "but we've got serious leverage. If Bradley's got any political aspirations left, we can end his hopes with one phone call."

"But you're right," Jen said. "Everything is still circumstantial."

"We know Shevchuk, Turchenko, and Tropov were contractors, and we know Bradley had a serious motive. But we can't connect them yet."

"Keep working it till you can." Ruiz picked up his pen and turned his attention to the paperwork on his desk.

We knew that was our exit cue.

———————— , ————————

Dave Zepeda was in the squad wrapping things up for the day. He was involved in the case, but not as deeply as the rest of us. We thought his relative distance might give him some perspective that we couldn't find. I gave him a summary of what I thought he knew and ran down what little new information we had.

"I'm completely fuckin' lost," Dave said.

"What part don't you get?" I asked.

"What part? The whole damn thing. Russians, politicians, Ukrainians, special ops, Jolly Green Giants. Come on. You think anybody could follow this?"

He wasn't just being difficult. One of the most important aspects of any homicide investigation is shaping the evidence into a cohesive narrative. People—lieutenants, captains, district attorneys, juries—need a story, and it has to be clear and easy to follow. We knew laying it out for him would be our first stab at selling the story to an audience.

I rolled our large dry-erase board to a good angle for Dave to see from his desk. Across the top edge, I wrote the names of the first victims—*Sara, Bailey,* and *Jacob*—in blue ink.

"Okay," I said, "here's where it starts. Three victims." Along the right edge of the board, I made a tight column in black that read, top to bottom, *The Congressman, Bradley, Kroll, Campos, et al.* "They were related to some very powerful people. At this point, we don't have any evidence linking any of the names on the right to the crimes. There is a motive, though."

Jen picked up the ball. "There are rumors that Bradley Benton the Third had been considering a run for congress, either succeeding his father or running in an adjacent district. We know Sara was planning to divorce Bradley because of infidelity and possibly even some criminal behavior. There was a floor safe stolen from the crime scene that contained hard evidence that would have been very damaging to Bradley both in the divorce and in his campaign."

"So anyone in the column on the right had a reason to want the contents of the safe," Dave said.

"Exactly." I picked up a red marker, and underneath the first set of names, I wrote *Turchenko* and *Shevchuk.* "Here's what we know. These two, the Ukrainians, committed the actual murders. They've got records. Mostly petty Eastern European organized crime stuff, but some violence. Not hard to buy this escalation. And we've got conclusive physical evidence and a confession. Rock solid."

Dave said, "So you could close it there."

"We could." I still had the red marker in my hand. Below *Turchenko* and *Shevchuk*, I scrawled another name. "But these two didn't act alone. Turchenko claims they were hired by another guy. A Russian smuggler named Anton Tropov."

"That's the guy who Danny almost took his head off with the shotgun, right?"

"Not quite," Jen said. "That was Yevgeny. This is Anton. They're cousins."

"Cousins?"

"Yeah, but Yevgeny's not in this," I said. "Not as far as we know."

"All right," he said. "So Anton, the Russian, hires the two Ukrainians to take out the Benton family."

"Right."

"But he doesn't have a motive."

"No," Jen said.

"Maybe he wanted the safe. Blackmail the Bentons."

"Could be. But how would he know about it?"

"Good question," Dave said. "You sweat him about it?"

"No, Anton's gone. We can't find him. And now there are new players in the game." In green, the only color I had left, I wrote *Shooter* and *Driver* on the left edge of the board. Then I drew a red line through *Driver*.

"Damn," Dave said.

Jen agreed. "Yeah."

"The shooter killed Shevchuk; then when the driver botched the getaway, he killed him, too."

Dave thought about it. "Maybe Anton hired a couple of button men so the Ukrainians couldn't roll on him. Now he's trying to stay out of the heat."

"Possibly." Careful not to write over any of the names, I drew a line connecting the column on the left to the column on the right. "But maybe not. This is entirely circumstantial, but the congressman and Kroll, his chief of staff, both served in the air force special ops unit."

"Pararescue," Jen added.

"The green footprints," Dave said. "So you think someone in the column on the right hired all these goons to make the evidence in the safe disappear?"

Jen and I looked at each other and then back at him.

He made a little whistling noise and said, "That's a real clusterfuck. You should pin it on Anton and the Ukrainians and call it a day." He stood up and put on his coat. "I'm going home. You two have fun with that."

After work that evening, I had an appointment with my physical therapist.

During our session, Brookes made approving noises and nodded every now and then. When we finished, she said, "What have you been doing? You seem looser. There's less tightness in your neck and shoulder."

"Just the usual. The regular exercises. I think work is helping." I thought for a moment about going into detail about the specific ways in which it was helping, but I still wasn't comfortable talking about it.

"Has the pain level been lower overall since the last time you were here?"

"A bit, yes." As long I have innocent murder victims to think about.

"Did you get a guitar?"

"Well—"

"You better not say no."

"Kind of."

"What does that mean? How do you kind of get a guitar?"

"I didn't get a guitar, I got a—"

"I knew it."

"I got a banjo."

"A banjo? Who gets a banjo?"

"A friend gave it to me." I explained to her about Harlan, about his illness, about the gift.

"He's right," she said.

"About what?"

"The banjo. It will work."

Outside of her office, in my car, feeling relaxed and with my pain only a low hum in the background of my awareness, I thought about calling it a day. Going home and relaxing. Maybe watching one of the Netflix DVDs that had been gathering dust on the shelf under the TV for the last few months.

It didn't take long to convince myself that even though that sounded tempting, it would be better not to allow my awareness to drift too far away from the case. I decided I'd treat myself to carne asada at Enrique's and then get back to it. I left messages for Patrick and Jen, asking if they'd like to join me.

As I drove east on Broadway, I thought about where to go next. We needed to talk to Bradley. If there'd been even a slight chance of getting a crack at a real interrogation, I would have jumped at it. But in his condition and with his level of legal representation, there was no way we were going to get that kind of crack at him.

Still, after I turned off PCH onto Loynes and into the shopping center where the restaurant was located, I gave Campos a call.

"Detective Beckett, hello," he said. "It's been so long since I've heard from you I was starting to get worried."

"Thank you for your concern, Julian. I'm calling to see how Bradley's doing."

"Still struggling quite a bit, I'm afraid. But he is improving. Not a great deal, mind you, but some."

"I'm glad to hear that. Do you think he's ready to try our conversation again?"

"I'll certainly ask him, Detective."

"Please do," I said. "Is he still staying at his parents' house?"

"He spent a bit of time at his own house, but it was too painful for him. He'll be staying with his family for the time being."

"Thanks for your help, Julian."

I hung up and went inside to put my name in for a table. Enrique's wife, Michelle, greeted me and said, "You look like you're in a good mood tonight. Haven't you been coming in for breakfast lately?"

"Yes, I have. It's wonderful. Best in Long Beach."

"I hope you're telling people that."

"Every chance I get."

"Good. It hasn't quite caught on yet."

"I'll keep spreading the word." Even though I didn't like the thought of having to wait to be seated every morning, too.

———————— , ————————

Twenty minutes later, while I was sitting on the carved wooden bench reading the "Ask a Mexican" column in the *OC Weekly* and waiting to be seated, I saw Patrick's Mini pull into the lot and squeeze into a spot between a Range Rover and a Chevy Silverado.

Just as he was about to sit next to me on the bench, the hostess leaned out the door and called my name.

"Perfect timing," Patrick said.

They seated us at a booth in the back, and we ordered without looking at the menus.

"Anything to report?" I asked him.

"Yes," he said.

"What?"

"I'm not sure yet, but I've got a mountain of data to sort through. Cell phone records, location logs, personnel records from Sternow and Byrne. Even some case files. Their security is nowhere near what it should be. There's got to be something worthwhile in there."

"How do we find it?"

"I've got some programs running, searching all of it for a few dozen keywords and terms. Names, addresses, numbers, e-mail, stuff like that. That will help with some of it. I'll do some other data crunching, too. That won't get everything, though."

"What will?"

"The only way to catch everything is going through it page by page."

"How many pages are there?"

"About a hundred thousand so far."

Before I could respond, the waiter was at our table with the food. "Be careful," he said. "These plates are very hot."

Seven

AT HOME THAT NIGHT, AFTER I'D GONE OVER THE CASE FILES
looking for any connections we might have missed, and after I
had watched what I think was my favorite video of Bailey—the one
where she read *Horton Hears a Who!* to Sara, who was behind the
camera saying to her daughter every few pages, "Sound it out"—
three more times, I sat in the living room and strummed the strings
of the banjo with the back of the nail on the middle finger of my
right hand. I practiced hitting each string by itself, then in various
combinations. There was really no purpose to it, and I had no idea
what I was doing. But as I gradually became more adept at hitting
the string I was aiming at, I noticed something that surprised me.

I was beginning to like the sound.

But it didn't do anything for the pain that was coiling up my
arm and into my deltoid and trapezius muscles. I microwaved the
hydroculator for four and a half minutes, wrapped it in a hand
towel, then went back to the couch and draped it around my neck.
It was too hot, but I fought the burn and left it in place because its
pain was different, and sometimes a different pain is welcome, if
only because the novelty itself is a kind of relief.

As the heat dissipated, it penetrated into my muscles, and the
burning sharpness flattened out into a dull and heavy ache.

I turned on Craig Ferguson, drank three glasses of Grey
Goose and orange juice, and when I felt the alcohol beginning to
take hold, I went to bed.

It was sometime close to three when I went to sleep. I knew because the *BBC World Service* broadcast on KPCC had ended and I had listened to Steve Inskeep and Renee Montagne knock off a couple of *Morning Edition* stories each before my awareness began to fade and I finally nodded off.

When I'd been asleep just long enough for the dream of the saw to return—this time with Megan and my father standing in for Bailey and Jacob and imploring me to cut away their pain—my phone rang. In the midst of the hazy half consciousness that resulted from being jarred awake in the middle of a dream, I thought I heard Lieutenant Ruiz telling me that the Long Beach Harbor Patrol had found Anton Tropov's body. He repeated himself and my attention sharpened and my feet were on the floor and I was fumbling for the light switch.

Less than half an hour later, I was standing on the harbor's edge not far from Tropov's warehouse. Ruiz had kept things quiet. There were only eight people at the scene. Jen would be number nine when she arrived.

The body was stretched out on the asphalt. He hadn't been in the water long. There was no doubt it was Anton. He must have come back to his home turf and found someone waiting.

The officer who had found him had been responding to a report of a gunshot. Judging by the center mass through-and-through wound and the tissue damage caused by the round, it had almost certainly come from a rifle. Was it a sniper?

"Who called in the report?" I asked Ruiz.

"A guy working late up the block."

"Anybody talk to him yet?"

"No, Stan's with him. Waiting for one of us."

"You have Stan's cell number on your phone?"

"Yeah, why?"

"Get him for me."

"You don't want to interview him face to face?"

"No time."

"What do you mean?"

"I have an idea."

The lieutenant saw something in my face that convinced him not to ask any more questions. Ruiz dialed and handed me his phone.

Stanley Burke is a veteran uniform with more than twenty years on the job. Back in my uniform days, I'd shared a cruiser with him on a few occasions.

"Danny?" he said.

"Yeah. Can I talk to the guy?"

"Sure." He spoke to the witness before he took the phone away from his ear so I would know the man's name. "Mr. Santiago, a detective would like to speak to you."

"Hello? What can I do for you?" Santiago had a firmness and confidence in his voice. And an alertness, too, one I wouldn't have expected at four in the morning.

I introduced myself and told him I needed his help.

"First, would you just describe what you heard?"

"A rifle shot, coming from the east."

"A rifle, specifically?"

"Yes."

"How can you be sure it was a rifle and not some other kind of gun?"

"I was in the war. I know a rifle shot when I hear one."

Good, I thought. If I'd had time, I would have asked what war. I was guessing Vietnam. "And you said it came from the east?"

"Yes."

"What did you do when you heard the sound?"

"I turned off the light in front and went outside to take a look."

Santiago was smart enough to make himself less of a target before checking things out. Good. "When you went outside, did you see or hear anything else?"

"No. We're far enough away from most of the overnight harbor traffic that it's pretty quiet here."

"Did you see any headlights or hear any cars close by?"

"No. Nothing."

"How long did you stay outside?"

"Two or three minutes. I wanted to be sure there was nothing else going on."

"And there wasn't?"

"Nope."

"Do you think you would have heard a car a block away?"

"I think so."

"How about two?"

"Depends on the car. Maybe."

"Mr. Santiago, thank you; you've been a tremendous help."

I hung up and gave the lieutenant back his phone.

I took a look around. The edge of the canal was fairly open, at least ten yards from the nearest building. There were structures in every direction. Dozens of ideal places for someone to watch Tropov's property without being seen.

"What is it, Danny?"

"Nobody rushed to get out of here. Whoever shot Tropov wasn't in any hurry to flee the scene."

"Sniper," he said.

"Yeah. He wasn't close enough to confirm the kill."

"So what's your idea?"

"Call an ambulance. We have a gunshot victim who needs to be rushed to the hospital."

In addition to the ambulance, he called the deputy chief, who in turn called an administrator at Long Beach Memorial. Anton Tropov would be rushed to the trauma center. The records would indicate he was in critical condition.

"So what's the point of this, exactly?" Jen asked.

"Well, it gives us the chance to plant information. If they think Anton's still alive, maybe they'll try to hit him again."

"Who are 'they'?"

"Whoever hired Anton and his two thugs."

"You think they'll try to get to him in the hospital?"

"Maybe."

"That's a long shot, isn't it?"

"Yeah. Patrick thinks it might shake some information loose."

"What kind of information?"

"He's monitoring Bradley and the congressman and Kroll. Phones and computers. And Sternow and Byrne. Maybe we'll get something."

"And the lieutenant went for this?"

I nodded.

"Are we really this desperate?"

A sharp pain stabbed at the base of my neck. Jen saw me tense up and raise my shoulder toward my ear. "Seven," she said. She saw all the confirmation she needed in my expression. "Did it come out of nowhere," she asked, "or was it already there and it just got worse?"

"It was there. But I wasn't as aware of it."

"Is the pain constant? Is it only your awareness that changes?"

"It's partly the awareness. But it gets worse when I focus on it."

"I'm sorry, Danny."

"I know."

My BlackBerry rang. I saw Patrick's name on the screen. "What's up?"

"Twenty minutes after Ruiz called for the ambulance, Roger Kroll made a phone call and sent a text message."

"Who'd he call?"

"A number that I don't have yet."

"What about the text?"

"He sent it to Margaret Benton." When I didn't reply for several seconds, he added, "Are you still there?"

"Yeah," I said. "I didn't expect that. Do you know what it said?"

"Yeah. He told her, 'We have a problem.'"

"Did she answer?"

"Yep. Just said, 'Fix it.'"

———————— , ————————

"For all we know," Ruiz said, "they could be talking about a toilet in the mansion."

"They could," I said. "But they're not."

"So you're thinking she's the shot caller?"

"We have the earlier phone records showing a lot of contact between them. Maybe there's something else going on. We don't know. Maybe she's the one pulling the strings."

"What do we do with it?"

"We find more evidence."

"More? You don't have *any* yet. All you have are illegally obtained phone records."

"We have more than that."

"Not that you can use."

He was right.

And by the time Jen and I got to Patrick's place, we had a whole bunch more we couldn't use.

"I'm not sure where I should start," he said.

"Can we backtrack and find any previous text messages between Kroll and Mrs. Benton?" Jen asked.

"We've already got the records. They go back about two years. More than a few, but not a huge number. I'm still working on the contents. The older they are, the harder they are to find."

Jen nodded.

"My first thought," I said, "was some kind of relationship."

Patrick said, "Well, it is *some* kind of a relationship."

"Just not the kind I was thinking of."

"Even if they hired Tropov and the stooges, they still could be fucking each other," Jen said.

"Good point," Patrick said.

"Maybe the texts will tell us something." I looked at the stacks of papers on his desk. "What else did you find?"

"I told you last night I have access to S and B's personnel files? Don't know what to do with them exactly yet. They have fingerprints on file for all the PMF guys. I'm figuring out a way to run the driver's prints against what they have without leaving any tracks."

Jen thought about that for a moment. "Think they'd go in-house for something like that?"

"Maybe not," I said. "But let's hope so. If they didn't make any more mistakes, we're in trouble."

———————— , ————————

It wasn't even noon yet, but we'd already been on the clock for nearly eight hours. Jen looked tired.

"You want to go home, get some sleep?" I asked.

"No, I'm okay."

"At least take a long lunch. Get a little rest."

She nodded.

"Come back at three or four."

"We're almost there, Danny."

"Yeah," I said. I didn't know where "there" was, but I knew she was right. "Go sleep."

After she left, I started tossing things around in my head. I was surprised Anton would have gone back to his warehouse. Every experience I'd had with him seemed to indicate he was too smart for a rookie mistake like that. Especially with Yevgeny watching his back. There must have been a reason that he'd taken that kind of chance.

What could it have been?

I was still trying to answer that question when Patrick called. He'd left a few hours earlier to get back to his data.

"What's up?" I asked.

"I've got something," he said.

Three

THE FACE WAS NOT MUCH MORE THAN A BLUR, REALLY, reflected in the rearview mirror of the Tahoe that Shevchuk's killers had been driving. Patrick gave me a long and complicated explanation of how he had been able to recover the deleted photo from a mirror image of the flash memory of the driver's iPhone. I got lost somewhere in the second or third sentence.

"How can we be sure this is the Tahoe?"

"Well, we can't sure it's *the* Tahoe, but we know it's *a* Tahoe." He opened a file and showed me a dozen photos of rearview mirrors. "These are all from the same year and trim level they were driving. If you look close, you can see the shape and proportions are the same." He moused around the screen for few seconds and pulled three of the pictures into a line under the blurred face. He was right. The mirrors were all identical.

"How did you find all those?"

"Everything's out there. You just need to know where to look."

I was impressed. And he knew it.

"And you said you got this from a copy of the phone?"

"Yeah, that's the best part. The phone itself is still in evidence. I didn't have to break the chain of custody."

That meant that, unlike most of the other evidence Patrick had gathered, one of the techs at the department would be able to duplicate his results, and this would be admissible in court and valid evidence for warrants and other investigative purposes. If we could only match the photo to an actual face.

When I asked him about that, he said, "I used a facial-recognition program to run against the Sternow and Byrne personnel files but didn't get any hits." He saw the disappointment in my expression and went on. "Don't give up yet. The program I have is fairly basic, so I'm upgrading to a much better program. I've also got a guy who can enhance the image better than I can. We'll also have a lot more resources we can use whenever we go on the official record with this and can run it against the state and federal databases."

"No way to do that sooner?"

"I could access them, but that's way dicey. We leave a footprint with the feds, and we're going to be in way deeper than anything we've been digging into so far. I don't think we're ready to go there, are we?"

That was the first time since we'd started down this path that Patrick had hesitated. He was much more familiar with the territory than I was. I deferred. "You understand the implications of what we're doing a lot better than I do. You're in the driver's seat on this."

"I like the sound of that," he said, smiling in the blue light of his computer display.

———————— · ————————

Jen and I were back at our desks when I described him. "Dark hair, short beard, features on the sharp side. Hard to be much more specific."

"Could you pick him out of a lineup?" she asked.

"Depends on who else was in it. Maybe."

"Patrick thinks the techs will come up with the same image?"

"He seemed confident of that."

"How long did he think they'd take?"

"Couldn't say. Depends on how they're prioritizing things."

"So we've got an indefinite window until it goes into the reports."

I nodded. "I thought about talking to the techs, see if we could slow things down, but I didn't want to get anyone else involved."

"Might not be so bad."

"It would give us access to more data and make coming up with a match a lot more likely."

"What would we lose?" she asked.

I'd already considered that question and had an answer ready for her. "If he's still around, and we match him, he's likely to disappear."

"How do we know he hasn't already skipped?"

"Only Anton." There were a few angles to consider, but I was confident I'd figured them all out. "He might already be gone. If Anton was the contractor, the middleman, then he was probably the last loose end. The shooter and whoever's calling the shots might figure the mess is completely cleaned. Move on to whatever's next."

"That assumes a lot," Jen said. She was right.

"I know. That our theory is a slam dunk and that we've foreseen every possible variable."

"Think we have?"

"I doubt it."

"Me too."

"So where does that leave us?"

"With another needle in another haystack."

We talked briefly about tipping off the techs to the image on the iPhone, the exact opposite of what I had considered earlier, but decided to wait to see if Patrick could come up with something.

I dug back into the files and started looking for loose ends. A few minutes later, when I extended my hand toward the ceiling and pulled my raised elbow toward my head in an attempt to relieve the pain rising in my shoulder, Jen said, "What?"

"I hate this."

She waited for me to go on.

"Waiting. Every solid lead we're getting is coming from the fucking driver's iPhone and from Patrick's computer. I want to do something. I need to do something. I can't just sit here and wait. It's killing me."

"Then let's get out of here."

"And go where?"

"I've got an idea."

———————— , ————————

"*Yogurtland?*"

"You love Yogurtland," Jen said.

"I know. But it's not what I thought you had in mind."

"What were you expecting?"

"I don't know. I thought maybe we'd be kicking in a door or something."

We were sitting in lime-green chairs at the table closest to the window, looking out onto Second Street.

"You know," I said, "something exciting."

"Are you kidding?"

"What do you mean?"

"You're sitting there eating vanilla frozen yogurt topped with vanilla wafers and you honestly expect me to believe you want excitement?"

She had a point. So I used the pink plastic spoon to shovel another bite into my mouth and didn't say anything else.

———————— , ————————

"How are the schools?" I asked the real-estate lady. She had shoes with heels so high they made my calves hurt, shoulder-length blonde hair that didn't move when she turned her head, and smelled like a Sephora store. Her name was Shelly.

We'd stopped by a property on Fifth Street in Belmont Heights. They called it a duplex even though it really wasn't one. I didn't know what style it was—maybe a little bit Craftsmany mixed in with contemporary suburb? I did know it was a really nice three bedroom/two bath with a guesthouse in back, but it was way out of Jen's price range. Which was why I was having some fun with Shelly.

"Excellent schools," she said. "Fremont is only a few blocks away, and that's the best elementary school in Long Beach. Do you have any children yet?"

"Not yet," I said.

I couldn't tell if Jen's examination of the insides of the kitchen cabinets was out of genuine interest or just a way to pretend that she didn't hear me.

When we had introduced ourselves and told Shelly we were LBPD detectives, she'd seemed pleased and asked if we had met on the job. I told her we had and decided to see how far Jen would let me go.

She hadn't acknowledged anything yet. She seemed too engrossed in the inspection of the house.

"How long have you two been together?" Shelly asked.

"We've been partners for more than five years," I said.

Jen, still oblivious to our conversation, ran her hand across the marble countertop and took a look inside the stainless-steel dishwasher. Then she squatted down and looked at the tile work where it butted up against the bottom of the cabinets.

Shelly and I let her go. "And what's your current situation?" she asked.

"Oh," I said, "we're renting."

"Where?"

"Here in Long Beach." I was enjoying the vagueness game I was playing with Shelly and wondered how long I could string her along without actually telling a lie.

"So this will be your first house?"

"Neither of us has owned before."

Jen moved on through the laundry room, one of the baths, and all of the bedrooms before she said anything at all to us. When she was finally ready to talk, she said, "I like it. Can we take a look at the guesthouse?"

Shelly and I let our conversation drop and followed Jen through the rest of the property. The one-bedroom rear unit was every bit as nice as the front house. "How much do you think this would rent for?" Jen asked.

"It's so hard for people to buy right now," Shelly said. "The rents are going up. I think thirteen hundred would be a conservative guess."

Jen nodded, apparently in agreement. She seemed genuinely impressed with everything she'd seen. She traded contact information with Shelly and told her she'd call soon.

In the car, I said, "Are you really thinking about that one?"

"Yes," she said.

"It's almost seven hundred thousand. Isn't that way out of your price range?"

"If I could come up with a bit more for the down payment, with the rental income I could probably swing it."

"Do you really want a place so big?"

"I've been thinking," she said. "My dad's not doing too well. With Johnny gone to med school, they have a lot more house than they need. They could maybe use a smaller place."

I knew she was also thinking about the possibility of her mother being left alone in the big Gardena house she grew up in. She wouldn't say that out loud, though. Neither would I. Not surprisingly, I felt like a dick for joking around with Shelly.

"I'm sorry," I said.

"I know."

"You do?"

"Yeah. Why do you think I didn't give you any shit?"

We were in the car headed back downtown when the throwaway cell phone rang. I recognized the number.

"Good news, I hope," I said.

"Maybe. With the new software and enhanced photo recognition, we've got three possible matches in the Sternow and Byrne personnel files on the pic from the iPhone."

"Three? How many did you search it against?"

"As many as I could get my hands on. Over four thousand. Most of those were clerks and attorneys and paralegals. About seven hundred of those were the former PMF employees."

"Were all three matches from the mercenary pile?"

"Two were. We've got one air force vet and one with no military record who was already on the security payroll when S and B made the acquisition. Third guy's one of the mercs, former Army Ranger, no apparent air force connection."

"What do we do with the info?" I said. "How do we check these guys out and stay off the radar?"

"I'm working on that," Patrick said. "I'm trying to find out if I can get pictures of these guys through any other sources. Facebook, Flikr, anything online."

"Because then we don't have to worry about anybody asking how we made the connection."

"Bingo."

After we detoured by Patrick's loft, where we picked up hard copies of the info on the three possibles, we headed back to the squad room.

"How much do you want to know?" Jen asked the lieutenant.

"You're going to have to be the judge of that."

"How come she gets to be the judge?"

They both went on as if I hadn't spoken at all.

"We found some data in the phone," Jen said. "We can use it. It might lead us to the Seal Beach shooter. And it's going to be good info. Stuff we can use."

"Going to be?" he asked.

Jen nodded but didn't go into any more detail.

"It won't be long before you have to move on some of this, will it?"

"No," I said.

He gave us a look weighted with concern. It was clear he wanted to say more, but we'd gone too far to talk openly about our information-gathering techniques to be any more forthcoming about things without implicating him as well. None of us was comfortable with the situation, so he told us to be careful and went back into his office.

―――――――――― , ――――――――――

"Only one of the three was in the air force," I said. "Patrick put it on a Post-it." I held up the file for Jen to see. "Should we start with him?"

I flipped open the file on Aaron Baker and started reading. Patrick had done all the background he could on him without going through any of the government databases like NCIC or ViCAP. With those, there would be the possibility of leaving traces that the FBI might be able to find. Still, he was able to come up with quite a bit of information. Baker had dropped out of community college in Arizona and joined the air force in the wake of 9/11 and had served for four years before deciding not to re-up and accepting a position with a private military company that specialized in airborne surveillance and security, called SkyHawk.

"SkyHawk?" Jen asked. "As opposed to what? LandHawk?"

"Redundant," I said. "He didn't have to deal with the name for long. Six months after he signed on, they merged with DefCorp International. Been with them ever since."

"What else? Any record?"

"Unmarried. Has a Corvette, a Range Rover, and a Kawasaki registered with the DMV. One drunk and disorderly charge in 2004. Looks like it was pled down from an assault beef. Did some community service. Spent most of the last decade in the Middle East. Only has a US address going back to '09. Moved to LA when Sternow and Byrne snapped up DefCorp."

"What do you think?" Jen asked.

"This isn't a lot to go on. Patrick included a bit more. Mostly Google hits. He's got a Facebook page with no pictures, says he likes Metallica. Can we bust him for that?" She smiled, and I handed her the open folder.

"What's this? 'The Kawa-Kazes'? Some kind of rice-burner biker club."

"Wait," I said. "I thought we couldn't say 'rice burner' anymore."

"No, *you* can't say 'rice burner' anymore. I can say it all I want."

"Oh, it's one of those things."

"Yeah. Get over it."

"Think this could be our guy?"

"I don't know. We don't even know if he was Pararescue."

"No, we don't."

"How about the other two guys?"

"Let's see," I said. "We know neither one of them was a PJ. One's a former Ranger." I shuffled the folders. "This one. Roger Bell."

"What else is in there?"

"Records similar to Baker's. Although, he was already in the army. Joined in '98. Re-upped in '02, again in '06. Signed on with DefCorp in 2010. Sounds more like career military. Ex-wife and two kids. No criminal record. He was delinquent on his child support twice—second time, the year before he went private."

"Maybe he just needed the bigger paycheck."

"Think he needed an even bigger one? Signed on for some private wet work?"

"Wet work?"

"Yeah. It means assas—"

"I know what it means. I thought you gave up on Tom Clancy novels."

"The old ones are pretty good."

"Sure. How about number three?"

"Peter Jarman. No military service for him. Degree in political science from UCLA in '94. Looks like a pretty normal guy."

"How long has he been with S and B?"

"Twelve years."

"What did he do in between graduation and the law firm?"

"Don't know. Nothing in the file on that."

I spread the three folders on the table between us like giant playing cards and considered them. There didn't seem to be anything at all that would lead in one direction or another. We could dig deeper and start using some of our other resources to check them out, but that would be likely to tip off Young and Goodman.

"Should we talk to them?"

"How do we do that without tipping our hand?"

"We make some shit up."

———————— , ————————

Aaron Baker lived on the top floor of a condo complex two blocks in from the beach on the southern edge of Santa Monica, just north of the city's border with Venice. We parked on the street, and just as we were deciding if we wanted to buzz Baker's unit, a tall balding man in a Radiohead T-shirt led an energetic golden retriever out of the gate, and we slipped in behind him. He looked over his shoulder at us, but I gave an authoritative smile and an officious nod, and his dog pulled him down the street. It's surprising the kind of thing you can get away with if you act like a cop.

We got out of the elevator on the third floor and caught a few glimpses of the sun setting on the Pacific Ocean as we walked to Baker's door. I gave the door a triple rap with the knuckles on my left hand. My right was resting on my belt in front of my right hip. After a few seconds, I repeated the knock and said loudly enough for the next-door neighbor to hear, "Aaron Baker?"

The door opened on a safety chain, and an eye peeked around the edge. "Yes?"

"Mr. Baker? We're with the Long Beach Police Department. Could we have a few words with you?" We held up our badges.

"Just a moment," he said and shut the door. I heard him move away and then come back. We had known he'd be armed and might even answer a knock at his door with a weapon in his hand. Jen and I couldn't blame him—we'd both done the same thing more times than we could count. At least more than I could count. She's better at math than I am.

I whispered, "Stashing a gun?"

She nodded.

We heard him behind the door and saw a shadow move across the glass bricks to the right of the door, then the knob turning and a very soft squeak in the bottom hinge as he opened the door, keeping most of his body behind it. His manner was friendly, but he was being cautious, ready to slam the door and head back to wherever he'd hidden the gun.

"Hello," I said, amiably. "I'm Detective Danny Beckett, and this is Detective Jennifer Tanaka."

Baker nodded. "What can I help you with?" He stepped back, giving us as wide a berth as he could without it seeming obvious, and gestured toward a black leather sofa in the living room. The walls were eggshell, the floors hardwood, and the view was even better than it had been from outside. Sternow & Byrne was paying him well.

We settled onto the couch, and he took a seat in a matching chair. "You're a member of a motorcycle club," Jen said. "Is that correct?"

He looked puzzled.

"The Kawa-Kazes?" I said.

"Oh," he said. "I suppose you could call it that. It's really just a bunch of guys with motorcycles and a Facebook page. Haven't even ridden with anybody for a while."

"Do you know Larry Yamagata?" Jen asked.

"The name doesn't ring a bell."

"He was shot a few days ago, and his bike, a Kawasaki Ninja"—I made a show of checking my notes for the model designation I'd copied off the motorcycle company's website—"Ten-R was stolen."

"That's a good bike. I can see somebody killing for one."

Of course you can, I thought. *You're a fucking mercenary.*
"Would you mind looking at few pictures?" I asked.

"Sure," he said. The more he realized we weren't asking about anything he was connected to, the more relaxed he became.

I flipped open a file folder and showed him a photo of a man's chest with a tattoo that read KAWA-KAZE, in a font that had been modeled on Japanese kanji. It was easy to find with a Google search. We had dozens to choose from. Apparently, helmet-head Kawasaki fans lack imagination.

"Guy was serious, I guess," Baker said.

"Look familiar at all?" Jen asked.

"Nope. Turned out there were other guys calling themselves that, too. We weren't as clever as we thought we were. Never seen that tattoo."

I lifted the top photo to reveal another. The green footprints tat on the arm of the SUV driver. This was what we'd been leading up to. Jen was as focused on Baker as I was.

"Dude was a poser." He recognized the tattoo and knew it shouldn't have been on the driver's arm, but that was it. No twitches, no pauses, no uncertainty, no discernable micro-expressions, no red flags of any kind.

"What do you mean?"

"You don't know about the green footprints?"

"What about them?" I said. "We saw the color and thought it looked like Kawasaki green. Figured there was some kind of motorcycle connection."

"No. That's an air force Pararescue thing."

"Pararescue?"

"That's the air force version of the Green Berets or the SEALs."

"Really," Jen said. "This guy was special forces?"

"No," Baker said. He leaned forward, enthusiastic, pleased with himself. Maybe even showing off a little. "He wasn't. If you're Pararescue, you get the footprints on your ass. This guy was a tool. A wannabe."

"Oh, wow," I said. "That really helps."

"No sweat," Baker said. He looked directly at Jen. "Can I do anything else for you guys?"

She just smiled at him, tilted her head, and said, "I can't think of anything."

He smirked, completely oblivious to the fact that he was the only real tool anywhere in the vicinity.

———————— . ————————

The price we paid for the beauty of the sunset was rush hour traffic on the 405 back to Long Beach. Jen was driving, though, so I didn't mind.

"How do you want to go at the Ranger?" I asked.

"The Kawa-Kaze thing just jumped right out at us. Didn't really have to think about it."

"True," I said. "We can just go with a body in the neighborhood."

"He's in Pasadena?"

"Yeah."

"In a nice part of town?"

"Isn't Pasadena all nice parts?"

"I don't know," she said. "If we go in talking about a body, he might think twice about it when none of the neighbors bring it up."

"True." In Long Beach, murder is common enough and the population dense enough that we could make up a murder and no one would really think twice about it. Pasadena, as far as we knew, was in a different category. You can't always get away with stories like that in areas with low crime rates. "We're not going to fight the traffic tonight anyway. Let's sleep on it and see if we can come up with an angle tomorrow."

We drove in silence for a few miles, and just when we were passing LAX, my throwaway cell rang.

"Patrick," I said.

There was no reply.

"Patrick?" I repeated. "Hello?" I looked at the display. His name and number were there, and the line was still open. I tried again. "Hello?"

I hung up and redialed his number. The generic voice mail greeting answered.

"That was weird," I said.

"Try mine," Jen said, fishing the phone from her jacket pocket with her left hand.

I tried on her cell.

"No," I said. "Straight to voice mail again."

"Want to stop by his place?" she asked.

"I don't know," I said. "Probably just the crappy phone. We can try back in a while. How about we get something to eat and wait for the traffic to lighten up?"

"What are you thinking?"

"There's a CPK in Manhattan Beach."

"Really? CPK?"

"Yeah. It's right by the Apple Store."

"The truth comes out."

"I'm thinking about an iPad." It was one of the few tech toys that I'd wanted but hadn't actually gotten for myself during my leave.

"Didn't you just get a new MacBook?"

"That was months ago."

We went to the China Grill instead; then she indulged my techno lust. After oohing and aahing over all the merchandise and playing Angry Birds on the relatively large screen of an iPad for the better part of an hour, it was a challenge to talk myself out of spending a thousand dollars on shiny things I didn't need. Only the surety of Jen giving me shit about it all the way back to Long Beach gave me the strength to hold off.

"I think I'm jealous of Patrick," I said as we were getting back on the 405.

"How do you mean?"

"I want to be a hacker when I grow up."

"You were practically a Luddite before your leave," she said. "When did you send your first text message? A year ago?"

"I had a lot of time on my hands."

"Learning how to make an iTunes playlist doesn't make you Steve Jobs."

"I know that. I was thinking more of the Woz, anyway."

Her eyes narrowed, and I could see her decide not to indulge me any further.

After Patrick's throwaway went straight to voice mail again, I said, "Screw this. I'm just going to try his real phone."

"You think you should? He might not like it. He was pretty adamant about not using official hardware."

"Well, I won't say anything I shouldn't."

It didn't matter what I said, though, because I got another message prompt. This time I had to wait for six rings, though. "You ever see Patrick without his phone?"

"No."

"Still want to stop by his place?" I asked.

_____ , _____

Later that night, at the hospital, even though Jen tried to convince me otherwise, I wouldn't be able to stop myself from laying blame on my own seemingly infinite childishness and self-indulgence.

Nine

HOW MANY THINGS IN LIFE ARE DIVIDING LINES THAT separate the before from the after? I keep thinking I've encountered what surely must be the last of these, the final split, the ultimate separation. The first, of course, was the death of my father. Then the graduations—high school, college, the academy, becoming a cop, getting married, making detective, Megan's death, the onset of my chronic pain. Befores and afters. How many more would there be? How many more times could something happen that would make me think, This is it, things will never be the same again?

Driving south, we started to worry. I added two more voice mails and three text messages to Patrick's various inboxes.

"That's not like him," I said.

"I know," Jen said. "He's even texted me once from court."

"How'd he manage that?"

"He does it without looking at his phone. You've never seen him?"

"No."

"Yeah. Doesn't even need to take it out of his jacket pocket."

"Really?"

The headlights of the cars behind us reflected in the rearview mirror cast a bar of light across her eyes, and I could see the concern in them as she nodded. She'd partnered with him for almost a year. That was the first time I'd really thought about it. It had never occurred to me how close they must have become.

"I'm sure it's nothing to worry about," I said.

She didn't say anything.

I speed dialed Lieutenant Ruiz and waited for him to answer. When he did, I asked, "Have you heard from Patrick in the last few hours?"

"No," he said. "Why?"

We knew it was wrong even before we stopped the car.

"Drive past," I said to Jen as we approached Patrick's loft. "Check the side." When we saw that the big roll-up door facing the street was closed, she made a U-turn and parked on the other side of the street, just far enough away that no one would be able to see the cruiser from the front windows or the door.

Patrick's Mini was parked out front, but there were no lights on inside. Jen drew her Glock and started across the street.

"Wait," I said quietly. "Pop the trunk."

I took the Remington 870 out of the war bag inside and racked the slide to chamber a round. "Let's go."

We approached the door in a wide curve and stacked on the left side. I nudged the door with the muzzle of my pistol.

"Unlocked," I whispered.

"Wait for backup?" she asked.

Part of me was hoping we'd go inside and find Patrick in the dark, staring at one of his screens, headphones on, engrossed in a game of *Gears of War*. The other part couldn't stop worrying about what else might be inside.

I shook my head, crouched down, pushed the door open, and went inside. There was a light switch over my left shoulder, but I left it as it was. If I turned it on, it would give anyone in the expanse of the warehouse a perfect target.

When my eyes began to adjust to the darkness in the front room, I pulled the door open for Jen and she followed me inside. We took flanking positions on either side of the doorway leading into the short hallway.

I made eye contact with her, and when I saw that she was ready, I began down the hallway. Hugging the wall, I leaned into the stock of the Remington. The kitchen and bathroom looked clear, although, in the darkness, I couldn't be positive. I knew Jen had my back, so I kept moving.

A few short steps in front of me, the hall opened into the large expanse of the warehouse. All I could see was darkness.

Behind me, I heard Jen move into the kitchen, then the bathroom, to be sure we wouldn't be surprised from behind.

If I remembered correctly, there was a light switch just around the corner that was wired to turn on half a dozen lights around the edges of the large space.

When Jen was at my heels, I turned to her and whispered, "Lights."

She gave me a single nod.

I reached up and tried to find the switch with my fingers.

The adrenaline was pumping at full force, and I could feel my hands shaking.

I took two deep breaths and slid my hand around the wall. I could have sworn I'd seen Patrick turn on the lights there, but all I could feel was the empty wall.

No lights.

I shook my head to tell Jen what she had already figured out.

She took the SureFire flashlight out of her pocket and held it up.

I nodded and motioned for her to move to the right of the door, then pointed at myself and gestured to the left.

When we were in position, she crouched low and raised her left hand high before hitting the flashlight's thumb switch.

At the same time, I flicked on the Remington's fore end–mounted tactical light.

We moved the spots around the big space, looking for movement or anything out of place.

Nothing.

When we knew we'd seen everything we could from that position, we began to move.

Not more than ten feet from the door, Jen said, "Danny," and her beam of light stopped on the far side of the loft.

Patrick's computer setup had been trashed. As we moved closer, we could see someone had taken great pains to see that nothing would be salvageable. I was still looking at the mess when I heard Jen gasp.

She was already kneeling next to him before I even understood what had caused her exclamation.

On the floor, with his hands and feet bound and strips of duct tape across his mouth and eyes, was Patrick's motionless body.

From the evidence at the scene that Dave and Marty gathered while we waited at the hospital, and the reports of the paramedics and the emergency room doctor, we knew that he had been Tasered and had hit his head on the edge of one of the computer tables as he fell. He was unconscious when he was bound and gagged. If not for the head injury, the assault would have been relatively minor.

But the trauma was serious—a severe concussion and a cracked skull led to a subdural hematoma and brain herniation. He was in a coma, and the doctors were unsure of his prognosis.

Had he been found sooner, the surgeon said, he could have been more positive. As it was, we'd have to wait and see.

"Stop it, Danny," Jen said.

"Stop what?"

"It wasn't your fault."

I wanted to argue with her, but I knew doing so would be self-indulgent, and that was exactly what I was blaming myself for already. I didn't believe it was my fault Patrick was attacked, but I knew that if I hadn't been dicking around, we would have gone to his house sooner.

"What should we do?" I asked.

"The lieutenant's on the way. Let him call it."

When he got there half an hour later, he told us we could stay at the hospital, go work the scene, or even go home and try to get some sleep. Which, of course, wasn't any help at all. Jen decided to stay.

"Is it okay if I go see how Dave and Marty are doing?"

"Yeah," she said. "One of us should. I'll call you as soon as there's any news."

With that, I drove the ten minutes back to Patrick's loft.

There were four cruisers, a Crime Scene Detail van, and two unmarked LBPD vehicles. The one I was in made three.

I badged a rookie I didn't know, and he let me inside.

"Danny," Marty said as he saw me walk toward him, "what's the latest?"

Dave joined us, and I told them everything I knew about Patrick's condition.

"He'll be fine," Dave grumbled. "He's a hardheaded bastard. He'll be fine."

I tried hard to believe him, and judging by the look on his face, Marty did, too.

"Detectives?"

The three of us turned back toward the door and looked up toward the voice. Above the front rooms was a second floor, kind of a loft within the loft. One of the crime scene technicians was looking down at us and waving. "I think there's something up here you should see," he said.

The only access was a steel ladder attached to wall in the corner.

"After you," Marty said.

I climbed up. "Hey, James," I said to the tech. When he looked at me oddly, I second-guessed myself. "I'm sorry. Jim?"

"Ben," he said.

Before I could apologize again, Marty stepped off the ladder. "Hey, Ben," he said. "What do you have?"

"Right over here," he said, gesturing to a three-foot-square metal access hatch. "I hope it's okay," Ben said. "I used Detective Glenn's keys to open this."

"Why?" Marty asked. We felt awkward snooping through our colleague's things. None of us were sure how much privacy we should afford him. It wasn't a stretch to assume Patrick's attack was connected to the Benton investigation, and he had been assaulted and was in critical condition. It was a stupid thing to worry about, but cops always get uncomfortable when one of our own is on the other side of an investigation. Fortunately, though, Ben had a good answer.

"I was following this." He motioned for us to step closer, and he ran his hand along the joint where the wall met the low ceiling of the loft. "Feel up here," he said.

I did. There was a ridge of spackle that filled in the right angle of the joint. As I followed it with my fingers, I could see the unusual convex curve where the seam should have been sharper and more angular.

"What's this?" I asked.

"There's a wire underneath," Ben said. "Runs out here to the edge."

"What's there?"

"Take a look."

I leaned out over the railing and looked at the edge of the joint. There was a shallow hole that was perhaps a quarter of an inch across with something black inset into the opening. "What am I looking at?"

"A lens," he said.

Marty and I looked at him expectantly.

"The wire runs into the wall and inside."

"What's in there?"

"Take a look."

I got down on my hands and knees and crawled halfway into the hatch. The first thing I noticed was how clean it was. There was no dust on the floor, no cobwebs hanging from the studs. It didn't even smell musty. Just inside was a rack of what looked like computer equipment. I think Ben expected me to recognize what I was looking at. I didn't. As I backed up out of the hole, I said, "You're going to have to help me out with that, too."

"It's a video control unit hooked up to a couple of hard drives."

"Surveillance?" Marty asked.

"Yeah," Ben said.

"Did it get what happened here?"

"Power's on and everything's running, so I'm guessing yes."

"Guessing?"

"Can't tell for sure. Security's tight. Didn't want to risk damaging any of the data."

"It's connected directly to the camera?" I asked. "Why not use wireless?"

"Six cameras," Ben said. "And they're all hardwired. Closed circuit. With wireless, if somebody had the right frequency and they were close enough, they could intercept the signal. With wires, no one's going to see anything you don't want them to."

"Where are the other cameras?"

"I don't know yet. I'll follow the wires and find them."

"This hardware, it's not the kind of thing somebody would plant here, right? It's for security?"

"Right. Detective Glenn knew his tech. This is his."

Marty started down the ladder. While I was waiting for him to clear the bottom, I turned back to Ben and said, "Good work. This is big."

He looked pleased, and I hoped that helped to make up for my mistake with his name.

"Thanks," he said. "That really means a lot coming from you, Detective Ionesco."

When I got down to the bottom of the ladder, Marty asked, "What's so funny?"

Dave, Marty, and I gathered around the wreckage of Patrick's computer equipment. "They destroyed everything. Took the hard drives, ripped them right out of the machines. Weren't messing around," Dave said.

"Who do you suppose 'they' were?" Marty asked.

"Not the shooter from the SUV," I said.

Dave's brow furrowed. "Why do you say that?"

"He shot the driver at the first sign of trouble. Whoever did this was trying to avoid violence. Used a Taser. Patrick's only critical because he hit his head on the edge of the table on the way to the floor. They probably didn't even know how bad he was when they tied him up."

He considered it. "Maybe. Maybe they just didn't want to up the ante by killing a cop."

I thought about that. Dave might have been right, but I didn't think so. There was so much blood on the shooter's hands at that point that the added weight of a cop on top of everything else wouldn't make that much of a difference.

But.

We needed the video from the surveillance unit.

"Why do you suppose he has such a heavy-duty camera setup?" Jen asked.

"I don't know. He had a lot of computer equipment. Must have been worth a lot. Maybe to protect it?"

"Could be." She thought for a moment. "You don't think he could have put it in just since we went off the grid, do you?"

"I doubt it. It was a serious installation. Not the kind of thing you'd do on the fly."

"Think the techs will be able to crack the security?"

"They said they could; they just couldn't say when. The more skilled he is, the longer it'll be."

We sat in silence. The KABC news was on the TV in the waiting room, but the sound was turned down. About ten minutes in, there was an update on the Benton case. I watched a reporter standing in front of Bradley and Sara's house in Bixby Knolls talk into the camera; then they cut to a video of Bailey and Jacob. The same one that Oliver Woods had leaked. All the stations were using it now. The report didn't last long. There was nothing new for them to say.

———————— , ————————

Jen insisted that I go home and try to rest. When I got there, though, I was so wired that I knew sleep would be hard to come by. The pain had been worsening in my arm and shoulder for several hours, and by midnight I couldn't think of anything else. I took two Vicodin, put my iPod in the dock, set it on shuffle, and sat in the darkness of my living room, looking out the window at the quiet and empty street.

After Johnny and Bruce—who are always in heavy rotation because I have so much of their music in my collection—the shuffle surprised me with Tom Waits's "House Where Nobody Lives." I hit the REPEAT button and let it play four or five times. It was the perfect song for wallowing.

I waited for the meds to kick in and the progression of the pain to slow and hopefully even back up a bit. It didn't.

A few minutes after one, I took another pill and forced myself to sit down at the dining room table and watch a video of Bailey and Jacob. That didn't work, either.

I thought about calling Jen, but on the off chance that she'd managed to find any rest at the hospital, I didn't want to disturb her. She'd said she'd let me know if there was any news, and I had no doubt that she would.

After I moved on from Tom, Arcade Fire tried to cheer me up with "Antichrist Television Blues." That didn't work, either.

I turned the iPod off and picked up the banjo. Five minutes of random finger picking did nothing.

The pain was still as strong as it had been all night. The third Vicodin hadn't dulled it, but it had left me feeling off center and mildly nauseous.

It seemed that I stood in the kitchen for a very long time looking at the Grey Goose on the counter, but, in reality, I doubt that I took more than a minute to reach for the bottle.

My cell phone seemed much louder than usual when it woke me. The morning sun was bright through the living-room window, and I was slumped uncomfortably over the arm of the sofa.

It was Jen's ringtone.

"Hey," I said.

"Hey."

I waited for her.

"They say he's not getting any worse."

"That's good, right?"

"Not as good as him waking up."

"That's true. Did you sleep at all?"

"A little. They let me crash on a cot in one of their break rooms. You in the squad?"

"Not yet. Still at home."

"Were you sleeping?"

"Yeah."

"Shit. Sorry I woke you up. I just figured…" Her voice trailed off.

She didn't need to finish. It was 7:40. I couldn't remember the last time I'd slept so late. Then I wondered if I should think of the unconsciousness I'd just experienced as sleep. It didn't seem like a good precedent to set.

"Don't worry about it. I'm on the way in right now. Once I have updates on everything, I'll head over there. Want me to bring you a change of clothes?"

"If you wouldn't mind staying for a little while, maybe I'll take a break."

"Sure thing."

——————— , ———————

"Good news," Ben said.

"Tell me." I'd stopped to check in with him on the way up to the squad. I flipped open the top of the pink box and offered him a donut.

He looked inside. "Four vanilla crullers?"

"Yeah."

"Why no chocolate?"

"There's a chocolate bar and two cake."

"But no chocolate crullers?"

"No. Sorry. Have a vanilla."

His face screwed up into what looked like a very uncomfortable expression. "I'll just have a glazed. Wouldn't want to short anybody."

"Please." I raised the box toward him. He took one.

"That's good," he said.

"So what's the news?"

"The video recordings."

"Go on."

"It doesn't look like Detective Glenn was worried about anybody finding the equipment."

"Then why the whole closed-circuit thing?"

"He *was* worried about somebody picking up the signal. Hacking in. Getting a free show."

"Okay." He could see I wasn't following.

"What that means is I didn't have to figure out his security. I was able to bypass it and just remove the hard drives and access them with our equipment here."

"That's great. What did you find?"

"Nothing yet. He had six cameras and enough space for four or five days' worth of recording. Going to have to scan it all manually."

"How long?"

"A few hours, I'll have everything that matters ready for you to look at."

———————— , ————————

Jen checked in with the doctor one more time before she agreed to let me take over her watch.

"He said Patrick's doing a bit better. The pressure in his head is going down. That's a good sign." She didn't sound convinced, though. "I'm just going to get cleaned up and change; then I'll be back, okay?"

"Sure," I said. "Maybe just lie down for a few minutes, too."

"Maybe."

When she hugged me, I pulled her head into my shoulder and let her rest it there for a long time.

After she left, I checked in with the nurse on duty and told her I was there for Patrick. She told me the doctor would be checking on him before too long and they'd let me know if there were any changes in his condition.

I sat down in the waiting room and got out my Kindle. The only things I had on it that I hadn't read were *The Passage*, a postapocalyptic vampire book, and *Room*, a novel narrated by a five-year-old who had never set foot outside the storage in which he and his kidnapped mother were held hostage. Both were on a bunch of the end-of-the-year best book lists. While I was trying to decide which one to start on, my memory got the best of me and I started thinking about Jen holding vigil here for Patrick. It had been almost fourteen months since she'd done the same for me.

Seeing her waiting had made me think of that experience, but I shoved it down in the back of my mind. I didn't want to think about it. And I didn't want to think about how hard it must have been for her. It was only just beginning to dawn on me that I'd been so caught up in my own pain and recovery that I hadn't really given much thought to her. At least not about how she must have struggled. And I hadn't given much consideration to her partnership with Patrick. I'd never thought of it as more than temporary, a transitory relationship that wouldn't amount to anything of significance in the long run. But every month I was out on leave, every time the next surgery didn't quite go as far as we'd hoped, every extension of my medical leave—four months to six, to nine, to thirteen—had been another step for them.

At what point, I wondered, did it start to feel like a long-term thing rather than a transitory, just-until-Danny-gets-back-on-his-feet deal?

Jen and I had four years together before I went out on leave. That was a long partnership. Sure, Marty and Dave had us beat by quite a stretch, but that was at least in part because the lieutenant was old-school and liked what he got from teams who really had the opportunity to get to know one another well and learn each other's moves and manners. How much of that had Jen and Patrick been able to do?

Was I stepping in the middle of that? Did Jen resent it? Did Patrick? I had assumed that I'd walk right back into the job at exactly the place I'd been forced to leave it. Was I wrong to think I could do that? Was it even possible?

Before I knew it, I was simmering in a swill of guilt and jealousy.

Self indulgently, I tried to remember to blame my self-indulgence for Patrick being here.

When I finally turned on the Kindle, I went for *The Passage* because I like postapocalyptic stuff even more than I hate vampires.

Jen came back a few hours later, but the world still hadn't ended. It was a long book.

"You can take off," she said. She looked rested and as if she'd gotten a second wind and hoisted the weight she carried into a more manageable position.

"You talk to Marty and Dave?"

"Yeah."

"Seem like they're on top of things?"

She nodded.

"How about if I stay a while?"

———————— , ————————

The next morning, the doctor gave us an update. The pressure appeared to be back to normal levels and the swelling had gone down considerably. He was out of danger. "We'll need to wait and see if there are any lingering effects."

"Like what?" she asked.

"Well, traumatic brain injury can have a number of ramifications," he said. "Memory loss, impaired function, primarily things like that. Because he was unconscious for more than six hours, the chances are greater that there will be some lasting consequences."

"Lasting?" I said, aware that Jen didn't want to ask the hard question. "You mean permanent?"

"It's possible."

"Thanks."

He went back to doing whatever he'd been doing, and I wondered how many people he'd have to give bad news to today. I thought about how hard it is to tell a person that someone they love is dead. At least he gets to give people good news once in a while.

"What do you think?" I said. "Want to go back to the station with me, or stay here?"

"You think Ben's got the video ready?"

"He said a couple of hours. It's been more than three."

"You mind going?"

"Not a bit."

————————— , —————————

"Run it again, would you?" I said to Ben.

He did, and I watched a man in jeans, a dark jacket, and a ski mask with a dark object in his extended hands move quickly across the loft toward Patrick, who appeared to be completely absorbed in his work at one of his computers. It was a wide-angle shot that distorted the field of view, particularly around the edges. When the man was about fifteen feet away, Patrick either heard the intruder or was drawn to the motion, because he stood up, turned toward the intruder, and reached for his holstered pistol. The man stopped and fired the Taser in his hands. Patrick's body tensed in the distinctive convulsion caused by electroshock weapons and then collapsed. His head recoiled and snapped backward as it impacted the edge of his desk. The intruder closed the distance between them, dragged Patrick out from behind his desk and tables, and bound and gagged him. When he finished with that, he went to work on the computers.

"You said you had it from two other angles as well?"

"Yes," Ben said. He showed me those, too. The second record-ing was from the upstairs camera he'd shown me the night before, and it gave us a better view of Patrick, but we were only able to see the intruder's back. The third came from a camera mounted on the opposite of the loft and came fairly close to reversing the angle of the one we'd just watched.

"This is fantastic coverage," I said.

"Yeah," he said.

"Never had three angles on a crime before."

"That's not all."

"What else?"

"Detective Glenn had a camera outside, too."

"Show me."

He tapped at his keyboard, and I saw a view of the street and part of the parking lot outside of Patrick's place. A Honda Accord pulled up to the curb and parked about thirty yards north of the loft. It was partially obscured by some tree branches, but we could see the man who accosted Patrick get out and walk calmly toward the front door. It looked liked he put the mask on while his face was out of view.

"Nothing on the face?"

"No, but I did find something interesting on the car. It was confiscated three days ago in a DEA drug raid. It's supposed to be impounded in Santa Ana."

"Supposed to be? Do we know if it is?"

"Yeah, it's there now. And according to the lot's records, it never left."

"Can you put everything you just showed me on a disc?"

"Already did. And made a couple of extras, too." He handed me three DVDs in plastic jewel cases. "I'm going to stay on these. See if we can find anything else."

As soon as I got back upstairs, I slipped the DVD into my computer and cued up the footage. I watched each angle again and then began to focus on them one at a time. It was the third time through the first angle Ben had shown me—the wide-angle view from across the room—that I spotted them. I wasn't sure at first, so I went through the other angles a few times each. When I was absolutely positive, I called Jen.

"How's he doing?" I asked.

"About the same as when you left. He's out of danger, but he still hasn't woken up."

"How about you?"

"I'm doing okay," she said. She'd said that to half a dozen people in the last eighteen hours. This was the first time I believed her.

"Good," I said. "Because I need some backup."

One

"THE SHOES?" JEN ASKED.

"Yeah. New Balance Nine Fifty-Fives. We talked about them. Remember I told you about meeting him at The Potholder?"

"He was wearing them?"

"Yeah. I used to have a pair just like his. Then they changed the model, and neither one of us liked the new version."

"Is that enough?"

"There's the car, too." I told her about the impound lot in Santa Ana.

"Is that the same one the Orange County Sheriff's Department uses?"

I nodded. "Santa Ana PD, too. If we dig around there, we might be able to firm things up a bit."

"We put him at the lot or in the car, it's solid," she said. "Want to head over there?"

"We know they've got video, right?"

"Yeah."

"Why don't we skip the preliminaries and go right for a warrant?"

"I'll call Bob."

By dinnertime we were in the lieutenant's office showing him the footage Patrick's camera had picked up outside his loft of Goodman getting into the car. The time codes from both sources lined up perfectly, putting him at the scene less than an hour after he'd left the impound lot.

"He's at the Westin?" Ruiz asked.

"Yeah," I said.

"Grab him before he gets wind of the warrant."

The hotel was only a few blocks away from the station. I was only half joking when I suggested to Jen that we should walk. Dave and Marty hadn't signed out for the day, so they and four uniforms joined us.

"You suppose we're going in heavy?" Marty asked.

"No," I said. "He only used a Taser on Patrick, but he could be getting desperate, feeling cornered. Better to hit him hard with a lot of force so he doesn't get any stupid ideas."

"Shock and awe," Dave said from the backseat. I looked at him in the rearview mirror, and the setting sun angling onto his face made the laugh lines etched into his face look like creases in ancient leather.

The Westin's director of security was a former LBPD sergeant who had taken his twenty and gone private. He met us at the desk.

Marty had ridden with him back in the day.

"Sarge," Marty said, extending his hand.

They shook and gave each other a pat on the elbow with their free hands.

"Good to see you," he said, giving the rest of us a single nod.

I stepped forward, and he didn't have to ask which one of us was the lead. "He's upstairs?"

"Yeah," he said. "Just had the front desk do a courtesy check. He said everything was fine."

"Any chance that might have tipped him?"

"Got a man on the door, just in case."

"You want to lead us up?"

We took two elevators to the eighth floor.

He rode with the uniforms.

Down the hall from Goodman's room, he gave me a master key card. "Works just like a regular one, slide it into the slot, pull it out, wait for the little green light, and you're good to go."

"I know how hotel key cards work, Sarge," I said.

"Well, you can't ever be sure with detectives."

The uniforms got a grin out of that, and to be honest, the rest of us did, too.

We stacked up on either side of the door, Dave on my shoulder and Marty on Jen's. We unholstered our weapons.

"Ready?" I whispered, making brief eye contact with each person close to the door. When I had unanimous nods, I slipped the key into the door, pushed it open, and shouted, "Agent Goodman! Police! We're coming inside!"

The room was off-white with lots of wood and earth-toned upholstery and accents. It was also empty.

"Goodman!" I shouted. "Police!"

I moved inside. The crew followed. Something was wrong. He'd answered the phone ten minutes earlier. Was he barricaded in the bathroom? The door, to my right as I came in, was closed. I nodded in that direction, and Jen moved into position behind me, facing it and giving me cover to check out the rest of the room.

"Goodman?" I said, moving across the room and around the king-size bed.

He wasn't there. The closet, across from a sink and mirror, flanked the entryway to the bathroom. Jen moved aside to let me in first.

I said his name again as I tried the knob. It wouldn't turn. "Locked," I said.

We backed out of the room into the hallway.

"Sarge," I said, "the bathroom's locked. You have anything we can use on it?"

"You hear anything from inside?" he asked.

I shook my head.

"Just kick it. It won't take much. Otherwise, we'll have to wait five minutes for maintenance."

Back inside, I lifted my knee and drove my heel into the door just below the knob. The latch popped open and the door recoiled hard against the wall, giving me a brief glimpse of Goodman's brain matter and blood spattered on the wall over the toilet before it bounced back and swung back into the jamb again.

I nudged it with my toe to reveal the scene again. Goodman's body was leaning back over the toilet tank, with his head tilted toward the wall in way that didn't allow us to see the worst of the damage. Only a small red hole under his chin was visible. If not for the spray of blood and viscera fanned on the eggshell wallpaper, it might be possible he suffered nothing worse than a particularly nasty shaving wound. Although, there were a few bits of fluffy white material clinging to his jaw.

On the floor next to the toilet I saw his Sig service pistol and a pillow from the bed, and I realized how he'd done it.

"He put the pillow under his chin," I said to Jen, who was looking around me into the bathroom.

She finished my thought. "And pressed the muzzle into it. That's why the guard didn't hear."

We backed out of the room and asked one of the uniforms to call the Crime Scene Detail and the ME.

She gave a nod and started talking into the radio mic clipped to her shoulder.

"Sarge?"

"Yeah, Danny?"

"You get a lot of noise complaints?"

"Almost none. Great soundproofing. Best in Long Beach."

We didn't have much to investigate at the scene. We bagged Goodman's phone, his laptop, and all of his other personal effects. It seemed, unlike most of what we'd been investigating, completely clear what had happened. The call from the front desk had tipped him, and that was all he'd needed.

Carter, the ME, had the body laid out and ready to be put into the body bag when I asked him to wait. "Can you roll him over?"

"Sure. What are you looking for?"

"I need to look at his ass."

Goodman had been wearing a T-shirt and his suit pants. No shoes or belt. Carter tugged down on the waist of his gray wool slacks and exposed his cheeks. On the right one were two green footprints. No apparent aesthetic value.

———————— , ————————

"Does his partner, Young, have a room here, too?" I asked the sergeant.

"Not that I know of. Goodman checked in with me as a courtesy. Imagine he would have mentioned another agent staying in the hotel."

"Thanks," I said, leaving him. Jen was just down the hall. "What should we do about the other one?"

"Young?"

"Yeah. Don't know where he's staying."

"Think he was in it with his partner?"

"No sign of him on any of the video. You'd think if he were involved, he'd be there for backup."

"You'd think."

"But you don't?"

"I'm worried he knows something. We give him a heads-up, he might spook."

"You have an idea, don't you?"

"Where's the evidence we booked?"

———————— , ————————

Twenty minutes later, Special Agent Young was downstairs in the lobby bar looking for Goodman. He was green, but he was sharp enough to realize something was wrong when he saw us approaching him instead.

"Detectives, hello."

We nodded our greetings.

"Are you meeting Agent Goodman here as well?"

"No," I said.

"Must be a coincidence, then."

Jen said, "No, it's not. We sent you the text message."

The small amount of cordiality that had been lightening his expression disappeared. "Where?" he said.

"Back at the station."

"Should I get my car?"

"We'll give you a ride."

None of us said another word until we were seated at the table in the Homicide interview room. We pulled a third chair in from next door so we could all sit. There wasn't much point in trying anything tricky with Special Agent Young. The FBI had made sure he had even better interrogation training than we did.

Jen started. "Would you like to have someone from the LA office here for this?"

"No," Young said. "Tell me what's going on."

We did. In detail. Starting with Patrick's attack and finishing with Goodman on the toilet.

"Why do you suppose he killed himself?" I asked.

"*Why?*" he said indignantly. "You really need to ask? He assaulted a police officer. His career was over and he was going to jail. The real question is why did he throw a twenty-five-year career away? That's what I'd like to know."

"Do you have any ideas?"

"Nothing specific. He hated that we were here. Hated everything we were doing for the congressman. They went back a long way. Someone had to pull some strings to get us here, and

Goodman wasn't happy about it. There was some serious resentment there, but he did it anyway. That's all I know. I've been trying to figure out what was going on, too. I'm just spending every day in the Federal Building going through old case files."

"For Goodman?" I asked. "Did he have you looking for something specific?"

"No, for the LA special agent in charge. Different stuff every day. Just busywork to keep me out of Goodman's way."

"Where are you staying?"

"I have a sister who lives nearby."

"Didn't like the Westin?"

"No. Looks great. Too great. They usually put us at the Courtyard, someplace like that. Goodman was, I don't know, overreaching? Said just because he had to do a shit job, it didn't mean he had to stay in a shithole."

We spent another forty-five minutes with him, and when we were done, both Jen and I were convinced he didn't have any idea what Goodman had been doing.

Young was on his way back to his sister's house, and Jen and I had just sat down at our desks when Ruiz came out of his office and said, "Patrick's awake."

Two

BY THE TIME WE GOT TO LONG BEACH MEMORIAL, PATRICK HAD been conscious for more than two hours. They let Jen in for a few minutes, but the rest of us had to wait until morning. When she came out, she told me he wasn't able to do much but nod and blink before he fell asleep. Then she hugged me and we both went home. I knew it would be the first good night of rest she'd had since Patrick had been in there. I didn't bother hoping for the same for myself.

———————— , ————————

"Hey, guys," he said when we came in early the next day. The morning sun was angling in through the window of his room. There were two other beds, but they were both empty. "The doctor told me what happened to my head. You know who did it?" His voice sounded a bit ragged, and he looked tired, but he seemed like himself. I hoped that was a good sign.

We told him.

"Goodman? Really?"

"For what it's worth, it didn't look like he wanted to hurt you. Your head hit the table on the way down."

"Yeah," Patrick said. "The motherfucker just wanted to Taser me and remove my eyebrows with duct tape."

"They're not entirely gone," Jen said.

"Not entirely? That's not making me feel much better."

"We only got him because of your surveillance system," I said.

"Good thing I put it in, then."

"When did you install it?" Jen asked.

"Soon as I moved in. Remember I had that break-in at my old place?"

I didn't, but Jen nodded.

"Figured better safe than sorry."

"Too bad we lost all the data," I said.

"What do you mean? We didn't lose any data. Only about twenty thousand dollars' worth of hardware," he said, with enough dejection in his voice to bring the mood in the room almost as low as had been when he was comatose.

"Wait," I said. "What do you mean we didn't lose any data? Goodman took all your hard drives and storage devices. We don't know what he did with them. We definitely lost it."

"Oh my god," Patrick said, "when was the last time you backed up your computer?"

I was taken by surprise and didn't know how to answer. "What? Why? What does that have to do with anything?"

"Jen, when was the last time you backed up?"

"Last time I used it. Backed up automatically. Just like you showed me." She clearly enjoyed ganging up on me.

"Wait," I said, too caught up in my thoughts to enjoy the fun they were having at my expense. "They didn't get the data?"

"No, they got it, so they'll know what we know. But we have it, too. Everything on my system backed up automatically every thirty minutes to multiple remote servers."

"That's good," I said. "So we've got everything up until the time of the attack?"

"And everything since," Patrick said. "Haven't you ever heard of the cloud?"

I had, so I assumed he meant that he had the surveillance programs running on systems other than the one that Goodman had trashed.

"How can we access it?"

"Got a laptop?"

I went out to the car and got mine for him. He'd only been on it a few minutes before a nurse came in and told us to leave because Patrick needed to rest. He'd already opened and book-marked two sites in Firefox for me. The first was one I recognized. It kept a real-time record of phone calls, text messages, and e-mails we were tracking. The other was unfamiliar. It looked like a Google Maps page.

"What's this?"

"My MacBook has GPS. The marker there on the map? That's where it is." He tapped a red marker just above Ocean Boulevard.

I looked more closely. "That looks like the Westin." I turned to Jen. "Think it's in his car?"

The nurse had had enough. "I'm serious," she said. "He needs to rest."

"I've been asleep for days," Patrick said, but she wouldn't budge. If we wanted to stay, it looked like we'd have to draw our weapons.

I closed the MacBook and tucked it under my arm.

Patrick didn't look like he wanted to let it go.

"We'll bring one of yours as soon as we can," Jen said.

"Does that work?" he said, looking at the clock radio on the table next to his bed.

I said, "Sure. You want me to put on *Morning Becomes Eclectic*?"

"I'm not a hipster."

———————————— , ————————————

Most of the activity at the hotel crime scene had passed, but there were still two technicians and a few uniforms tying up the loose ends. Nichols was still there. Watching. Waiting until he could clear everything out and get back to business as usual.

"Hey, Sarge," I said.

"Danny." He gave me half a nod. "What did you forget?"

"Anybody been down to the garage to check out his car yet?"

"We took one of the uniforms down to tag it for a tow to the impound."

"The truck come yet?"

"I don't think so." He took his cell phone out of the pocket of his dark-blue suit and hit a speed-dial number.

"Anybody pick up the fed's car yet?" He listened. "Well, if they show up before we get there, don't let them hook it up." He turned back to us. "Let's go."

In the elevator on the way down, he said, "What's this all about?"

"Can't say much," I replied.

"What can you say?"

"We think he was dirty," Jen said. "Deep into some bad shit."

"The Seal Beach thing or the congressman's family?" he asked.

"Yeah," I said.

Jen frowned at me.

When he said, "Well, which one?" I knew I hadn't said too much.

The doors opened and the three of us stepped out into the dank concrete emptiness of the underground parking structure.

"You have his keys?" he asked.

We didn't, so he stopped by a small office filled with video monitors displaying a dozen views of the garage. Every few seconds, the feeds would switch to different cameras, but the shots looked so similar that if I hadn't been paying close attention, I wouldn't have noticed the change. There was an empty chair facing the screens.

"This the place you have to come when you screw up?" I asked.

"One of them, but this isn't even close to the worst," the sergeant said. "Remind me when we're done. I'll take you down to check out the boilers and the laundry. It's just like hell, but with more humidity and a bleach-scented air freshener." He opened an equipment locker and took out a slim jim, then closed the door and led us out into the mostly empty rows of parking spaces.

"Slow day?" I asked.

"Slow year," he said.

We walked eight rows over and halfway down the ramp to the next level, where we found a black Crown Vic parked by itself in a corner, with a giant Pacific Islander standing next to it. He wore what must have been a sixty long navy-blue blazer with the Westin insignia over the breast pocket and name badge that read, *Manuia*. He looked unhappy.

Nichols nodded at him and slipped the slim jim in between the driver's side window and top edge of the door trim. With a few practiced pulls, he popped the door open, reached inside, and released the trunk latch. "We'll give you two a little space," he said and led the guard a few yards away.

Jen lifted the trunk lid and said, "Danny?"

I stepped around to the back of the vehicle and saw a standard-issue Rubbermaid Roughneck fourteen-gallon storage box, not at all unlike those we use every day for evidence. Jen snapped the lid off the container. The innards of Patrick's computers, including his apparently undamaged MacBook Pro, were there waiting for us.

———————— , ————————

Special Agent Young's sister lived in Rossmoor, just across the Orange County line, in a nice suburban split-level four bedroom. She had two kids, who were off in another part of the house playing a video game that sounded like *Guitar Hero* or *Rock Band*. I couldn't tell which.

"I'm not sure," Young said.

"Goodman's stink is going to come off," I said. "This is the best thing you can do to try to get it off of you."

"It's a just a phone call," Jen said.

He thought about it some more. He was wearing a T-shirt and jeans and drinking a Heineken. It was still obvious he was an FBI agent. He might as well have had it branded on his forehead.

"I think I should run it by the LA SAC," he said.

"You really want to do that?" Jen asked, her voice thick with concern.

"Why shouldn't I?" It was clear he wasn't used to situations that didn't follow the playbook clearly and closely. Sure, Goodman was an asshole, but he certainly understood the real world a great deal better than his junior partner. On the other hand, the people at the Westin were still trying to remove the stains Goodman's brains had left on the toilet wall.

"He might say no, and then you won't have any way to mitigate the circumstances with Goodman."

I backed her play. "I know we're not feds. But bureaucracies are bureaucracies, and law enforcement's law enforcement. The brass is going to be looking for ways to cover their asses and cut their losses. Either you come up with a way to get in front of this thing or you're going to find yourself in the Bismarck field office."

Jen raised an eyebrow at me. I'd just thrown down more clichés in one sentence than she heard all month. But Young was green enough for it to work. We could both see he was starting to come around.

"You really think it will do some good?" he asked.

"Absolutely," Jen said. "It's not just about squaring what Goodman did. There are six people dead, here. If this works, we'll close half a dozen open murders and nail the people responsible."

"Okay," he said, "I'll do it."

In the car on the way back to the station, I said, "Isn't it seven?"

When we realized we had to count the victims on our fingers to get the number right, the heaviness between us seemed powerful enough to pull us down into some deep and unfathomable darkness.

———————— , ————————

"Who'd you talk to in SWAT?" Ruiz asked. "Phillips?"

I nodded. "He said go to the house first, set up, then make the call. Be sure there's no possible way to let them get there ahead of us."

"And Young'll do it from there?"

"Yeah. Then he'll leave his phone and clear out, just in case they've got a way to track it."

"Think they do?"

"Patrick was able to."

He thought it over. "When? Tomorrow?"

"That's what we're thinking," Jen said. "Makes sense with the story we're selling."

"Plus, it gives us tonight to get the whole surveillance package set up," I added.

"Tell Phillips it's a go," he said.

———————— , ————————

We were in the den of the Benton house, and I kept looking back at the wall with too many photos of Bradley and not enough of Sara and Bailey and Jacob.

"Why didn't he have more pictures of his family?" Young asked.

"I don't know," I said. "I've been wondering about that from the beginning."

Phillips and two other SWAT officers were in the house with us. They'd wired the place for pictures and sound. The two officers would stay there with us. There were also spotters on the street and in the alley. Phillips and the rest of the team would be set up across the street and two doors down in a bank-owned vacant house that had been on the market for months. Two empty houses on a street in a neighborhood like this one is a rarity. The residents must have been mortified by the hits their property values must have been taking. Multiple murders were even worse.

"We're ready to go," Phillips said. "You guys good?"

We all nodded. Young had been fully rehearsed. He'd be making one or, more likely, two calls, then leaving his FBI Ford in the driveway and heading out through the alley behind the garage to wait with the rest of the team.

Young swallowed and took a single deep breath, then used Goodman's phone to dial Kroll's number.

When the call was answered, Young said, "Hello, Mr. Kroll. This is Special Agent Young. Agent Goodman's partner?"

Jen and I were huddled around a receiver that Phillips was holding between us so we could all lean in and hear the other end of the conversation.

"Hello," Kroll said. "I'm very sorry for your loss. It's a real shame."

"Yes," Young said, "it is."

"It's a real tragedy when the stresses of the job overwhelm such devoted public servants as Agent Goodman."

"You're right, sir, it is."

Kroll paused briefly, to see if Young would continue, and when he didn't, said, "How can I help you, son?"

"Well," Young said, "I have some things here. Some...uh... personal effects of Goodman's?" A pause. "He didn't have a chance to deliver them. I was hoping you might know what to do?" He was selling it well. His performance made him sound even more immature and green than he actually was. "Mr. Kroll? What should I do with this stuff?"

There was silence on the other end of the line. It seemed as if it lasted for hours. Later, the recording of the conversation would clock it at seven seconds.

Finally, Kroll spoke with an empty and unconvincing certitude. "I'm afraid I don't have any idea what you're talking about."

"But, sir, I really don't know what to do with these things."

"I'm afraid I can't help you with that. If there's anything else we can do for you or the bureau, please don't hesitate to contact our office."

"Sir, I—"

"I'm sorry for your loss, Agent Young. Very sorry." Kroll didn't give him time to answer before ending the call.

"Just like you said," Young said to me.

"Make the second call," I told him.

He dialed Kroll's number again, and as we'd expected, the call went straight to voice mail.

Young's voice had a slight quavering stutter as he spoke. It made me think he had potential. "Mr. Kroll? I know you couldn't help before. But I really hope you can now. Goodman said I should trust you." He waited a few seconds, as if he were summoning his courage. "I'm going to take those things of his to Bradley Benton's house. In Bixby Knolls? I know it's empty. I'm going to wait there for two hours. I'll be in the den. Right inside the door off the backyard. If anyone comes, they can have Goodman's things. If not, well, then"—another practiced pause—"well, then I'll have to give them to the special agent in charge in LA. Help me out, okay, Mr. Kroll? I'm sure this is what Goodman would have wanted me to do." He waited a few more seconds, as if he weren't sure if there was anything else to be said, and ended the call.

"How was that?" Young's voice was firm, and all the traces of uncertainty had vanished.

"Spot on," Jen said.

"Let's go," Phillips said.

Young followed him out into the yard, and the two SWAT officers took up their positions upstairs, one watching the front of the house and one the back.

Jen and I both had radios with wireless earpieces and open mics. "Phillips? You hear us okay?"

"Yeah," he said, his voice sounding small and tinny in my right ear. "We got you. We're just about in place. How about you guys upstairs?"

"Front's clear."

"Back's clear, too."

"Okay," Phillips said, "now we just sit and wait."

I reminded myself not to forget that everything we said would be going out to the rest of the team and be recorded as well.

"You have the Taser?" Jen asked me.

On the way, I'd made a point of getting the stun gun out of the war bag in the trunk of my Camry. I told Jen that, with the way all of our suspects had been winding up dead, I wanted to keep this one alive if we could.

But my hand was resting on the butt of the Glock on my right hip, not the electroshock weapon in my coat pocket.

The pictures on the wall were same ones I'd spent so much time studying the day of the murders. I saw all the same images, but read into them completely different interpretations. Context is everything.

In the photos of Bradley, so many of them in so many places with so many people, where I'd seen arrogance and superiority, now I just saw the pathetic, broken man who couldn't go for more than ten minutes without the regret and sorrow overtaking him and reducing him to tears. As much as I wanted to take satisfaction in his misery, it was hard to do so. Even if he wasn't responsible for the death of his wife and children as I had so wanted to believe he was, he had still committed at least three counts of sexual assault, and probably more. Wasn't that enough for me to revel in his pain? I thought about the life of privilege and entitlement in which he'd been raised, and while it wasn't enough to absolve him in my mind, it was enough to allow me to take pleasure in his suffering. I had wanted to believe him evil, a monster capable of willful, cold-blooded infanticide, when really he was just one more fucked-up and spoiled child.

There were a few photos of Bradley and his father. If there were evil here, that's where it truly found its place. Congressman Benton was the connecting tissue, but I was convinced Margaret Benton was pulling the strings through Kroll and his underlings and using all the strength that Sternow & Byrne had put within their reach. It all came back to the green footprints. Air force Pararescue. The congressman, Kroll, Goodman, even the SUV driver who wanted so badly to fit in that his envy earned him a bullet to the back of his head. I was willing to bet whoever came through the back door would have the tattoo right where it belonged.

I looked at the shot of Sara and the children that had moved me so much the first night and wondered what, if anything, we had accomplished for them. Had we brought them justice? Was there even such a thing? What could possibly balance the scales for the loss of a mother and her two young children? One of the men who had actually perpetrated the crimes had been dealt with to the full extent of the law; the other had left his brains splashed on an ATM in Seal Beach. Was that justice? How about those truly responsible for the crime? Anton was certainly one of them. His body had been rotting in the harbor when we'd pulled him out. Justice? I don't know. Would whoever came through the door get us any closer to Kroll and the congressman? And even if it did, what would that mean for Jacob and Bailey and Sara?

I turned to see Jen leaning casually against the wall with a serene expression on her face. Her left hand was clasped over her right, which held her Glock, her index finger resting on the side of the trigger guard.

"What are you thinking about?" I asked.

"Nothing."

I looked at her. "Really?"

She nodded.

"Wish I could do that."

"You can."

"How?"

"It's easy." She let a slight smile play across her face. "Just go study martial arts for twenty years."

I smiled, too. "Phillips? We got anything yet?"

"Nope. Don't worry. We'll holler when we do."

The clock said it had been fifty minutes since Young had made the call. I was already pacing the room.

"If you're going to keep moving," Jen said, "do it farther away from the windows. He might pick up the motion."

She was right.

I sat down on an arm of the sofa, careful to keep weight on the balls of my feet so I could be up quickly if anyone saw anything. I thought about unholstering my pistol but decided against it. I didn't have Jen's Zen-master calm, so I worried I'd get too comfortable and lose the edge with a gun in my hand.

Again and again, I wished I were better at waiting.

"You used to be lot better at this," she said to me.

"I know."

"What happened?"

It hadn't occurred to me until she asked, but I was surprised to realize that I knew the answer to her question. "I spent more than a year waiting for something that never came."

"On a scale of one to ten," she said.

For just a moment, I was upset that she mentioned the pain. I realized, though, that she knew what she was doing. She could sense the level of my pain more clearly and accurately than I could myself. The ache in my arm and shoulder was distant and dull. My awareness was where it needed to be.

In the moment.

In the room.

I was ready. And for the first time since I'd come back to active duty, I knew I could do what needed to be done.

"What's that line in *Hamlet*?" I asked. "'If it be now...'" I tried to remember how it went.

"Seriously? *Hamlet*?"

"I can't remember exactly how it goes, but the last part is 'the readiness is all.'"

"You're ready?" she asked.

I looked at her and knew she could see it in my face.

Then we waited for two and half hours for absolutely nothing to happen.

————————— , —————————

"How much longer should we keep it up?" Jen asked.

"As long as we can," I said. "How long can we go, Phillips?"

There was no reply. We hadn't checked in for a while.

"Phillips?" I said again.

"The radios are dead." Jen took the receiver out of her pocket with her left hand and fiddled with the controls. "Nothing except a little bit of static," she said.

"Can anyone hear me?" I asked.

Nothing.

"Coincidence?"

She answered with a single shake of her head.

I pointed up at the ceiling.

She nodded.

I held up a finger. My Glock was in my right hand, and I backed into the corner farthest from the outside door. With my left thumb, I managed a clumsy text to Phillips: *lost rdio wht shold we doo?*

We didn't wait for him to reply.

I took the lead and started across the den to the inside door leading into the great room and the rest of the house. The lights were off and the gray sky outside did little to diffuse the dimness of the light. I took a position on the right side and looked through the door to the left as far as I could without crossing the threshold. Then I repeated the process from the opposite side. I nodded to Jen and then stepped through the door.

I didn't see where he'd come from.

Before I knew what was happening, I was on the floor, my gun was no longer in my hands, and my ears were ringing. When I tried to stand up, dizziness overtook me and I fell back to the floor with a weight that seemed much heavier than my own.

To my left, I heard the sounds of a struggle and concentrated my vision on the commotion.

"Shoot him," I said without being sure if I could even hear myself speaking.

My focus was returning, and I saw two figures silhouetted against the white curtains of the large front window.

They were both in fighter's crouches, and it looked as though he was backed up into a corner.

Jen was standing in his way.

He closed in on her, but she stopped him with a kick to his knee.

He backed up and then feinted left, but Jen didn't take the bait. He hooked with his right, but Jen blocked it and connected with a hard left jab and then a right open-handed strike to his neck. He stumbled back and got his bearings, then lunged hard at her.

She moved in toward him, twisted and bent at the waist, and threw him to the floor with a force that reverberated strongly enough for me to feel the vibrations through the hardwood slats all the way across the room.

She rotated upward, still grasping his wrist in both of her hands, then spun again, turning him facedown on the floor. She yanked and twisted his arm, and I heard a meaty snap.

I was expecting a scream. It didn't come. I found my balance and wobbled to my feet.

By the time I made it across the room, she had stepped over him without ever releasing the wristlock and brought her foot down hard on his other hand, then cuffed him with his face in a puddle of his own blood.

We heard Phillips and the rest of the tactical team kicking in the front door.

"Jarman," I said, looking down at him and recognizing his face from the iPhone image and our facial recognition match, battered and swollen as it was.

He spit some blood on the floor. A tooth went with it.

"Is that all you've got left?"

He rolled over looked up at me with anger in his eyes.

I fired the Taser into his face.

When he stopped convulsing, I squatted down and grabbed his web belt above the hips, pulled his pants down, and rolled him up onto his hip.

Half a dozen SWAT officers leaned in and looked at the tattoo on his ass.

"I'm not sure that's proper procedure," Phillips said.

No matter how hard I tried, I couldn't return his grin.

PART FIVE: PROGNOSIS

―――――――――――― , ――――――――――――

That's how it is on this bitch of an earth.
　　　　　　—Samuel Beckett, Waiting for Godot

Two

WHEN JARMAN WOKE UP IN THE SECURITY WARD OF LONG Beach Memorial, he had casts on both arms, one for his shattered left wrist, the other for his right elbow, which, when the EMTs had started working on him, had been bent at a ninety-degree angle in the wrong direction. One of his legs was elevated as well. Jen had done a job on one of his knees. His face was a swollen, discolored mass of bruises and inflammation. There were two bandages—one on his cheek and one on his forehead—where the Taser electrodes had hit him.

On a scale of one to ten, I thought.

And I wanted nothing more than to hurt him even more. He saw me smile, and although it was really impossible to tell with his face in the condition that it was in, I genuinely wanted to believe that he found it disturbing. I stared at him until he tried to talk.

His voice was slurred and muffled, but I think he said, "I don't have anything to say to you."

"Really? You're going to be stand-up after everything that happened? You know Kroll sold you out, right?" I watched his eye. Of course Kroll hadn't sold him out. I wanted to shake something loose. Get him to give us something we could use to add credence to our best theory. Or even to help us come up with a new one.

He was buying it. I could see the seeds of doubt in his squint.

"That's right. We've got you cold on Shevchuk and on Porter." The coroner had been able to, finally, ID the SUV driver. "And on Anton Tropov, too. Kroll told the DA the whole story. You're going down hard. Unless…"

The "unless" got his attention, but he tried not to let me see it. He hardened his expression as much as he could. Tried for a thousand-yard stare. I wondered if his one good eye meant he could only go five hundred.

I stopped talking again. Made him bring the conversation back to me.

"Unless what?" he mumbled.

"You know what. You want to talk to us?"

He turned his face an inch or two toward the window. It was the closest he could come to storming out of the room.

"Okay. I get it. *Semper Fidelis*, and all that." I let that sit for a few seconds. "No, wait. That's the marines, right? Does the air force have a thing like that? A motto?"

He made a vague grunt.

"Isn't it *Aim High* or something like that? Doesn't have quite the same ring to it, does it?"

He was still quiet.

"How about Pararescue? PJs, right? You've got to have something, right? Something for when you're all drunk and trying to pick up chicks? To impress the wannabes?"

It looked like he was clenching his jaw.

"Nothing? It seems like you'd have something to say when the SEALs or Green Berets tell you that calling yourselves 'PJs' makes you sound like a bunch of pussies."

He angled his face back to me, and I could see the rage in his uncovered eye.

"What, you're not pussies?" I finished that sentence with a snicker. I could feel him wanting to talk, to fight. But he couldn't. "You got your ass kicked by a girl you outweigh by seventy-five pounds. You really believe you're not a pussy?"

I couldn't have stopped pushing his buttons at that point even if I had wanted to.

"I saw your ass tattoo. Green footprints. I get it. I do. Maybe you're right. Maybe you aren't a pussy, after all."

There was a question in his eye. He thought I was changing my tactic. But he still didn't have anything to say.

"I think I get Porter. He was...uh...What was he again?" I made a show of flipping through my notebook. After half a dozen pages, I pretended like I couldn't find what I was looking for and snapped it shut. "He was in some kind of logistics unit, right? What does that mean? He drove a forklift or something?"

He exhaled through his nose. Was that indignation?

"An asswipe like that has no business with that tattoo."

He wanted to say something, but I could see him struggling to hold back.

"The dicktard didn't even know enough," I said, "not to put it on his fucking arm."

He didn't say anything, but his expression at least confirmed that theory. Porter was a poser wannabe, and it had gotten him killed.

"Is that why you did him like that? I know he blew the getaway, but that wasn't all of it, was it? If he'd been a real PJ, you wouldn't have dropped him like that, would you?"

I wasn't sure, but under the bruises, his face seemed to grow redder. He wanted to tell me. He needed to. I could see it, and even more, I could feel it. I just didn't know if I could push him hard enough.

"Did that make it easier? That he fucked up? I can see how you justified Tropov and Shevchuk. They were low-life shitbags. But no matter how incompetent Porter was, he was still on your team. That means something, doesn't it?"

It did.

And we both knew it.

He'd found his resolve.

Or maybe he'd just remembered his counter-interrogation training.

That was it.

He wasn't going to give us anything else we could use. All I could do at that point was rub salt in his wounds. So I did.

"*That others may live,*" I said.

He tried to lunge for me and let out a cry filled with anguish. He was only able to move a few inches, but that was enough that he almost fell out of bed. I caught him by the cast on his right arm, put my other hand on his shoulder, and shoved harder than I needed to in order to get him back into bed.

I knew it caused him great pain, but he didn't make another sound.

_____ , _____

In the next room, Jen, Marty, and the lieutenant had been watching the video feed of my interview with Jarman.

"That others may live?" Ruiz asked.

"Never ask a question you don't know the answer to," Marty said.

Ruiz looked puzzled.

"That's the real USAF Pararescue motto," Jen said.

"I wish I were in a better mood," Ruiz said. "Maybe I could appreciate the irony."

_____ , _____

Jen and I were at our desks a few hours later working on reports.

She looked up from her MacBook and said, "Is this as far as we can take it?"

Neither one of us had given voice to the idea that Peter Jarman could be the last link in the chain and that we might not be able to make a connection to Kroll or Margaret Benton or anyone else. Molly was the only one who was willing to talk, and she had suspicions, too, but nothing anywhere close to solid.

We were out of leads.

I couldn't accept it, though.

"No," I said, "it's not."

Her face held an enigmatic expression that I couldn't quite read. I wanted to think that it was hopefulness, that she just needed me to give her a little pep talk to get her back in the game, but I wasn't naive enough to convince myself of that. The reality was more likely that she had found some small bit of amusement in my total and complete inability to accept the truth.

Three

THE PHONE CALL TOOK ME BY SURPRISE. MY BLACKBERRY only displayed a phone number with a Long Beach area code. No name. I fought my inclination to hit *DECLINE* and answered it.

"Beckett," I said, trying to sound mildly annoyed, just in case I wanted to get off the line. It wasn't much of a stretch.

"Hello, Danny Beckett." The voice had a familiar Eastern European inflection. It took me a few seconds to place it, but I did.

I didn't bother trying to hide my surprise. "What could you possibly want?"

"We should have a talk, you and I."

"I'm listening."

"Not on the phone. Not that kind of talk."

I agreed to meet him that evening at the harbor. On Pier B Street, close to the edge of the inner harbor.

About a block away from where we'd found Anton's body.

I ended the call.

And wondered how to handle it.

———————— · ————————

The night air was still and cold and heavy with the industrial smell of the harbor when I got out of my car across the street from Anton's warehouse. It was only about a block away from the meeting place. I looked around. No sign of him, but there were a thousand places he could be hiding. I wondered if he was watching me.

I called Jen.

"You're there right now?" she asked, the exasperation thick in her voice.

"Yeah."

"Why'd you even bother calling me?"

"Just in case."

"Just in case of what? In case somebody finds you floating in the harbor tomorrow?"

"No, I just wanted to—"

"I don't fucking believe you."

She ended the call.

That went well, I thought.

I put my phone away, brushed my hand across the grip of my Glock, and started walking toward the water's edge.

Soon, I saw a figure I couldn't yet recognize step out from behind a dirty-gray shipping container. He was silhouetted against the pier lights that gleamed from the other side of the channel.

He kept his hands in his pockets. Probably just to make me nervous.

I wasn't in the mood to dick around. My hand slipped under my coat, and I drew my gun, switched on the tactical light, and lit up Yevgeny Tropov's face.

Fear might have flashed in his eyes, but if it did, it disappeared too quickly for me to be sure. By the time I could focus clearly, his expression was all dull arrogance.

"You going to shoot me, Danny Beckett?"

"I wish." I turned off the light and lowered my gun. "What do you want?"

"Some information," he said.

"And you think I'm going to give it to you?"

"Yes."

"I'm not giving you shit."

He smiled his cocky little Russian smile. "I think you will."

"What makes you think so?"

"Your investigation is not so well, yes?"

"It's just fine."

"Don't embarrass yourself by saying things we both know are untrue."

I didn't respond to that.

"All your murders, you have the triggermen, but not the people who made them happen. That's why I think you will want to help me."

I was curious. And he knew it. "Do you know something?"

"No," he said. "But you do."

He was right. I had no proof and probably never would, but I believed that Margaret Benton and Roger Kroll had conspired to kill Sara Benton. And that every murder that followed had resulted either directly or indirectly from their actions. They had more blood on their hands in this than anyone else.

"I don't have any idea what you're talking about," I said.

"That's okay, Danny. You can pretend however you want it to be. I just have to ask you a few questions."

I waited.

"I know what you think of me," he said. "I do. So I'm sure it will surprise you to know I need to be sure of certain things before I take action."

"Take action? What are you talking about?"

"It's the mother and her boyfriend, yes? They are the ones responsible."

That was it.

The moment I knew.

I turned my head and looked at the water.

"Nothing to say?" he asked.

The digital recorder in my pocket felt heavy against my chest. I took it out and hurled it into the water. The splash was small and quiet.

I could feel him smiling as I walked away.

———————— , ————————

Jen's rented Infiniti was parked between my car and a silver Taurus. She leaned against the fender and watched me walk toward her. The closer I got, the more I could make out the disappointment in her eyes.

"Hey," I said.

"Hey."

Marty Locklin stepped out of the shadows between two shipping containers with a scoped AR 15 in his hands. He looked at me, looked at Jen, opened the back driver's-side door on the Ford, took out a black ballistic nylon case, slipped the rifle into it, looked at the two of us, gave us a single nod, got behind the wheel, and drove away, all without a word.

We watched him go and then stood there in the weighted silence for what seemed like a very long time.

"You hungry?" she asked.

"I could eat."

Ten

NINETY-FOUR DAYS LATER, AFTER ENRIQUE'S HAD SUCCUMBED to the lack of interest in its morning menu and stopped opening before lunch and I had fallen into a deep and profound mourning for the world's most amazing breakfast burrito; after Jen had signed the mortgage on her new home and started warming her parents to the idea of moving to Long Beach, after Patrick had healed enough to return to the squad from his modified desk duty and he'd grown back enough hair so that the shaved spots in his scalp were no longer visible; after Harlan had his surgery and most of his first course of chemo and had somehow forged a stronger relationship with his daughter than they had ever had before; after Bailey and Jacob had lessened the frequency of their nighttime visits to once or twice a week and had stopped imploring me to find a way to use my father's saw to cut away their pain in addition to my own; after I had started to let them go and long for another case that would compel my attention powerfully enough to awaken my obsession and assuage my pain to even the smallest of degrees, we heard the news that I had been expecting.

On their way home from a very successful fundraiser for his upcoming reelection campaign, the congressman and Margaret Benton were both killed when their Mercedes-Benz was struck by a hit-and-run driver as they drove north on the 405. And even though I knew better, the Benton curse was also held responsible a week later when Roger Kroll passed away after an accidental overdose of prescription painkillers and sleep medication.

"What do you know about all of this?" Jen had just gotten off the phone with an acquaintance from the Huntington Beach PD who'd looked into the Kroll case for her. She'd also talked to the California Highway Patrol, who had jurisdiction over the investigation of the Bentons' deaths. There were irregularities in both cases, she'd found out, but nothing anyone believed was worth pursuing.

"Nothing," I said, trying to take some comfort in the knowledge that I did not, in fact, know anything at all about the deaths.

But I suspected things. She saw that.

And even though I wanted to know, even though I needed to know, I couldn't bear to ask her if I was able to see the disappointment in her eyes so clearly—the disappointment that pained me more than my injuries ever had—because she wasn't able to hide it, or because she didn't even want to try.

Five

"Jesus," I said to Harlan as he handed me another beer. "I thought you moved like an old man before." He'd insisted on getting up and going into the kitchen to get me another Sam Adams even though he wasn't drinking any himself.

"I am an old man," he said. "I earned this hobble."

The surgery had gone well, the doctors said. If the chemo did what they expected it to do, he'd be out of the woods. For a while, at least.

"Where's Cynthia today?"

"I don't know. She's a grown woman. I'm trying to give her some space."

I wondered if that was how he'd drifted away from her the first time around, but I didn't say anything. But maybe I was wrong and it was a good sign that he was trying to respect her needs.

"You been practicing?" he said.

"Practicing what?"

"The banjo," he said. "Don't go pretending like you don't know what I'm talking about."

"No, not really."

"Goddamnit, Danny. Why won't you take this seriously?" He started to stand up again but stopped with a grunt. He put his hand on his side and sank back down into the couch.

"You okay?" I asked.

He nodded.

"What do you need? I'll get it."

"Go back to my bedroom and get me the banjo on the stand by my bed."

I looked at him.

"Go on," he said. "Do it."

As I walked down the hallway, I glanced into the guestroom that Cynthia was using. Next to the window on the far wall hung a pencil sketch of her father. I'd never seen it there before and wondered if she'd drawn it. If so, she'd managed to capture the odd sardonic warmth of his expression just about perfectly.

In his room, I tried not to but couldn't resist my natural inclination to nose around a bit. He kept things neat and orderly. The row of medicine bottles on his nightstand was arranged by size. I pulled open the drawer just enough to see the walnut grip of the Smith & Wesson Model 66 he had pointed at me the first time we met.

The banjo was perched upright in an oak stand. It looked even nicer than the one he had given me. Polished dark wood, carving on the neck, mother-of-pearl inlays on the fretboard, gold plating on some of the hardware. I couldn't help but wonder how much that one was worth.

"What the hell you doing in there?" Harlan shouted from the living room.

"Looking for your dirty magazines."

I removed the banjo as carefully as I could and took it back to Harlan in the living room.

He plopped it down into his lap with a practiced smoothness that actually surprised me a bit.

"You didn't bring my picks?" he asked.

"What picks?"

"Never mind."

He eyeballed me, turned up the corner of his mouth, and started plucking out a surprisingly delicate and tender melody that became more complicated and more somber as it went along. He never looked at his hands, and his gaze drifted somewhere far away.

He was good. I didn't need to know much about music to know that.

When he finished, I said, "Wow."

He smiled.

"I thought you couldn't play anymore," I said. "Because of the pain. It doesn't hurt?"

"It does. But the pain's different now."

I nodded.

He handed the banjo to me, and I got up to put it back in his bedroom.

"Sit down," he said.

"Sorry, I thought you were done."

"I am," he said. "But you're just starting."

Acknowledgments

Perhaps some novels result from the efforts of a lone author laboring in solitude. *The Pain Scale* did not. My most sincere and heartfelt thanks to:

Nicole Gharda, the best partner anyone could ever have.

David Aimerito, who always helps me see the art.

Jeff Dilts, who was always there when the chips were down.

Paul Tayyar and LeeAnne Langton, who not only helped Danny Beckett into the world but continued to help him grow.

Shaun Morey, who looked at some rambling fragments and helped me see a novel (and who keeps the coffee flowing).

Gary Phillips and Naomi Hirahara, who took me seriously even before I did.

Eileen Klink, Stephen Cooper, Bill Mohr, Gerry Locklin, and my colleagues in the Department of English at CSULB, whose support and mentorship has been and continues to be invaluable.

Richard Klink and Derek Pacifico, who helped me get the details right.

Zachary "Thug" Locklin, who always knows how to pass the time in 702.

Enrique and Michelle Perez, who make the best Mexican food in Long Beach and who will, I fervently hope, someday bring back the universe's most amazing breakfast burrito.

Barry Hunn, who, in reality, is even nicer, more generous, and more knowledgeable about banjos than he seems to be in the preceding pages.

Andrew Bartlett, Alex Carr, Jacque Ben-Zekry, and the rest of the amazing crew at the Zon.

And finally, to Sharon Dilts, my mother, whose own struggle with chronic pain was the impetus for this novel.

About the Author

 As a child, Tyler Dilts dreamed of following in the footsteps of his policeman father. Though his career goals changed over time, he never lost interest in the daily work of homicide detectives. Today he teaches at California State University in Long Beach, and his writing has appeared in the *Los Angeles Times*, *The Chronicle of Higher Education*, *The Best American Mystery Stories*, and numerous other publications. He is the author of *A King of Infinite Space*, the first in the Long Beach Homicide series.